DEADLY
TOUCH

HEATHER GRAHAM

DEADLY TOUCH

mira

ISBN-13: 978-0-7783-6095-7

Deadly Touch

Mira
22 Adelaide St. West, 40th Floor
Toronto, Ontario M5H 4E3, Canada
BookClubbish.com

Printed in U.S.A.

For cousins, near and far,
those we're born with,
and those we're privileged to acquire through marriage.

For Kristin Ann Stock, with deepest thanks for her wonderful support.

Jonelle Garofoli and Keith Pozzessere, and my husband, Dennis,
with thanks for the incredible (and massive!) family he brought to me,
descendants of the Martinelli, Pozzessere, Mero and D'Onofrio families.

And for one last and never least: my biological cousin, Pat DeVuono,
whose mom was the Irish side, my big cousin when I was little,
the coolest musician ever, and now the only one who can correct my memories
regarding my own past and the tales Granny told us. Like the one about
the leprechauns, or how "if we be misbehavin',
the banshees be comin' for us in the outhouse."

She did it well. We were teenagers before we realized
we didn't have an outhouse.

I am grateful to and for all!

DEADLY
TOUCH

PROLOGUE

Thirteen years ago

"Imagine, if you will! There are those who fear the creatures of our great Everglades—not a swamp—but a river of grass, one that houses alligators and in certain places crocodiles, as well. Though, frankly," the storyteller said, pausing to smile, "the true plague we endure can most often be mammoth mosquitoes. Some think the skunk ape is real. But, my dear friends, I have a tale to tell you that will chill your blood, and that is of the cursed pirates who roam the Everglades. Watch for the sails of their lost ship upon this river of grass for they are doomed to sail it forever!"

Raina found herself feeling as if her blood was somehow chilling even in the almost-warmth of the night. In a few days it would be spring, but a late storm had settled over the north of the country, and here, in the very southern end of the mainland of South Florida, the temperature had dipped to a cool fifty degrees that night. Maybe that was causing the chills?

But the storyteller was good. He was young—maybe eighteen or so. He was extremely good-looking with fantastic cheekbones common in both the Miccosukee and Seminole tribes of Florida, startling gold-green eyes far more common in someone of Northern European descent and a fine smile that wrapped it all up with a rugged charm. But then, she was just going on fourteen. She and her girlfriends were here on a field trip to camp out for a night in the Everglades and had whispered about him and giggled, thinking he was pretty hot. One of the older men—Jeremy Gray, a superfriendly and informative member of the Miccosukee tribe—had given a speech on the effects of people thinking they could "humanely" release pythons and boas in the Everglades and how those predators threatened the natural flow of life there. The danger being that many native species might soon be wiped out.

Raina had been excited about their field trip from the beginning. Yes, she was afraid of killer creatures and not at all fond of mosquitoes, but she had always loved the region, so wild with beautiful birds and a haunting, nostalgic beauty when sunset came.

She loved all of it.

And especially this storyteller. His name was Axel Tiger—a mixture of ethnicity as intriguing as his appearance. She wasn't sure if he was Miccosukee or Seminole, since both tribes were here to talk about the Everglades and their culture, history and future.

Like the other girls, she just knew that he was hot.

"The pirates were a bloodthirsty crew believed to have been trolling these waters in the late 1600s and into the early years of the 1700s. When a British merchantman came into their sights, they chased it down the coast and through the keys and close to the tip of the mainland where our great sea of grass meets with the bay. They gave no quarter. Hey, they were angry! They had to chase the ship for days! And to that end, they decided the entire crew—left alive after the fierce battle to take her—would walk the plank. The pirate captain especially hated the merchantman captain. The young captain's wife was aboard, and as he forced her to watch her husband walk the plank—chained at his wrists lest he somehow swim to shore—she looked up to the heavens and cried out, 'Curse these bloody pirates! Dear Lord above, curse these brutal creatures until the end of time!'"

Axel Tiger was dramatic, stooping low and walking between the campfire and the campers, hands laced behind his back, his eyes alive with mischief.

"And so!" he said suddenly, causing several to jump and then giggle. "The captain's lady's words were heard, they say. A mammoth storm rolled across the Atlantic to the Caribbean, and despite the seafaring talents of the pirates, the waves rose and fell and rose and fell...and *slam*! The pirates—and all their stolen treasure—were rent apart and tossed into the far corners of the air and sea. It's said that hour by hour, day by day, more bodies piled up on the southern tip of the Glades, trapping the cursed souls of the pirates to roam the waterways and the hammocks, high points and mud and muck and sawgrass. They say sometimes when the moon rises high and even when it does not—even when the glory of the sunset fades into the shadow of night—the pirate ship itself can be seen sailing over our river of grass, the pirates manning her doomed forever."

There was silence. Raina, wedged between her friends, stared at him. He was smiling—secretly pleased, she imagined, that he had brought them all to silence.

The campfire snapped and crackled.

He looked at them, still waiting. "Hey, they're ghosts. At least they don't get mosquito bites!"

Someone giggled. The stories were over. They could head to their tents for the night.

"That was a bit of fun, folks!" Axel Tiger reminded them as they burst into applause and began to rise. "There's so much more about this amazing ecosystem you'll be learning tomorrow. Yeah, we have mosquitoes, alligators, crocs and snakes—but it's still amazing. Tomorrow, you'll learn how these wildlands saved a people—and how the Native Americans came to be here, and how we all finally came to be at peace today."

He moved on, talking to a small group of men, including one of the tribal members who had taught them about culture and ecology that day, Jeremy Gray.

She stared after him a minute and then—not wanting to hear about having a crush on the man—she quickly turned to her friends. They were all talking about him, though, comparing him to various movie stars.

She was in one of the little pup tents at the campground with her friend Lucia, who was laughing with Mya and Elly. Mya had a crush on Tate Fielding, who was standing with some of the other boys, including Jordan Rivera—another slightly older guy beloved by almost every girl at school. Jordan and Tate were two of the coolest guys and best friends. Tate's dad was a partner in a law firm, and both Tate and Jordan planned on being big-time lawyers one day.

Raina thought being Jordan had to be easier than being Tate—Tate's dad could be exceptionally hard on him. And Tate was sometimes embarrassed by him. His dad tended to be around a lot. Tate had grumbled to Raina once that his dad didn't ever seem to trust anyone—he'd even driven out to the school encampment, as if he didn't trust the school, the United States government, the state of Florida or a soul within the Miccosukee tribe.

"There are some intriguing young men over there. Smokin' hot for sure! We could slip into that conversation," Mya whispered.

"Yes!" Elly said. She giggled. "And look—there's Mr. Fielding. Tate's been ignoring him—but he's finally leaving. Guess he's not a fan of the mosquitoes!"

But Mrs. Oster, their science teacher, came hurrying by, shooing the boys into their tents for the night. She was giving Mr. Peters, the gym teacher, a very stern look, indicating he had to get his young charges under control. Mrs. Oster was vivacious and usually fun, but she could be stern, too.

It had been a long day; they should have been tired. They were, but all a little bit frightened, as well. Being in the Everglades made them wary, even if they did have mosquito protection and adults guarding them, not to mention Timothy, the massive rottweiler, a dog that—so they'd been told—somehow knew to warn people about snakes and alligators, should they come too close.

Personally, Raina found the dog to be wonderfully warm and cuddly. But she could see how snakes and alligators would feel different.

They giggled more but then obeyed. They were attending a magnet school and those who didn't follow the rules could be easily replaced. In the tent, Lucia brushed her hair, hoping she wouldn't find too many bugs in it, and swore she'd never sleep.

But just minutes after Lucia's head touched the pillow attached to her sleeping bag, she was very softly snoring.

Raina couldn't sleep so easily. For a while she stared at the tent's ceiling, watching the way the fire danced on the canvas of their tent.

But then Timothy let out a little "Woof!" and she sprang to her feet, staring at Lucia.

Lucia softly snored on.

It was nothing, Raina was sure. She didn't want to wake Lucia, but she knew she wasn't going to sleep herself. She hesitantly stepped from her tent.

★ ★ ★

Axel saw the group of men standing just down from the camping area. His good friend, Jeremy Gray, was among them, along with two Miccosukee patrolmen and an older officer from the Miami-Dade County Police.

He glanced around the campground. The kids had been ordered to bed by their chaperones. They'd been a good audience, interested in ecology, culture and the Miccosukee and Seminole tribes of Florida. He'd enjoyed working with them.

There were always guards on duty when groups like this camped out. The Miccosukee force always managed a few volunteers.

Miami-Dade police didn't show up that often.

But he knew as much as he loved his strange homeland—well, what he saw as his homeland, though he'd been born in Baptist Hospital, Miami—that, over the centuries, the Everglades had a history of being used for sinister deeds.

Far beyond the long-ago murder spree of the pirates, over a hundred and fifty bodies had been found in the Everglades since the 1960s. Seeing the Miami-Dade cop, he was afraid it signaled yet another disappearance.

He would prove to be correct.

He walked over to the group.

"Hey, Axel, how are you doing? You must be heading off to some Ivy League school before long."

Axel realized he knew the older county policeman who had spoken. Vinnie Magruder's patrol was out in this region and he was friends with a lot of the Miccosukee police.

"No, sir. I'm going into the marines, then I'll go to college," Axel told him.

"Well, good plan," Vinnie said, glancing at Jeremy and the two Miccosukee policemen who were there.

"My folks are both good with it, thanks. What's going on?" Axel asked.

"A Kendall area woman is missing. Fran Castle. I found a car deserted on the Trail, on the embankment between here and the casino, near one of the power stations where there's no guardrail. Found it right around two o'clock. Sounds like she and a friend were at the Miccosukee casino and then suddenly the friend couldn't find her. Not necessarily a big deal—until I found the car." He hesitated, shrugged and sighed deeply. "They've got cops and dogs working the area. They'll skirt north and west after. I was just letting all these guys know to be on the lookout. We'll be searching county land, tribal land, state and federal. Makes me sick, the crime that goes on here. Killers and sickos think they can make people disappear and get away with it. Well, I intend to put a stop to that. You haven't seen or heard anything?"

"You think...she's dead? Killed and dumped?"

"I, uh, sorry—I mean, she could be lost out here somewhere. Or she could have just left her car—illegally, where it is—not knowing. She could've just taken off."

"I'm only out here to tell tales to the school group," Axel said. He shook his head and added, "I wish I could help. If something bad has happened, if there are more search groups starting up, I'd be happy to join in. I, too, hate that people think they can use this land to hide their crimes and get away with them. It has to be stopped. Hopefully, this woman is found alive and well."

"Hopefully. We're just a little jaded and worried. The Everglades. One-point-five million acres. It's a wonder and a danger if people don't know what they're doing." Vinnie paused, shaking his head. "Anyway. Keep an eye on the kids, huh? But for now, don't say anything. Who knows? Maybe someone met her and they decided the Seminole Hard Rock had better payouts and they headed to Broward County."

Axel didn't think he believed it. But he also agreed not to

tell. The kids on the school trip were filled with the wonder of the Glades—ecology, fast airboats and even alligators.

"I'll stay by the fire, keep the dog company and watch out for the kids," Axel said. He turned and walked away.

He was afraid the missing woman would remain just that—missing. Fran Castle. He wished with all his heart he could help. That they would find her. That she would be okay.

He doubted it. Too often, far too often, someone disappeared in the Glades only for an unwary fisherman to find remnants of him or her—what had once been a living, laughing human being.

Axel was suddenly even more determined to stick to his plan. He would join the military. And he knew that someday, somehow, some way, he would help hunt for the people who did such things.

In fact, he already had a pretty good idea as to exactly what he wanted to do—and to whom he'd go when he was ready.

He was there. Hunkered by the fire, stroking the dog. "It's all right, my friend," she heard him tell the animal. "Bad things do happen, but tonight you're on guard duty for this group of kids. Strange night. But you are the best dog, always on guard. And look! I have a bit of jerky treat right here in my pocket."

He frowned suddenly, glancing over toward Raina, aware she stood just outside her tent, though she hadn't moved or made a sound.

"Hi. You okay?" he asked softly. "Raina, right?"

She nodded.

"Yes." She croaked out the word.

A bit of a fog had fallen. The moon was full, or just about so, and it cast a strange glimmer over their little clearing, the wetlands, waterways and tree-laden hammocks.

Was it him? Had he been such a wonderful storyteller that his story had come to life?

There was a rich field of sawgrass stretching behind him, caught in an eerie glow between the fog and the moonlight.

And she saw it, sailing upon...the sawgrass and wetlands.

Idiot—she certainly had yet to get a high school degree, much less her college degree! She knew great old-fashioned sailing ships could not be on a sea of grass!

But the dog whined again. Axel Tiger looked out across the land beyond them as she had.

He turned back to her.

"You see it," he said softly, a note of surprise in his voice.

She could barely form words. She whispered, "The ship."

"The night, the fire, the fog," he said. "But there's nothing to fear. If pirates roam, they do so praying. They pray they might somehow find their way to atonement. Some say they learned the hard way and now they guard the Glades, doing what they can to stop evil from occurring. I'm being whimsical. You need to go back to sleep. It's a great program they've got going for your group in the morning. You'll want to be awake for it."

He looked back at what appeared to be an endless sea of grass bathed in fog and the strange glow of moonlight.

He saw the ship. She knew he saw the damned ship. He'd even asked if she'd seen it, and now...now he wanted it to be a vision cast within her imagination.

He looked back at her again.

"Please, don't be afraid. Timothy and I are here, and we have a few Miccosukee police on duty just over there at that picnic table. You're safe. Don't worry, we're all watching. I'm watching. Go back to bed."

There was little choice. She nodded and slipped back into her tent. She laid down, but she stayed awake and stared at the canvas, at the fire dancing again.

Two things kept rushing through her mind.

The ship. She'd seen the ship.

He'd known her name. No big deal; he probably knew all their names. This was an amazing program.

Eventually, she slept. She woke with the sun and the sound of laughter and conversation. It was time to start the day.

The program was wonderful. She loved learning the history of the area, what needed to be protected, how the entire ecosystem worked. She loved learning about the different Native American tribes that had come to Florida, and how the Seminole and Miccosukee had settled the Everglades.

She loved it all...

But in her heart, she felt she had touched something and then lost it.

She didn't see the pirate ship again.

Nor did she see Axel Tiger again. As in all things, memories faded as the years went by and she became a college graduate.

And stepped out into the world.

CHAPTER ONE

Now

She was found—what remained of her—on the south-side embankment by the road and the canal that stretched the length of the Tamiami Trail, just about ten miles west of the casino.

It wasn't surprising she had been partially consumed. What was surprising seemed to be that she had been almost neatly bitten in half.

The top half remained; the bottom half did not.

"This is how we found her. Exactly how we found her," Detective Nigel Ferrer, Miami-Dade Homicide, told Axel. At his side, Andrew Osceola of the Miccosukee Tribal Police shook his head.

"We haven't touched anything," he said, echoing Nigel. "No one has touched anything. Even Doc Warner said that since you were on the way, he'd hold off for a minute."

Axel nodded and hunkered down by the body. He was somewhat surprised his old friends were so courteously resolved he become involved as quickly and completely as possible.

He wasn't a medical examiner. He had, however, seen his share of murders and the sad state in which a body—recently a viable human being—might be found.

The Everglades beckoned to nature lovers and bird-watchers, but also offered a tempting place to dump a body. The miles of wetlands were hardly ever traversed fully, and numerous creatures survived off carrion, plus trees, grasses and brush that all but enveloped any form—living and dead.

"We would have found her, anyway—without the tip from the so-called psychic," Nigel said.

"Vultures," Andrew added quietly. "Of course, they'll come for anything. A dead possum, roadkill..."

His voice faded. They were not looking at any kind of roadkill.

Axel nodded and gave his attention to the body. Flies were swarming around them.

As Andrew had noted, the sky was alive with vultures.

But at least this woman had been found. And that gave them a far better chance of finding her killer than the women who went missing, never to be found.

The victim had been in her midthirties, he thought, but even that was difficult to judge. Even the prettiest little birds that flitted about down here were fond of soft tissue. That meant they'd gone for the eyes, the lips and the line at the waist where the body had somehow been severed.

"Never seen an alligator do anything like that," Andrew noted.

"But they will eat what's already dead when they're hungry enough. Don't need to drown a body when it's—"

"Gator can only snap down," Nigel said. "Usually lies in wait, mouth open."

"When it hunts on shore, it finds prey, opens its mouth and snaps. I'd say improbable, but possible. Snapped down on her, dragged off the bottom half. It's not like he's going to think about it and say, *Uh-oh, I only got half, better grab that other part, too*," Andrew said. "And what with all the constrictor snakes we've got around here now, food is scarce."

Axel saw Dr. Warner standing with his medical bag in hand, stoic as he waited, but surely growing impatient.

He looked at the body again. There were points he could note without the bottom half of her body. She was naked except for remnants of her clothing—Axel thought her clothing had been destroyed by birds or other scavenging creatures, rather than having been torn by a human hand. A ring of blood sat around her throat like a necklace. There were abrasions on her wrists; she had been bound at one time. Most probably by rope. The abrasion marks were rough. Someone had held her against her will, but with the bottom half of the body gone, they wouldn't know about sexual assault unless Dr. Warner found telltale fluids elsewhere on the body. Most evidence would have been heavily compromised.

The Everglades, as Axel knew too well, could swallow many a sin like a massive, stygian, dark hole.

He stood and looked at the tribal policeman and the homicide detective, both men he had known since he'd been a child. They had each decided on different paths to law enforcement, all headed in the direction where they thought they might serve best.

Nigel and Andrew had often worked together. As a Miccosukee officer, Andrew had passed all the state certification requirements and then been commissioned by the United States Department of the Interior, Indian Bureau Affairs *and* by the National Park Service as well as the US Fish and Wildlife Service. Complicated, but while a homicide detective would be called in by Miami-Dade on this, the eastern side of the Trail, Andrew would remain part of the force of the investigation.

Axel knew that during the years he had been at the academy with Adam Harrison's Krewe of Hunters unit, his two old friends had been working many a case together.

Two bodies in oil drums—case solved, traced back to a drug ring.

A domestic situation. Murder at a campground.

The capture of felons involved in a murder-for-hire case, caught as they tried to hide in the great southern section of the river of grass.

Axel knew as much as he did about the cases because the three of them had kept up and also made use of each other—listening, being sounding boards, offering theories or suggestions from afar. Sometimes the distance could lend a different perspective—like a bird's-eye view when others were on the ground. And he'd come down himself, just a year or so ago, on the oil drum case.

And now, they were together. The pattern emerging suggested there was a cold and calculating killer on the loose. A serial killer, but not the usual kind. Sane and organized. Aware of the density of the Everglades, the ability of the land, the foliage and the animals to destroy evidence, allowing the killing to go on and on with the bodies leaving nothing for investigators to use in their search for justice.

Dr. Keith Warner came striding over.

"Let me take a look at her," he said simply, hunkering down as Axel stepped back. "You've noted the obvious. She was bound. Throat slit. I'm not seeing any obvious defensive wounds, but under these circumstances, I won't know until the body is cleaned. There will be things I won't be able to tell you. But before any of you ask, yes, at first glance I'm going to suggest it might be the same killer—or a killer working in tandem with whoever killed your last victim. Axel, you weren't here for that one, but I'm assuming that you were already in the area and that's why you were able to get here so fast. You're usually still with the feds up in the capital area, right?"

"I'm still a fed," Axel said. "And yes, I was already here."

He'd been sent down when Andrew and Nigel had gotten together and quietly communicated with Axel's superior, Jackson Crow. He knew they wished the vocation he had chosen was nearer but they were also aware the Krewe of Hunters was a different and special unit, and probably right where Axel needed to be.

While Andrew was a Miccosukee and had grown up on tribal land, Nigel's background was an odd mix that would defy any ancestry chart to determine. He had grown up just east of the Miccosukee lands—his family had owned a farm in unincorporated Miami-Dade County.

Axel had been the one to come and go between both worlds. Two of his grandparents were both Native American. Axel knew he'd been a lucky kid because they were still alive when he was young, ready to tell him tales—some truth, some exaggerated—about his forefathers. The sides of his family had blended easily, so he'd been encouraged to enjoy his relations with both societies.

Thus, as kids, with their parents all friends, Nigel, Andrew and Axel had become fast friends, as well.

They all knew Dr. Warner, too. While Axel had never been with the police for either the county or the tribe, he'd come down on an invitation before as a federal investigator on a drug case that had crossed state lines.

The police photographer was still snapping pictures.

"Okay, so let me try to get this straight. Nigel, you were first informed about the victim because a woman called the police department and claimed she'd seen a woman out here in the Everglades? She said off Tamiami Trail and described exactly where?"

"Yes, that's it. They're holding her now," Nigel said. "You

see where we are, unless someone got an urge to stop right here and crawl through the wild grass to the canal, there was no way to have seen this victim. And she told us just how far east from the Hawk and O'Reilly Tour Company, and west from the Miccosukee Resort and Gaming Casino, she could be found. The caller *had* to know something about the murder or been involved with the murder to know with such precision."

"Okay, so she called in and—"

"And my captain called me," Nigel said. "I called Andrew and he had one of his men who was out patrolling come, too."

"And you said the Miami-Dade force picked her up?" Axel said.

"Yes, no problem. She didn't lie. They didn't have to search for her. She gave them her address. I'm not sure if she's brash and overconfident or totally idiotic or insane. They're getting a bunch of gibberish out of her."

"Where was she address-wise?" Axel asked.

"South Miami, not far from the hospital off US 1," Nigel said. "That means nothing. From her area, you could just hop on the highway, hop onto the Trail, be here and back in an hour or less. Of course, around here, it could also take way more time depending on traffic. But Doc will tell us if we're right. We're pretty sure the victim was killed sometime late last night. Her remains are cold as ice." He winced. "Fluids are congealed. There was a tour bus out here yesterday and the driver made a stop here or near here for pictures and old Jimmy Bob was out fishing right around here, too. No body, then. He likes late-night fishing. There's never been a gator or a snake to scare him off. He started fishing the area about the same time he could crawl."

"Okay, then," Axel said, and he looked at Nigel. Miami-Dade had the lead on the homicide. "I'm still an assist out here. What I want to do first is talk to this woman. Can you make that happen for me? I want to talk to her alone. Can you arrange that?"

"If you can stop whoever is killing women and dumping them like this in the Everglades, I'll see you get ice cream with cherries on top, too," Nigel told him.

"Great. I'll head in. And by the way, I'm not a fan."

"Of?" Andrew asked, frowning. "Murder? None of us is a fan—"

"Of course not! I mean ice cream. I've never liked the stuff—or maraschino cherries for that matter." He hesitated, the past weighing on him. "Hey, Magruder's retired, right?"

"Yep. We sure miss Vinnie Magruder," Andrew said. "He finally gave it up. They say he fought retirement. Things weigh on you, you know?"

"That young woman from years ago—Fran Castle? They never found her, right?" Axel asked.

Andrew shook his head. "They never found her. And I think Vinnie always blamed himself. He's a good guy. He's living in a community down on Krome Avenue. He checks in now and then."

Axel nodded. "Thanks. What's the woman's name, by the way? The one who called this victim in."

Andrew referred to his phone.

"Raina. Raina Hamish," he said. "There's something familiar about that name."

Axel stiffened, staring at him in surprise. Years washed away. He couldn't have heard right. He remembered the bright, pretty girl, tall, slim and wide-eyed with enthusiasm for everything that was offered to her. She'd had amber eyes framed by wild auburn hair and a quick smile.

She was the one who'd seen the ship, the great pirate ship with its billowing sails, journeying through the river of grass and the clouds and the fog.

"You know her?" Nigel asked with surprise.

"Yeah, we met years ago. She was with the school camp at least one year that I recall," he said. "You two might remember I gave some speeches that year. It seemed she was interested in more than escaping the classroom. Anyway, I'm on my way. We'll keep in touch."

He started walking, then turned back.

"Nigel, no cameras when I'm with her. And no recordings."

Nigel paused to look at Andrew; Andrew nodded with a stoic and sage expression that would have done a mighty chief proud.

"We need her," Axel said softly.

"Right. I'm on it," Nigel said.

Axel headed to his car at the side of the road. Dr. Warner was instructing his assistants on the removal of the body.

The wind was beginning to blow. Long grasses and high trees bowed, as if they cried for the young woman, honoring her as best they could.

He headed back to the city, wondering just how Raina Hamish might come to know about a woman, dead and with her throat severed, on a canal embankment in the middle of the Everglades.

He was worried for her, though he knew nothing of the woman she might have become.

He was anxious—curious if he could make use of her in any way.

Because not everyone saw the pirate ship.

In fact, very few ever did.

"You put on a dress and then...you saw the victim?" Detective MacDonald demanded.

Yes. Raina Hamish had slipped into the changing room and tried on the blue dress she hoped to buy for the Children's Place fundraiser, and when she had looked in the mirror to check the fit, she hadn't seen her reflection. She had seen the dead woman. Lying on the embankment, face and body covered in blood, the soft, damp earth around her soaking up more of the crimson flow that had escaped her along with the last breaths of her life.

MacDonald was a tough cop. He didn't scream or yell or throw things around the interrogation room. He sat quietly. His eyes never averted from the sharp gaze he held on her. His hands were folded before him. He had iron-gray, close-cropped hair and his eyes were a riveting hazel. Raina had found herself staring hard back at those eyes—and fighting for control—so that she isolated every bit of color in them, the green that surrounded yellow sparks that turned to a brown as they reached the pupil.

Well, he could be hard. He could grill her until she passed out. But that wasn't going to happen because she had called her brother, Robert, who was a criminal attorney.

Usually for the prosecution.

But he was heading here now. She'd given up on trying to explain. She had never harmed another soul in her entire life, and it had never occurred to her that anyone might suspect her of having committed a murder.

Now she realized such an assumption had been not just naive but entirely stupid.

And in retrospect, maybe she wouldn't have believed herself. What she was saying sounded ridiculous even to her own ears. She knew where a body had been dumped, which to most people would surely suggest she had put it there or at least knew who else had.

"Yes. I know it's hard for you to believe me. And I wouldn't have called the police unless I believed...unless I believed it helpful. I've heard that several victims have been found over the past few months in the Everglades. I know it's ridiculous! But I also know various police departments have accepted the services of mediums and psychics. I'm not psychic—not usually. I've never had anything like this happen to me before."

"Trying on a dress and looking in a mirror and seeing the mutilated body of a woman. And the sign for the airboat ride company and a mile marker and the whole bit," MacDonald said as he shook his head slightly.

He was speaking skeptically, but she replied earnestly. "It wasn't as if I was looking in a mirror. It was more like a window. I'm from here, born at South Miami Hospital, and I've spent a lot of time out in the Everglades. I'm an animal trainer. I usually work with dogs, but I've also been called in to work with dolphins, horses, cats and even a few ferrets and skunks."

"Skunk whisperer, eh?"

She sighed, trying once again for patience. "I really like animals and I believe I am able to comprehend what causes certain behaviors," she said.

"Is that why you killed her? She was a meat-eater?"

This was getting worse and worse.

"I have nothing against meat-eaters. We are omnivores. I don't like the way we treat and kill many animals we use as food sources. But no, I don't think people working for slaughter houses need to be murdered in turn."

He leaned closer to her. "She's dead. She was found exactly as you said she would be. There was no way you could know that. Unless you knew her killer or killed her yourself."

Raina leaned back, suddenly angrier than she was frightened.

"I was with a client and a troubled K-9 pup until almost ten o'clock last night. The woman is with the Florida Department of Law Enforcement as is her dog, Jake. They came to me. I didn't leave my apartment after that. We have cameras, so you can check. I left my house at nine this morning to go dress shopping. And then I called in what I saw, and the next thing I knew, I was being picked up. You can check out every move I made—something I assume you're already doing. There was no way I would have had time to get out to the Everglades."

"She's right, you know," a voice said.

Both Raina and Detective MacDonald started. They'd been so intent on one another that they hadn't heard the door quietly open.

They both stared at the man who had entered.

Raina let out a soft gasp.

She knew him.

She hadn't seen him in years and years, and he had definitely changed, but it was him.

Axel? Axel Tiger? The storyteller she had met deep in the Everglades years and years ago?

"Special Agent Tiger. To, uh, what do we owe the...pleasure?" MacDonald asked warily.

Special Agent?

Her mind was working in ridiculous circles. Axel. Here, now, in a blue suit, older, a man, filled out...special agent. Agent of what? Special—why?

"Hey. Yeah, you know we were called in," Axel said quietly, handing MacDonald a paper—something official.

Very official.

MacDonald shot her a hostile and suspicious look and rose, indicating Axel should take the chair.

"Knock yourself out, my friend."

She wasn't sure how sincere the "my friend" part of his words might be.

But Axel nodded, thanked him and took the chair, watching grimly until MacDonald had left the interrogation room.

When the door closed, he turned to Raina. She was surely staring at him just like a stereotypical deer in the headlights.

"Hello, Raina."

She continued to stare. He gave her a weary grimace.

"I'm FBI now," he explained. She hadn't asked the question. Maybe he could read her mind.

She managed a nod. And then because she was worn down and exhausted and hating herself, she added simply, "Dear God, I did not do this, nor do I know who did. I called because I thought I could help." Her voice was barely a whisper.

"I realize that," he said.

Was he trying to trick her? She thought of all the shows she had seen on investigations and questioning. Was this good cop versus bad cop?

She didn't reply.

"And I know," he continued, "you're wishing you'd never called. But you have done us a tremendous service. We both know the Everglades. We understand the landscape is brutal and that a body can be consumed by the creatures, the water and the vegetation there with amazing speed and certainty."

"I shouldn't have called," she said.

"'The only thing necessary for the triumph of evil is for good men to do nothing,'" he quoted. "You did the right thing."

"I don't believe your colleagues see it that way."

"But I do. I know you've told your story again and again, but would you tell it one more time for me? I will listen with an entirely open mind, I promise you."

Raina stared at him, incredulous that a boy from her past was suddenly here now in a somber deep-blue suit. He wore it well. His features had matured, as had his frame. He was more striking than he had been in his youth.

"I understand you grew up to be an animal trainer?" he asked.

"Dogs, mainly. But other animals, too. Mammals, that is," she added. "The occasional bird."

"They say you're the best."

"I don't know who 'they' might be, but I have a good work

ethic and I love all creatures." She winced. "Including human creatures. Mostly."

That brought a real smile to his lips.

"And you grew up to be an FBI agent?" she asked.

He nodded. "I joined the military, managed a college degree that way, and then a friend led me toward the academy and the bureau." He looked at her kindly. "So, what brought you in today?"

"I was planning on attending a fundraiser for a children's foundation on Friday night. I'm speaking, and I was trying to find the right dress to wear. There's a place I like on Sunset near the mall that carries local designs. Anyway, I tried on a dress, looked in the mirror and, instead of my reflection, I saw the crime scene. I know how ridiculous that sounds. But I'd heard that the body of a woman was recently found in the Everglades—or what remained of her. And a few months back, the remains of a man were discovered in a similar state. When I saw that..." She paused, looking down, wincing.

"You're a decent human being. When you saw her lying there, you had to call."

She looked up at him. "You believe I saw her in the mirror?"

He nodded at her gravely.

She sat back, staring at him skeptically. "Is this an act? If not, aren't you worried about what your colleagues are going to think when they listen to the recording?"

"We're not being recorded."

It seemed he was telling the truth.

He stood and said, "Come on. I'm going to get you out of here. Except I need you to do me a favor. Will you come with me to where the body was found?"

Again, she looked at him as if he'd lost his mind. She shook her head slowly and her voice came out as a whisper again.

"I really don't want to see—"

"The body is gone," he said softly.

"I don't know how that can help," she said.

"I don't, either, but it's worth a shot. We don't know what's going on. Let's face it, the Everglades is an area that's unique and wonderful in many ways with a fantastic history, but it also has a history of bodies being dumped. You heard about the latest victims. We believe these murders are related, we just don't know how. At least, not yet." He was quiet a beat, watching her before he continued. "I work with a special unit of the bureau. We are willing to look in just about any direction—with open minds. Have you ever had something like this happen to you before? The mirror thing?"

"No!"

"Then, who knows? To me, that suggests there's a reason you did this time. You might be able to really help."

He was serious, she realized.

Either that or she was being played.

"Two things," he continued. "I know I'm asking a lot. I know you have a life. What I'd like is to return to the dress shop. We'll purchase the dress."

She frowned. "You want me to put it back on? No, no, no, no, no!"

The door opened again; it was Detective MacDonald. There were a few seconds when she feared he was coming in to officially arrest her, then she saw her older brother, Robert, had arrived.

Raina adored her brother. He was tall and lean with hair redder than hers that he kept neatly and closely cropped. He was a prosecuting attorney for the county, but he managed to keep that separate from his life. He was married, a great dad who attended T-ball every weekend, and had maintained a sense of humor.

"I'm here to advise my sister of her legal rights. Oh, wait, you people have nothing. She tried to help you. You have nothing against her," he said.

Raina expected MacDonald to launch into the fact she'd known the exact location of the victim's body.

He didn't get a chance.

Axel had risen.

"Robert, Raina is entirely free to go. But I've asked for her help."

"Axel!" Robert said with surprise.

Raina looked at the two. They knew one another.

"I'm really not up to speed here," Robert said, addressing Axel. "I came because Raina called. Another body in the Everglades?"

Axel nodded.

"And Raina can help?"

"Only if she's willing."

No.

No, no, no. She wasn't willing.

But then she remembered why she had called in the first place. Someone had been cruelly murdered. And she was annoyed that Axel's quoting Edmund Burke had gotten into her head. If she did nothing... Was she helping evil? Turning her back on the poor woman she'd seen in the mirror?

"Raina," Axel said quietly. "Please. We could really use your help."

She looked at her brother.

"Kiddo, your call. But he's one of the good guys."

MacDonald let out a snort and left the room.

"You two know each other?" she asked. Axel was five or six years older than she was; her brother only had her by three.

"We've worked a case together before," Robert said. "He found some evidence it seemed no one else could."

Great. If not in awe of the man, her brother greatly admired him.

"Are you scheduled with clients today?" Axel asked politely.

She was frowning again. She needed to say she was busy—already late for a training session.

She wasn't. She tried not to frown. She had purposely kept the day clear, thinking she was going to work with Titan, her Belgian shepherd, for the little show they'd be doing at the fundraiser. But it wouldn't have been much work. Titan was an amazing dog. He seemed to understand when they were doing something important and he loved children. He'd be at his best.

And she had till Friday night.

But the dress!

He wanted her to put it back on. He wanted to buy the damned thing. Fine, then. They'd buy it. She'd put it on, and then she'd burn it!

She lifted her hands, tempted to touch her face and smooth out the wrinkles she had surely put there permanently.

"You'll come with me?" Axel asked.

Again, she looked at Robert.

Some protector!

He seemed all for it.

"Um, I guess," she said softly.

Robert looked at Axel. "I'll leave her in your hands, then."

That was it. She stood. "Robert, I don't need to be left in anyone's hands, thank you. I'll do what I can to help. But please, that was—"

"Sorry! Sorry!" Robert said. "It's just, well, I have to get back to work. I was worried—"

"Thank you. And I'm fine."

Her brother grinned. "Love you, sis! I'm out of here."

He was gone, and suddenly she was alone with Axel again.

"Come on," he said.

"We just walk out of here?"

"We just walk out of here."

She nodded. He waited, holding the door open for her. She walked out the door, and then through the station, anxious to be outside, afraid someone was going to stop them, that robotic or alien arms would reach out and drag her back.

Some of the officers did watch them as they left.

But they stepped outside at last. It was summer and the sun was high overhead, so bright she blinked against it. She hadn't known how cold she had been until she felt the warmth of it on her skin.

A hot summer's day. Humid. The kind they often whined about.

And it was perfect and beautiful.

"I'm across in the lot," Axel said, indicating where he was parked.

They walked together. And then, when they reached the car, she turned around to stare at him.

"I don't get it. No one believed me. The more I tried to explain, the more I doubted myself. The more ridiculous I sounded. But you believed me. Why?"

He'd put sunglasses on and she couldn't see his eyes.

But she did see the slight twist to his lips.

"Because you saw it," he offered. "Because you saw the pirate ship, sailing over our great river of grass."

CHAPTER TWO

"Is that it?" Axel asked.

The friendly clerk in the dress store greeted Raina politely, probably assuming she had returned for the dress, unaware of Raina's reasons for abandoning it earlier. When she had seen what she had seen, she must not have screamed or done anything that alerted anyone to the fact something else might be going on.

She'd gotten out of the dress—and out of the store.

Now, watching her, Axel was certain she was hoping the dress had been sold, or it had mysteriously disappeared.

It had not. The clerk, a pretty round woman of about forty with a nice if slightly nervous smile, beamed with plastic pleasure when they approached her.

"I thought you'd be back. Oh, with the date this time, eh? Having him check it out?" the clerk asked. "It's perfect on her, just right with those curves, and that little waist. I had a feeling you'd be back. In fact, I was so certain, I set it aside! After I picked it up off the floor of the dressing room when you, uh, ran out," she added, a slight touch of reproach slipping into her voice.

"I'm so sorry. I realized I had, um, somewhere to be. But yes, we're back for the dress," Raina said.

"Wonderful, dear. I have it right here!" The friendly clerk turned around to a rack of clothing, riffled through it for a minute and produced a blue dress. She then asked with a wince, "Did you want to try it on again, dear?"

Axel glanced quickly at Raina. She didn't give away much, but she was going very pale, which was really something since her skin was like porcelain. Her hair was a dark auburn, framing the lightness of her complexion. Her eyes, he realized, he had remembered through the years. They weren't brown, green or even hazel, but rather a shade that was like a true amber, unusual and striking, and now, again, adding to the pale shade of her face.

"I—uh..."

She was stuttering, so Axel answered for her.

"We don't need her to try it again. We'll just take it."

"Oh, thank the good Lord!" the woman said, her words whispered and barely discernable.

Raina turned to stare at him, something incredulous in her expression now, a touch of color rising to her cheek. She moved awkwardly to ease her shoulder bag to the counter, ready to produce her credit card.

Axel smiled, not sure if his words would make it harder or ease a burden. "My gift to you, darling!" he said quickly, handing the woman one of his own credit cards.

The clerk took it, babbling away about how beautiful Raina was going to be and what a lovely couple they made. Raina just stood still, saying nothing.

But he needed more from the place. "This is a very special dress. I would imagine not many people have tried it on."

"The only woman I know of who tried it on is your lovely little lady here," the clerk said. "But I'm not always here, of course. There are three of us during the late shift and on

Saturdays and Sundays. Someone else may have tried it on. I don't know. But I assure you, there's nothing wrong with it. Clothing is often tried on. It's good to know it fits."

"Oh, I didn't think there was anything wrong with the dress."

He'd have to come back; maybe one of the clerks did remember who else had tried on the dress—perhaps his victim was even someone who came often.

If his suspicions were correct, the information could help identify the body.

Once they were outside, Raina said, "You know I will never ever in a thousand years really wear that thing," she said.

"Yes, I know."

"That was an expensive…"

"Tool," he told her. "It's a tool, and well worth it if it can help. Now, do you want to go to the local offices and try it on there? I didn't think you wanted to try it on in the shop again."

"No! I barely made it out of there looking halfway sane the first time."

"Then we'll head to the offices."

"Would it be possible for me to try it on somewhere a little more private?" she asked. She hesitated, wincing. "I, uh, I think my house will be the best place. It's not far. I don't know how much you remember about Miami, but it's just off Sunset and US 1, High Pines area."

"That's fine."

She looked at him. "I have a dog."

"Um, that's nice?"

"A big dog."

"Is he vicious?"

"No! Well, he's protective."

"I'm assuming I'll be fine if you introduce me."

She nodded. "Yes, exactly. He's just really big. He scares

some people, but I can assure you, he's an amazing, smart animal."

"Then he'll know if someone means you harm—and I don't."

They arrived at her house. It was a well-kept home, probably built in the 1950s, concrete block and stucco with a handsome stone fence around it and a carved wooden gate. The yard held a massive avocado tree to the one side and a few palms to the other.

She led him up the porch steps to the front door, talking nervously. "I love where I am. Easy access to everything I need. I bought it from my parents. They always wanted to move down to Key West and finally did a few years ago. I love Key West, too, but I like to stay closer to most of my clients with quick and easy access to an airport. Of course, Miami International is superbusy, we all know that. Come in... Hey, Titan!" she called.

The dog was already at the door, and as she'd said, it was big. It was a shepherd, Axel thought, though the animal's fur was pitch-black. He wasn't sure what kind, but he was the biggest shepherd Axel had ever seen.

The animal barked—a deep bark with a hint of a growl.

"It's all right, Titan. We have a guest."

Axel set his hands out for the dog to sniff. Titan backed away a bit, then looked at Raina, wildly wagging his tail.

"He's a Belgian shepherd," Raina told him. "A rescue. Someone bought him and decided he was too big. Anyway..."

She paused. Titan was sniffing Axel's fingers and wagging his tail. Axel barely had to bend to scratch the dog behind the ears. "Well, I guess you two will be fine," she said.

"He's great," Axel said. "And amazing for a rescue animal."

"He works with me, too."

"In your work as a trainer?"

She nodded. "Dogs are wonderful, but they're usually a

mirror of the way they're treated. I mean, sometimes aggression has been bred into them. But they're such amazing companions. Not that he's my only companion—I didn't mean it that way. Well, he is my only roommate. I just meant that—never mind. I went to college knowing what I wanted to do and my degree is in animal science. Lots of biology and psychology, really. Here I am, rambling away…"

"Because you don't want to put the dress on," he said. "Listen, I can't make you do this, and I wouldn't, either, but we're at a loss here, with no evidence chain to follow, and when I heard you had called the body in… I was hoping we could find something out. Anything."

"Because you believe I only saw the body in the mirror because I tried a dress on."

"Yes."

She looked at him doubtfully. The dress—on a hanger with a plastic wrap over it—was draped over his arm. He offered it to her.

She took it. "Okay, I'll just step in my room. There's a mirror in there. I'll put the dress on and then call when I'm ready."

"Thank you."

"Uh, make yourself at home. Can I get you anything?"

"I'm fine, thank you," he assured her, hunkering down. "I'll get to know Titan."

Raina disappeared into the bedroom. Titan watched her go, but kept a wary eye on Axel. He was happy enough to be scratched behind the ears.

"No one bare-handed would mess with her with you around, huh, buddy?" he said to the dog, looking around the house as he did.

It was nice. Not elegant, but nice. The living room furniture was handsomely coordinated in leather and tan fabric. The house had a fireplace with a mantel and he wondered if

it was maybe older than he thought. Despite Florida's reputation for heat, he could remember several winters when—if
only for a few days—the temperature had hit the low thirties. Now air-conditioning systems reversed for the sporadic
cold days, but many homes here had once been built with
fireplaces.

The mantel was filled with family pictures; her older
brother with a woman Axel assumed to be his wife, her parents with her and her brother when they were young, a few
pictures of dogs and one of Raina on a big, beautiful quarter horse.

The living room offered a hall to the left with bedrooms,
he assumed, since she had gone that way. Straight ahead was
a dining room and through that he could see the door to the
kitchen. Beyond that, a Florida-style family room with glass
windows that opened to the backyard.

He was still surveying the house and scratching the dog's
ears when both he and Titan heard a terrified scream.

Dog and man jumped as one and rushed to the bedroom.
Titan woofed. Axel shouted her name. "Raina!"

Two doors were open along the hallway, but one was
closed. He twisted the knob, instinct and logic telling him
she would have closed the door when she went in to change.

She was there, dead still in front of a full-length swivel
mirror, just staring in a dress that admittedly looked amazing on her.

He saw her reflection in the glass, the look of pure horror on her face.

He didn't see what she was seeing.

"Raina?" he said.

Trying to reach her, he almost tripped over Titan. The
dog was doing the same. At first, Raina didn't seem to see
either of them.

He caught her gently by the arms, turning her to him. She

still didn't seem to see him, but she didn't protest his hold. And she was suddenly grasping wildly for her back, for the zipper, anxious to get the garment off.

He was afraid that, as she struggled in his arms and he attempted to help her, Titan would get protective and attack him. But the big shepherd stayed seated nearby, whining, worried and anxious.

The zipper was down. Heedless of his touch, she shimmied out of the dress. She was clad in only her bra and panties. Throwing the dress across the room, she sobbed as she fell into his arms.

"You saw it again?" he asked softly.

"As if I was there. As if I could smell the blood," she whispered.

Then suddenly she seemed to realize how exposed she was, and in a relative stranger's arms. She pulled away and they both stared at each other. Awkward, to say the least.

There was a directional quilt at the foot of her bed. He grabbed it and wrapped it around her shoulders. She swallowed, nodding. He thought of it as a "thanks."

Titan thumped his tail on the floor and whined.

"Titan!" she said. She knelt down by the dog. "Sorry to scare you, boy. I'm good—really."

She wasn't. Titan's affection sent her toppling backward, losing the quilt. Axel offered her a hand and she accepted it with a wince and a quick, "Thank you."

She regained her balance and awkwardly retrieved her hand. "I'm sorry. This is all so bizarre. I swear I'm not just being dramatic or seeking attention. I like my life. At least, I did like my life. Wow. I'm rambling again. I don't know what is happening. Maybe this helped find a body. But it does nothing to help the woman. Or to catch the killer. I wish—"

"I know it's asking a lot, but are you still okay to take a ride out to the site with me?"

She stared at him.

She had a right to say no. He was asking a civilian to help in a murder investigation. One who was terrified by her own visions. She had every reason to back out, but instead she inhaled deeply, still staring at him. "Do you really think it would help? I mean, this mirror thing with the dress…it's ridiculous. And I'm not sure—"

"I'm not, either. And I know I'm asking a lot. I know you have a life and this has been…" He paused, grimacing. "Upsetting, to say the least. But—"

"Yes."

"Yes?"

"Yes," she repeated firmly. "I'm flexible until Friday evening. I have to be at a fundraiser. Titan and I are part of the entertainment for the night. If you want to go now, it's fine. I'm just going to put on some jeans."

He nodded. "I want you to be sure."

"I'm okay," she assured him. "I'm not going to lose it again, I promise. No more screaming or stumbling around. No matter what."

"Hey, anyone would scream if they saw what you did. I'll wait for you in the living room."

He turned and left the room. To his surprise, the dog padded out with him.

Maybe it was more important now for Titan to keep an eye on him than it was to watch out for his owner.

Raina joined them in a matter of minutes.

"House is nice," he told her.

"Thanks."

"You live alone?"

"With what I do, I prefer to live alone." She grimaced. "My clients usually have four legs and I work with them here sometimes. One of my friends, Lucia—actually you would've met her years ago, too—thought we'd make great roommates.

But while she loves Titan, she's afraid of a lot of other dogs. I knew it wouldn't work."

"I see," he said, and then couldn't resist asking, "Does your vocation make dating hard?"

She shrugged. "If you don't like animals—dogs especially—you probably don't want to be dating me." She turned the question around. "What about you? Does being a fed make it hard? Oh, are you married? I suppose I have no reason to assume…"

"No, I'm not married," he said. "And yeah, my vocation makes it a little difficult sometimes. Anyway, let's get going, shall we?"

"Of course." She headed for the door, and then swung back. "Titan, back soon. Guard the house, okay, boy?"

The dog woofed as if he'd understood her every word. He followed them to the door, but made no attempt to come out.

"That's a good dog," he told her.

She smiled. "Most dogs are good dogs. They just need good people. So, what's it like where you're living? What have you been doing the last decade or so?"

"Military, the academy, the FBI," he told her.

"Ah." She was quiet for a minute as they got into his rental car. When they were seated, she asked, "What about your family? From what I can recall, your dad was Miccosukee and your mom wasn't. Is that correct?"

"Good memory. One grandmother was a Miccosukee, and one grandfather was a Seminole. One grandfather was from Norway, and the other grandmother was from England."

She laughed. "All-American boy. Your dad had a couple of homes, right?"

"My mom and dad did, yes. Two homes, one on tribal land and another in Coconut Grove. He was in construction."

"Right, and your mom was a teacher. Are they still around here somewhere?"

"My dad passed away three years ago. My mother loves to come back and visit, but she moved to New York City. She had some cousins there and she's able to volunteer at a few schools, which she loves."

"That's nice for her. I'm sorry about your dad."

"Thanks." He hesitated. "He had a good life. He was older when I was born. I was able to be with him when he died, and so was my mom. Best that could be hoped for."

"I'm glad," she murmured.

She fell silent. The drive from her place to the Tamiami Trail and then straight out west wasn't bad. It was midday and while rush hour in the Miami area could be brutal, they managed to avoid it.

They were headed out on the Trail, crossing over onto Miccosukee reservation land, when she spoke again.

"I still don't get it. You believe what I saw. You didn't call the police to escort me to an institution. And you're bringing me out here."

He was silent. When he was about to speak, she broke in with, "And don't tell me about a ghostly pirate ship. I mean, such things are suggestive, right? A foggy night, deep in the Glades. One could imagine all kinds of things. Over and above the real things like the alligators and snakes. Boas and pythons stretching well over ten feet these days."

"And not native," he added.

She persisted. "Right. So?"

He looked ahead at the road. They were nearing the place where the body had been found, rolled almost to the water of the canal, hidden by bracken and brush and tree limbs and the natural fall of the embankment.

"Hey!" she said.

He glanced her way quickly. "In my line of work, I have seen all manner of things most people might not believe or accept. And I've discovered taking help in any form—however unbelievable others might think it—solves more cases than refusing to believe or follow leads that may not be what is customarily expected."

She was frustrated, he thought, but she fell silent suddenly.

They had arrived. There were still police cars there—one from Dade County and one belonging to the Miccosukee police. A lone forensics vehicle remained.

Axel looked carefully at Raina as they exited the car. She appeared level and fine with their arrival. Her head was high, as if she'd taken enough mockery for the day and was ready for anything.

He was glad the police cars remaining belonged to Andrew and Nigel. He introduced them to Raina and neither asked questions about her being there. They greeted her politely and then told Axel they were heading out shortly. The autopsy wouldn't be until the next day and the forensics team was just about finished.

As they moved down the embankment, Raina said quietly, "They didn't ask why I was here."

"They're old friends."

"And so they let you do what you want?"

"We've worked cases before."

"Ah. So they know you're weird?"

He smiled. "They know I'm weird." He glanced her way. "I've known them since I was a kid. We all knew we'd go into law enforcement. We just went different ways."

He thought she might say, "I see"—without really seeing anything at all.

She didn't. She just kept walking with him. She'd worn the right shoes for the area, short boots with gripping soles, but she still slipped on a strip of mud. He caught her quickly and she smiled and added, "Thanks. I don't really feel like wearing a lot of this swampy muck!"

Then they were at the site, and she went silent and dead still. He stayed close, but drew his hand away, watching her.

She closed her eyes. She saw something; he knew it by the way her body tensed.

But she didn't cry out. She opened her eyes at last and looked at him.

"You saw the killing—or the killer?" he asked hopefully.

Maybe that was way too much to hope for.

She shook her head. "No, but I saw her. The victim. She was scared, but I don't think she believed she was going to be killed. I think she thought she'd been kidnapped. She wasn't dead on the way out here. She was killed here. She wasn't in a trunk. I could see it or sense it or…something. I don't even know how to explain. But she was seated in the back seat of a car. She was bound and gagged, and something was over her head. Like a burlap bag. It had that burlap smell like the bags horse feed comes in." She stopped speaking. "She was led out here. I think it might have been something like a straight-edged razor that killed her—something supersharp. Right across the throat. Fast. She was almost dead before she knew she'd been hit." She looked at him incredulously. "How could I possibly know all this?"

"I don't have the answer to that," he told her. "I just know it is."

She nodded.

"Are you all right?"

"Yes. Absolutely. I'm puzzled and confused. And so sorry for the poor woman. She was so frightened in the car, but she didn't believe she was going to die. Maybe none of us ever believes we're going to die—until it happens. Maybe there's a way for me to see more. I'm not sure how, but maybe you know?"

He couldn't help but smile at that. "Nope. You're unique."

"Ah, but you saw the pirate ship!"

"I've never touched anything—or had anything touch me, like that dress—and had visions. Connections. Closest I've heard about is a friend whose fiancée saw events during a past-life regression. Which, honestly, most of the time, I do believe relies on the power of suggestion. Just as I think most mediums are brilliant showmen—or women."

"Oh. Okay, then."

"I'd like to have you speak with Andrew and Nigel. I think Nigel has headed back into the city, but Andrew has a place not far from here. Would you mind speaking with him?"

"No, of course not. As long as—"

"Trust me. He's not going to make fun of you."

"Because he's seen the pirate ship?"

"Maybe. He has seen it. And he's just not the kind of guy to mock others." Fearing she'd change her mind, he added, "He's got an unbelievable horse. Two horses actually—one he's had forever, a quarter horse, sweet guy. And he has a mustang. I don't know the whole history, but so wild he almost became glue. Andrew, of course, couldn't let that happen and bought the horse. Maybe you're a horse whisperer, too?"

"The key to animals is understanding them." She made a face. "We human beings are animals, too, and a bit more complex. But people, like animals, respond better to kindness than whips and chains. Okay, you've sold me. Let's go see this horse."

CHAPTER THREE

Andrew Osceola was still in uniform when they arrived at his house.

Raina had always felt that as a Miamian, she had appreciated the Everglades and knew something about the "great river of grass"—at least in her area, since it stretched north in the center of the state for over two hundred miles.

But she had no idea where she was. Some of the land was tribal, and some of it was part of Everglades National Park.

She assumed they were on tribal lands. Axel told her they weren't as remote as she thought when they arrived along a grit-and-stone drive to a house in what appeared to be the middle of nowhere. But Axel pointed her to another trail and told her that it led to one of the Miccosukee communities, not so far away, not even a mile.

A mile through the swampy Glades seemed like a fair distance to her!

But Andrew Osceola had a freshly painted and sprawling single-story house with a large tiled front porch and a path leading to the front door along with a large barn on his property.

It seemed very isolated to her.

"Honestly, it's not as isolated as it looks. His whole family is in the general area. Super people, but I think he needed a little space. And he has his horses."

"Ah," she said. Maybe Axel was a mind reader. They headed up the tiled path to the house. Andrew opened the door as they reached it.

"I was hoping you were coming," he told them.

Raina smiled weakly, accepting the hand he stretched out to her. She assumed he and Axel were about the same age. Like Axel, he was tall and fit. His handshake was firm. His cropped hair allowed for a short fringe of black to fall over his forehead and his eyes were dark brown. He was a handsome man, with a quick smile of sincere welcome.

"I can't believe he got you out here. But if I remember right, you came on some of the camping trips years ago, right?"

"I did," she said. "And with all the kids, I'm surprised you remember."

"You were interested in everything as I recall. Not everyone is, I get it. I was a kid, too. Sometimes that kind of trip is just a really cool getaway. And let's face it—half the kids would rather be at Disney World."

"I love it out here. Well, I wouldn't want to be in the middle of the Glades alone or anything, but the birds are beautiful and it's so close to the big city—and so far away."

"I love it, too. Come in!"

Raina didn't know what she was expecting as they stepped inside, but Andrew's house was a warm and contemporary home, filled with intriguing Native American art. She paused, studying a figurine.

"That's Sitting Bull. Done by a friend of mine."

"A Miccosukee?"

"No." Andrew grinned. "Not a Sioux, either. It was crafted

by an amazing Cheyenne woman who comes to a lot of our festivals. She's brilliant. I have one she did of Osceola, too. *The* Osceola, I mean…my name is Osceola."

"Osceola is your name?"

"Yes, tribal name. And—in this world of social security and medical insurance—surname!"

"A great name. As Osceola was evidently a great man."

"Captured under a flag of truce."

"I know."

"Of course you do!" Andrew said.

Axel cleared his throat. "Andrew, anything?"

"I was hoping you had something. But let's head to the office."

Raina followed the men through the living room with its comfortable sofas, chair, sculptures and artwork, through the dining room, kitchen and out to a family room with a faux fur rug on the floor, another hearth and a large desk and stacks of papers, neatly aligned.

There were comfortable leather chairs facing the desk and one behind it. Andrew took his seat, handing a stack of papers to Axel. "I'm sure you have copies of all these. You are probably ahead of me on studying what info we've got. Can't find a relationship between the victims. If someone was studying victimology, they'd be going nuts. Between the two we know of, nothing is alike. The killings are like execution-style with a knife, but—" he paused and looked at Raina "—what have you got?"

She looked at Axel apprehensively. How many people would believe this craziness?

He inclined a brow in her direction, silently asking if it was okay if he spoke for her.

She lowered her head in agreement. He was welcome to run with it.

"I think these are executions—or murders for convenience.

I don't think we have a serial killer on our hands, but rather someone—or some*ones*—with a clear agenda regarding people who need to be disposed of. Maybe this person started out with just one murder and then realized that killing people and dumping them in the Everglades worked. Nature is brutal on evidence. After a body has been out here for any length of time, the elements and creatures—not just our big, scary predators, but those tiny little bastards, bugs—take their toll. Raina saw our victim. She was in the back seat of a car. She was scared, but still hopeful. A burlap or canvas bag or something was over her head. She didn't know where she was going. She wasn't assaulted, she wasn't tortured—she was swiftly dispatched." He looked at Raina. "With a straight razor, we believe."

Andrew looked at him, nodding slowly. "Not a crazed serial killer, but a serial killer nonetheless. Someone who has discovered they can get rid of certain problems by getting rid of people."

"That's what I'm seeing with all this," Axel said.

"Hmm," Andrew said. "You haven't talked to Nigel yet, eh?"

"No, nor my offices. Figured after the hours you'd worked, we could find you here."

"We need to work on this," Andrew said.

He didn't seem to doubt anything that had been said, but it also seemed to Raina that he wanted to speak with Axel alone.

"A little off subject, but I hear you have a horse," she said.

He brightened, looking at her, and then frowned. "He's a bit of a wild thing. Did you want to go riding? I have an old quarter horse, too. Jacob. He's the sweetest thing in the world. And if you stay on the path between here and the village, you should be fine. Our resident gator, Big Ole Mac, isn't here—he has his home over at the visitor's village. But of course, you know not to pull an alligator's tail—"

"Trust me. I know not to pull an alligator's tail."

"And to watch out for—"

"Poisonous snakes—rattler, pygmy rattler, coral snake, Eastern diamondback, cottonmouth and southern cottonhead," Raina said. "And the new constrictors like pythons and boas. We're on a hardwood hammock between here and there, I imagine?"

He nodded, smiling.

"It isn't safe," Axel warned. "If you're going to ride around, you should be in the company of someone who knows the area well."

"I'll bet you ride well!" Andrew said.

"I'm okay. You won't see me at any rodeos," Raina said.

Andrew grinned.

"It's not safe, especially since we don't know what's going on around here," Axel said.

"I'll probably just meet the horses. Not to worry," Raina said.

She let out a breath of relief as she turned and fled, not really so sure she'd be fine if she ran across any of the creatures mentioned, but suddenly needing to be away. Both men seemed to believe in her.

Any sane person would think she was crazy.

Her footsteps carried her out of the house. She paused, suddenly envisioning a horror scene in which she encountered a half dozen alligators and a slew of poisonous snakes and constrictors awaiting her.

There wasn't a thing in the yard. She didn't even hear the buzz of a mosquito.

With a sigh she headed out to the giant barn, which surely housed the horses.

It did.

The barn offered a clean-swept floor and a tack-room office that was neat and clean, as well. There were stalls for several horses, but Andrew kept only two—the quarter horse, Jacob, and the mustang, Wild Thing. Each had a handsomely carved plaque on their door, announcing them.

"Hi, guys!" she said.

Both moved to greet her curiously, noses and necks sticking out over their stable doors.

She stroked both first, talking to them, just continuing conversation so they would become accustomed to her voice. Jacob was like a very big puppy dog.

Wild Thing was a little more reticent, but eventually came around.

She thought Jacob was a running quarter; he was a very big horse, buckskin in color.

Wild Thing was much smaller, bay in color and, Raina discovered, a lover of having the area right behind his ears scratched.

She had no concept of just how long she'd been there until she heard footsteps and turned to see Axel and Andrew come into the stable area.

"You seem to be doing just fine," Andrew said.

Axel was silent, walking over to join her. Evidently, the horses knew him. They both greeted him with snickers and whinnies. She quickly knew why. He had come bearing gifts, offering both of the horses apples before turning to Raina.

"Thank you," he said. "I'll get you home now."

"Um, okay." She turned to Andrew. "I loved meeting your horses and seeing your home. The horses are great, and your home is lovely."

"Why, thank you," Andrew said, smiling. "I'm sure I'll be seeing you again."

She started when she felt Axel's hand on her shoulder. She wasn't sure why. He'd taken her hand and held her several times.

Once when she'd been barely dressed.

"Sorry," she said. "I guess I'm jumpy."

"I didn't mean to startle you."

Andrew walked with them back to the car, opening the passenger-side door for her as Axel walked around to the driver's side.

Andrew closed the door, leaned down and told her again how good it had been to see her—even if the situation wasn't ideal.

Then he waved to Axel, and Axel eased the car out of the drive, along the small dirt-and-grit road, back to the Tamiami Trail.

"What is it?" he asked softly.

She turned to him with surprise. "Um—what?"

"You're silent and you look worried."

She shook her head. "You're just accepting all this. Andrew just accepted all this. I don't get it."

"We've learned over time."

"What did you talk about when I left? Assuming it wasn't confidential," she said.

"Just putting together what you said. It wouldn't have been that hard to dispose of a body the way the last woman was set down low on the embankment right by the water. Smarter, though, than pushing it into the water where it might have drifted. People fish along the canal. Where it was—not visible from the road, covered with bracken but set in a truly damp and watery area where alligators and other creatures roam— was still easily accessible. The others were discovered badly decomposed and deeper into the Glades. I'd wager whoever is doing this knows a fair amount about the Everglades. That would suggest someone who lives out here or someone who works out here or even someone who has spent a great deal of time out here and knows some of the back paths—like the way to Andrew's house. You don't have to be a ranger or native to study and know a place, but I do believe it's someone who has been local for years—local to Miami-Dade or Collier County at least, maybe closer, or maybe just someone who works here or visits here."

"That's vague."

"Vague is all we've got. I also feel there has to be a relationship between the victims. What it is—we're lost at the moment. We need identities on two. And we will get them. Then we start putting puzzle pieces together."

"Sometimes killers are never caught," she said softly.

"Not this one." He glanced her way. "I think the killer's thought pattern ran in that direction—dump bodies in the Glades. No way to connect them. Leave no evidence. Let nature be the clean-up crew. But still, I think this guy knows the Everglades, where people go and where they might go."

"But this last victim. He just had to pull off the road and get his victim close to the canal where there was a little mound over the embankment, just enough to hide it from the road."

"But people travel Tamiami Trail all day."

"Not so much at night. The killer would know when to do it."

She fell silent, shaking her head, wincing inwardly. She really had nothing to do with any of this. She'd tried on a dress.

"What will you do now?"

"I'm going to go back to the dress shop." He glanced her way. "I'm going to meet with every clerk they have and ask who was in the shop trying that dress on. We may not need help. We might soon know who she was. They might get a match on the victim's fingerprints or dental work. Tomorrow there will be an autopsy, and the forensic investigators may have something. I'll keep you up on everything if you like. And of course, if you think of anything else—"

"Of course!" she said. "I'm available. I mean, I work, but I'm clear until the fundraiser Friday night. I planned my time for it. I mean, Titan is great, but I always like to run him through the paces before we're part of something."

"What is the fundraiser again?" he asked.

"It's for something called the Children's Place," she told him. She hesitated, frowning. "Life is full of coincidences, isn't it?" she murmured.

"It is? What's the coincidence?"

"Well, the land and the buildings—which need lots of work—are on our way back. We can see it, if you like. Just make a right when you get to the Miccosukee Hotel and Casino.

"I'm delighted to be a part of this fundraiser. It rather hits two birds with one stone. Wait—that's a bad analogy. The property was bought by a rich philanthropist and donated to the organizers. It's going to be wonderful—a refuge for abused and abandoned animals and an education center for children—many of them homeless or orphans. I'm not in on the planning, but the kids will have the opportunity to interact with the animals. And there's a lot more. There will be reading programs, sports programs. It's brilliant. I believe most of the land was unincorporated Miami-Dade County. It's huge, tons of acreage. There are a few houses on it. I think, at one time, someone had wanted it to be a family compound. Anyway, the fundraiser is a dinner and an auction, and there are all kinds of businesses donating. You can see where they're breaking ground soon. The event is being held in Coral Gables, at a hotel right on Miracle Mile."

"I'd love to see where this place will be, and actually, would it possible for me to attend the fundraiser?"

"Yes, of course. One of my old friends is running it along with the organizers. In fact, she was camping with us way back when."

"It's Friday night?"

"At seven. I'll text you the details. Oh, I don't have your number."

"You need to have my number. And I need yours." He rattled off numbers and she fumbled in her bag for her phone, repeating them.

"Call me," he said. "Then you'll be in my phone."

She called him. He answered by pushing a button on the steering wheel. "Hey, turn up there, right?"

"Right," she said into the phone. Then she quickly hung up, shaking her head, and added, "We head right, and then down a half mile or so and take another little road."

He grinned.

When they reached the property, he pulled off the road and looked across the expanse of the grounds. In the rear, they could see the houses and a paddock and stables. They opened the doors and took a few steps away from the car.

"It's amazing it's here, really."

He glanced at her. "Not quite so amazing. We are on the edge of the Everglades."

"I have friends almost in the Everglades. Especially up in the western area of Broward County. They keep building farther and farther west."

He nodded. "Well, if this comes to fruition, it will be great. It is an wonderful piece of property—and almost in the Everglades. In fact, at one time, it might have been. When I was little, half of this property didn't exist out here. It was the sticks."

"Yeah," she said.

"Well, guess I'd better get you home," he said.

He walked around, opening the passenger-side door for her. She slid into the car, quiet as he started to drive.

He was silent for a few minutes. "Who is the friend?"

"Her name is Elly Taylor. She's an event coordinator. I went all the way through school with her—until college. But a lot

and become scientists. And some can touch what can't be seen. How—I have no idea. Nor do I think there is anyone out there at this moment who does completely understand something so very complex. We have worked with all of the many unusual methods to find the truth.

"I think I told you that one young woman, now a friend, went into a past-life regression and saw things that were impossible to see. She herself didn't go to the past—which I seldom believe, anyway, and trust me, I shouldn't be a doubting individual. But in her case, she could see and feel as another woman. Again, how? I have no idea. And we don't tell everyone our methods, or why we're interested in certain witnesses or individuals who can't be considered witnesses—physically. You saw what you saw, and you led police directly to a victim. We're not judge and jury, we're law enforcement. But for victims—and their families and others—justice is important. And we bring what methods we can to the prosecutors so they can find justice for the victims—the dead and the living.

"Oh, and we try to do so as quickly as possible, though quickly is often impossible. You've seen the news. There will always be a case solved decades after it happened. It can take days, months, even years. But in this case...this killer has been at it awhile. It needs to be solved as quickly as possible. Or more will die." He looked at her over his plate for a minute, gaging her reaction.

Then he shrugged.

"Good choice. The food is great. You should try eating yours."

If she hadn't been so hungry, she might not have eaten. She wasn't sure if she'd been chastised or not. And she was still uneasy. It had only been that morning when she had been at the police station with officers thinking she had to be guilty of something.

She picked up her fork again. The rice and meat were very good, so she concentrated on her food.

He winced suddenly, pausing to look at her again. "I'm sorry, sometimes there's no explanation for what we don't really understand. Even in my unit. We go with what we get. We don't hold the secrets of the universe, or life or death. Though I will tell you this—my work has led me to the definite assurance that there is more."

"I suppose that's good to know," she murmured.

"So a lot of you who went through the school system together are still friends, huh? That's nice. I feel like that's rare."

"You're still friends with Andrew and Detective Ferrer."

"I am. Good point. And I don't live here anymore. It will always be home, of course. And I'm glad when they send me here. But it doesn't mean you get to spend your weekends supporting the home teams with old friends." He offered her a dry grin.

"Do you support your home teams?"

He grinned. "Sure. Were a lot of these friends on that school field trip years ago?"

"Yes, as a matter of fact. Elly Taylor—running the event—was in my class when we came on that trip. I still see Mya Smith—she was Mya Myers then. And, of course, Lucia Hampton, Tate Fielding, Jordan Rivera and a few others. Tate and Jordan both went into law. They're a few years older. I think it was my first year at the school and they were juniors," she said. "Mya had a major crush on Tate. But she met Len Smith a few years later when he transferred in from the north, and they became an incredible couple, in love then, through different colleges and, now, as a married couple.

"I'm sure you'll have at least seen many of the others who will be in attendance. It has a lot of local support. Lucia is teaching at an inner-city school, and she's convinced a lot of kids on the road to bad places that their lives can be changed with a little bit of help—and exposure to something better than the crack houses they grew up in. Oh, and our old chaperones will be there—Loretta Oster and Frank Peters. Those two are still taking kids on field trips out to the Glades. I'm not sure who and how many, but I know we have representatives from both tribes—Seminole and Miccosukee—coming, too. Once it's up and running, I'm imagining airboat rides, ecology and Native culture will be involved in the programs and events offered."

"And you and Titan…perform?"

"I talk about the positive approach to training. And also about the fact that if you haven't read up on big snakes and don't want a pet who will grow to be many feet long, you shouldn't get one. The Everglades is not a good place to dump pets. Then I talk about my work with dogs, and Titan does a little math, a few tricks, interacts with a guest and sings. We lighten up the mood—make people happy to give money."

"Well, that sounds great. I'm glad I'm going to get to see it."

"Do you have a dog?"

"I did once." He glanced her way. "You might remember him. Great animal. My folks watched him while I was in the service."

"You don't have him anymore?"

"He made it to almost eighteen years old. Then he passed away."

"And you don't have a dog now?"

"I would love to have a dog. Right now, I don't. I have a cat. Friends—coworkers—look after him when I'm traveling. It works with a cat. I travel too much to have a dog."

"A cat," she repeated, amused.

"Cats are funny?"

"Cats are great," she said with a laugh. "Just—big, tall guy, FBI. I pictured you with a bull mastiff or a Great Dane or some such pet, not a kitten."

"Sheila's not a kitten. Full grown, very old cat. She's a Hemingway cat—you know, six toes. I adopted her before college. Someone had thrown her out on the Tamiami Trail. She was a kitten then, so I'm thinking she's about fourteen or so now. Still healthy."

Raina couldn't help but smile.

"Hey! There's nothing wrong with a rescue kitten!"

"I'm a huge believer in rescuing pets. I think it's great that you rescued her."

"So what are you smirking at?"

"I'm not smirking!"

"You are."

"No, no. I'm just smiling. Sheila—it just seems a bit odd for a pet. I mean, I've heard odder. I just didn't think you'd own a cat. Named Sheila."

"Hey. I had named her Sheena. You know, like a jungle cat. 'Sheena, Queen of the Jungle.' A lot of the little kids kept coming out with Sheila. I gave up and called her Sheila."

"I like it. Great cat name. What was your dog's name?"

"Timothy. Fantastic animal. He had belonged to a tribal member who was moving, and I always loved the dog, so at that time, my dad was still alive and he and my mom were in the area… Anyway, it's not important. The food here was great. Thank you for stopping with me."

"Thank you. It was great to eat. I'm happy to get the check—"

"No. My unit thanks you. I've got it, and I'll get you home."

He rose, seeking their server, who quickly saw them. In a minute, they were back out in his car, and soon they reached South Miami.

He didn't just leave her but hopped out of the car and came around. He stood there, thanking her again for all that she had done.

"I've probably ruined any chance of you seeing anyone at the dress shop. They close at nine and it's just after now."

"That's all right. I'll go by tomorrow if they haven't gotten anything yet from fingerprints or dental work. People call in missing persons. They might already have something. I'm going to get some sleep." He seemed to hesitate. "I'll call you tomorrow, and if you think of anything—"

"I really hope I don't."

"I understand. But if you do…"

"I'll call. I promise."

"Thank you."

He lingered; she thought he was about to say something else. Something he didn't want to say—or something awkward.

"I…well, it won't matter tomorrow. It might later."

"What?"

"You don't need to see an autopsy."

"No, I don't," she assured him.

"But maybe…"

"Maybe?"

"I might have you come to the morgue with me. If you're willing."

"I—I'd help in any way I could. But I don't see how. I don't believe I knew her. I really think I would know if I did. So…"

"Seems to me it's all in the touch," he said, and he hesitated again and then added softly, "All in your touch."

CHAPTER FOUR

"A pretty thing, she was," Brianna Adair, the clerk working the late shift at the dress shop Thursday night, told Axel. Brianna had informed him that she was from County Cork, but loving South Florida. A delightful lilt sounded in her voice as she spoke—and yet her Spanish sounded darned good when she spoke to a customer, as well, telling her she was welcome to try on several outfits and not to worry if she left them in the dressing room.

It wasn't a busy night and Brianna seemed to have a calm and easy temperament—perfect for dealing with the public.

She'd been somewhat skeptical when Axel had first asked her about others who had tried on the almost-pencil-line blue dress. But he had shown her his credentials and after assuring her the shop was in no trouble, he was just seeking help, she became determined to tell him all she could. He had a photo on his phone of the dress, so that there was no confusion which one they were talking about.

"Aye, yes, the last woman to try on the dress when I was working—before it was bought. So pretty and sweet and pleasant. The dress was a bit pricey, y'know, so it wasn't a surprise when she wanted to think it over. Not everyone can wear such a dress—that's why I remember so clearly. I believe the young woman was from somewhere near here or at least from the south of the country. She had that lovely drip to her voice. Definitely not Hispanic or Caribbean—or from New York," she added with a grin. "I have come to know that one well. Then again, anyone can lose an accent, eh?"

He smiled. "Sure. But I rather like accents—yours is lovely by the way."

"I do not have an accent," she assured him.

"Ah, yes, well…did you know the young woman? Had she been in before?"

"Yes, I think she was in once before a few weeks back."

"Did she buy anything? Maybe with a credit card?"

The woman was thoughtful for a moment. She shook her head. "As I recall, she bought a blouse on sale and paid cash. I remember because she told me it was her 'mad' money. She was lovely."

"Could you give a description of her to a sketch artist?" he asked.

Brianna was quickly worried. "Oh, dear, no—did the lass do something evil? I don't believe it, she was just too lovely."

"No, she didn't do anything like that. I'm just asking for help. You can refuse me."

"A fine young man like you? I think not! Certainly. I don't work in the morning—"

"I can have someone here in thirty minutes. Would you mind? I realize you're working, but I'd be delighted to buy you a late-night meal or snack or coffee or whatever you'd like at the café over there if you'd be willing to stay and give my artist a description."

She smiled. "You're buying me a late-night dinner—that will be lovely, dear lad. Oh! You're a government man, and I called you 'lad.' Forgive me."

"I found it quite charming," he assured her. "And thank you. Come by the café when you close."

"I will," she told him.

He stepped outside, pulling his cell phone from his pocket. He hesitated, and then called the local office, gratified that Jackson Crow and Adam Harrison had long ago done the groundwork. He wouldn't be questioned on a case when he'd been given the assignment to work with the local police.

And he knew just the artist he wanted.

Luckily, Casey McConnell was available.

"I tried to reach you all day yesterday!"

Elly's voice was dramatic, but then Elly was always a bit dramatic. It worked well for her. Raina had been with Elly a few times when she'd been describing a reception venue to a bride-to-be, and her enthusiasm and way of being a bit larger-than-life helped to enthuse others, as well.

"All day? Elly, I missed one call."

"Yes, but two days before the event! This is a biggie. And other than the band, you and Titan are the main entertainment."

"I think the band is the main attraction. Titan and I are a bit of fun."

"No, Titan is a dog. A lot of rescue animals may be helped by this, and Titan is a dog who makes…who makes all dogs look good."

"Titan and I are just fine, not to worry. We won't fail you, I promise. Hey, I know the importance of all this, too, Elly."

"Of course, of course."

"So?"

"I was just checking. What were you doing yesterday?"

There was no way to explain. Raina decided on an approach that wouldn't be a lie. "I ran into in an old friend. Or acquaintance. In fact, I need a favor. The acquaintance is Axel Tiger."

"Axel Tiger?"

"From years ago, the Everglades. The young man who was telling the story about the pirate ship and working with the Miccosukee guides and lecturers on that field trip—"

"Oh! I remember him! Axel Tiger." Elly giggled. "Like I know lots of people with the last name 'Tiger.' You know, I get some of the other names—Eagle, say. We have Eagles. We don't have any tigers in Florida."

"I guess some people called the panthers tigers. I'm not sure."

"How did you run into him? That's bizarre. I mean, were you running around in the Everglades yesterday?"

"No, I was trying on dresses...and he ran into me."

That was close enough to the truth.

"He ran into you while you were trying on a dress?" Elly asked. "Like, he was in the dressing room?"

Raina could hear the confusion and amusement in her friend's voice.

"No, no, come on, Elly, really! I ran into him after I tried on the dress. Anyway, would you mind if he comes to the fundraiser? I kind of already told him he could, since it's a fundraiser and all. I imagine he's a generous man, but—"

"He works for the federal government!" Elly said. She giggled. "He's a G-man! I don't imagine that government men make a lot of money. Oh, his work is prestigious enough—very, very cool, but—"

"Wait. How do you know?"

"Oh, I saw something in the paper on him a while back. He's with a special unit. It was an article on a truly bizarre case that was solved—after twenty-something years—by his unit. I can't believe I didn't point it out to you. Maybe you were out of state working at the time. I noticed it, of course. We all had a crush on him after that camping trip. Who would forget a guy like that? My Lord, yes, bring him! I'd love to see him. Imagine—what were we back then? Thirteen, four-teen? Wow, that's an age I don't want to be again. Crushes on everyone, bodies in overdrive. Anyway, I'm really excited about this event, Raina. It's almost like old home week in the best way. So many friends supporting such a great cause."

"I agree. And I promise you, Titan and I are ready."

"Tomorrow, then. I was just getting worried."

"It's no problem and thank you for thinking of me."

"Of course. I know you have Titan. But still…"

"I didn't mean to worry you. I just wound up doing a lot of running around."

"Cool. Hey, it must be really neat, meeting him as an adult. Is he still to die for?"

Raina hesitated. It was a common expression, but it seemed ironic at this moment.

She answered judiciously. "He's an impressive man."

"Okay, well, I guess I'll see for myself Friday night."

They finished the call and Raina looked at the phone, wincing. She was lucky. She had good friends, women she'd known for years and years. Somehow, they'd all segued into good and caring responsible adults. But she couldn't tell them the truth about this.

Titan emitted a loud "Woof!"

He was seeking her attention—or reminding her they had work to do. She smiled, set down her phone and gave her attention to the dog.

Casey McConnell joined Axel at the coffee shop a few minutes before the dress shop was due to close. She was a tiny woman, slim almost to the point of gaunt, but with bright blue eyes, long elegant fingers—and a master's touch with a pencil.

He'd known Casey a long time. She had been with the Metro police ever since he could remember. She was close to retirement age, but her renditions of the people she sketched were so accurate that no one wanted her to leave.

He rose to meet her; she had never been shy and she gave him a kiss on the cheek and a warm hug before sliding into the booth across from him.

"Our friend didn't want to come to the station?" Casey asked.

"She works right across the street, and I just saw her and asked her to do this. I thought I'd strike while the iron was hot," Axel said. "I'm sorry. I didn't mean to drag you out at night."

She smiled. "Oh, that's fine. You caught me in time. Vacation next week. Off to see my first great-grandchild."

"You can't possibly have a great-grandchild!"

"Flattery will get you everywhere. I'm definitely old enough for a great-grandchild," she said, and grinned. "I just look like a spring chicken!"

He lowered his head, smiling. Casey had fluffy silver hair—and more energy than a twenty-year-old.

She grew serious. "So, another body in the Everglades. I take it you don't think these are all separate cases?"

He shook his head. "Not this case or the one before it and the two before that. They were killed in the same fashion. Throats slit, but quickly, doesn't appear there was torture involved—something far more like execution-style. Did you see the last crime scene photos?"

"No. I didn't want to be influenced. You know how that goes. You can't make evidence meet your theory. You always have to fashion what you're doing—sketching, investigating—to what we know as facts. Okay, well, sketching is a bit different, but I didn't want to be swayed in any way from what your clerk was going to tell me."

"I like it," he told her. As he spoke, he saw Brianna Adair coming into the coffee shop. He rose, and when she arrived at the table, he introduced her to Casey. They chatted, seeming to hit it off right away. A good thing. That meant Brianna would speak with her easily.

He asked what the two would like, then ordered coffee all around with a sampling of the menu's little desserts. When their order arrived, Casey pulled out her sketchbook.

Brianna thought the woman from her shop had been about thirty. Slim. Her hair had been shoulder length and golden blond. Her face narrow. The nose small. Eyes large, brows arched and waxed or plucked perfectly. The young woman's mouth had been generous, her teeth had appeared to be perfect.

That might mean someone at the morgue had searched for a dental match, but if they had discovered one, they had yet to inform him.

The description went on as Casey sketched. Brianna instructed her. "The nose just a wee bit longer. Perfect. The mouth, a little wider, with a beautiful smile. Oh, and her eyes! They were majestically blue, like a bright day!"

The eyes...

Axel hadn't seen her eyes. They had been gone. Pecked away by carrion birds.

It saddened him, as it always did. Casey went on with the sketch; when she was done, she had created a likeness of a lovely, smiling young woman.

Axel was sure it was the young woman he had seen so horrifically destroyed on the bank of the canal in the Everglades.

"Thank you so much for your help," Axel told Brianna.

Brianna studied the likeness a moment longer and then looked at him. "You think that this girl might be...the Everglades victim?" she whispered.

"Possibly," he said. He wished that he could lie.

Raina spent about an hour working with Titan, though it wasn't necessary. Titan knew his part. It was something that occupied her and kept her mind somewhat busy.

Titan knew his drill. And he was very happy to please her just as he had always been. She'd gotten him as a rescue, and she could only assume whoever had left him at the shelter had simply not expected him to become such a big dog—though, in her mind, it had to have been apparent that he would grow quite large. But people left animals at shelters for all kinds of reasons, many of which angered her. But sometimes people just had no choice.

She was, naturally, friends with a lot of people who worked at animal shelters. She volunteered time herself but could only bear to work at "no kill" facilities.

At some point, she realized she was still practicing with Titan because she didn't want to think.

Today had surely been the longest day in history.

And a strange day. It had been years since she'd seen Axel Tiger—and even then, she'd only met him briefly.

But in that one day, it seemed he'd left quite an impression. She'd been fascinated by him when she'd been a teenager.

That fascination hadn't gone away.

Sleeping wasn't easy; she kept thinking about him.

He'd matured nicely.

And he'd believed her. He'd rushed right in—almost like a knight on a white horse—and rescued her when the police had been convinced she was somehow guilty.

Her brother had come to her rescue, too—and she hadn't remembered to call him and thank him—even if Axel had used his influence to get her released.

That, too, was worrisome. It still bothered her.

Thinking of her brother, she quickly gave him a call. She loved her brother. He was, in her mind, an amazing man. A kid in love with comics and superheroes, he had wanted to do his best to follow along that lead—putting bad guys away.

He'd worked hard through law school, apprenticed with

the system in Tallahassee and then returned home, quickly rising in the ranks at the county courts.

Robert told her he'd been trying to reach her, too. "You okay, kid? You didn't get back to me. I was concerned. Don't you do that to me again, young lady."

"I won't. I promise!"

"So, what happened?"

Raina took a deep breath. She tried to explain about the dress, muddling it terribly. But it seemed Robert hadn't worried excessively over not hearing from her because she'd been with Axel.

She did her best to be reassuring. She tried to segue to the fundraiser the coming night. When they ended the call, she let out a long sigh, hoping her brother didn't think she was losing her grip on reality and sanity. Of course he loved her. And he believed in her.

Axel simply believed her when she wasn't sure she believed it herself.

All because of a pirate ship she most likely imagined on a foggy night long ago.

She tossed and turned for a while, not wanting to admit she was anxious he call her.

She really just needed out of all this. Why, of all the dresses in the world, had she been compelled to try on that one?

And look in the mirror.

And see...

"Argh!" she spoke aloud.

Titan whined, sensing her mood.

"I'm so sorry, boy! We're going to sleep now, I promise!" she said.

The dog settled down. She lay awake a long time.

She slept at last. Deeply.

Axel could have stayed out with Andrew at his place or even with Nigel in Miami Springs. He knew he was welcome at either place anytime.

But sometimes he liked his own space. A place to come at night and go over what they knew and what they didn't know.

He had a hotel room between Raina's place and Andrew's, at the western edge of the city, not far from the Miccosukee casino. It was an average place, nondescript but decent, with breakfast included in the morning. It was large enough and offered a desk and plenty of outlets for phone and computers.

He sat down to read new information that had come in and reread the old case files.

The first two victims had been identified. The first had been a young widow who made her home on Miami Beach. She'd been well-liked, loved by her staff and appreciated by all the charities she was involved with.

No one knew what had happened to her. She'd gone to a bake sale to support a local Little League team, and she'd never come home.

Her car had been found in a strip mall parking lot with no video surveillance.

Police searched high and low. She was found almost a year ago, after she'd been missing for three months. Her body had been so badly decomposed in the Everglades that it had taken another three months before she'd been identified. She hadn't had enemies. No one could think of any reason why she should have been killed. Her name had been Hermione Shore. The cause of her death had been determined by the medical examiner who had found knife marks on a throat bone.

The second death had been that of a fifty-year-old man. Peter Scarborough. He, too, had taken forever to identify because sun, water, birds and other creatures had done quite a number on him.

Peter—finally identified through dental records from South Dakota—had been married, and his marriage had been in trouble. But his wife had been back in South Dakota, having not come to Florida when he'd moved. Naturally, she had been a prime suspect when his body was found and later identified. But everything on her had been investigated: movements, financials, phone—any possible means of her hiring a killer. And nothing suggested she had killed her husband or had paid anyone else to do so.

The third victim had signaled Axel's involvement. This one had been—through the medical examiner's report—in her early thirties. Little else had been determined. She had no implants of any kind. Dental records yielded nothing. They were still comparing the remains to missing-persons reports. Sadly, she matched many.

Reading further, the third victim had finally received a positive ID. They hadn't been able to identify her for months. She had been Alina Fairfield, a clothing designer, who traveled for a living but kept an apartment in Miami. Because she traveled so much, she hadn't been flagged as missing until recently, and the report on her had been filled out in the Orlando area.

Again, nicks on bone suggested the same thing—a slit throat.

He went over his notes again, comparing Hermione Shore and Peter Scarborough. Peter had just come to the area; Hermione had been a long-time resident. Peter had been making a living as a carpenter; Hermione had inherited her wealth but had been known for her generosity. One male; one female. No associations whatsoever that matched up. Nothing.

He went over and over the notes, knowing he was missing something.

And he found himself thinking of the night, long ago, when he'd first met Raina Hamish. When Vinnie Magruder had come out and told them all that the search was on for a young woman.

A young woman who was never found.

Odd that it had been the night he'd met Raina.

She'd been a kid. Now she wasn't. Now she was a beautiful young woman, a caring and responsible young woman as far as he could tell.

Fascinating.

And she seemed to have a very strange talent—or curse.

He gave up on the papers he was reading and rolled onto the bed, wincing slightly. This had to break.

He needed Raina. It was that simple. He needed her.

Raina answered the phone groggily. She thought that it was early.

It was not. She'd slept until after eleven.

"You up to coming to the morgue?" he asked.

"The morgue?"

He said quietly, "Where they keep the dead."

She hesitated; she really didn't want to see the morgue. She'd lived here all her life without ever having seen the morgue.

"I... I didn't know the woman," she said.

"We know who she was. A police artist did a sketch and we put it in the paper. A very distraught friend called in. I'm not expecting you to give us an identification, nor do I believe you knew her, though you may have. Are you free? Maybe I should just stop by."

"Stop by."

"I'm heading in your general direction."

He was heading in her general direction? She hadn't showered and her hair was wildly out of control.

Stupid things to be thinking.

He was coming because a woman was dead. Murdered.

"Of course. I'm here," she said.

She hung up and made a beeline for the shower.

Raina was evidently awaiting him nervously. She threw the door open as Axel arrived, dressed and ready, Titan by her side.

The dog barked and wagged his tail. Axel paused to give him a pat and looked at Raina.

"You okay with this?"

"No. But I'll do what I can. I mean, just don't forget, I need to be at that fundraiser tonight on time. But then, I'm guessing we're not going to stare at a body all day?"

He shook his head. "We'll be just a minute or two in the morgue."

"Why are we going exactly?"

He hesitated. She looked so worried. But he was determined to tell her the truth.

"Raina, when you see her, touch her, you may know something more."

"Touch her?"

"Nothing evil will befall you. But yes, touch her. You may see or feel something that might be helpful to us."

"How?"

"How did you know where the body was?"

"It was the dress. I've said that over and over—"

"It was the dress. Because she'd worn the dress." He was quiet a minute. "Raina, you have a very unusual gift."

"I don't want an unusual gift."

"We don't get to choose," he said softly. "I don't want to force you in any way. If you're uncomfortable, we don't have to do this."

"I'm uncomfortable, but I do have to do this."

"You don't—"

"Let's get this over with." She offered him a weird smile. "Hey. I don't want to spend the rest of my life afraid to try on clothing, right? I don't like any of this. I'm not comfortable with it." She paused, looking at him, and then shrugged, looking downward. "But I'm glad you're here. I think the police were ready to arrest me."

"Your brother would have never allowed that."

"Come on, let's do this!" She turned to the dog. "Titan, rest up. Busy night ahead!"

She headed down the walk toward his car. He followed quickly, opening the passenger-side door for her.

He walked around to the driver's side, and she hooked her seat belt and stared at him.

"I'm afraid to ask you this, and I understand you've seen weird things, really weird things, but how weird? You don't think that..."

"That what?"

"That this is going to be like a zombie movie? If I touch this poor woman, she's not going to bolt up and stare at me like the living dead, right? I mean, if she were alive, but we know she's not..."

Her voice trailed, her face filled with concern.

"She's not going to come back to life. But you have some kind of a connection. You saw her when you tried on a dress she'd tried on. I confirmed that, by the way. She was the last person to try on the dress before you did. If you touch her body, in your mind you might see even more."

"In my mind," she echoed.

What he was doing was not the least bit fair. People had a difficult enough time seeing their loved ones when they had died, even of natural causes. Police officers, agents, soldiers and others saw death far too often. They were accustomed to touching the dead frequently, hoping they might find a spark of life.

Raina was not involved in any kind of law enforcement. He was asking her to touch someone who had been murdered, her remains viciously altered by insects and birds.

He decided to be honest. As he drove, he filled her in.

"The Krewe of Hunters is a special unit—my unit. The main man behind it is Adam Harrison. I met him when I was young—when a hurricane had ripped our neighborhood all to shreds. He was friends with my grandfather, who had a fair amount of money and ran charity events. Adam was and still is often involved with several philanthropic endeavors. I also learned his son was 'special,' that he saw things. When his son died, he passed that special something on to his best friend."

He paused to let that sit with her for a moment.

Then he went on. "Adam spent years connecting with people who had gifts. He was big in Washington, DC, for that reason. Eventually, he formed the Krewe of Hunters—that's an unofficial name. We're officially a special unit. All the members go through the academy and must pass all the tests and receive the certifications required. But my team is hand-picked by Adam, and by a man named Jackson Crow, often recommended or brought in by others. The unit is quite big now—but small still, in comparison to the rest of the bureau."

They'd come to a traffic light, so he looked over at her for the next part. "I see the dead. Those who choose to be seen. Some souls remain behind because—as lore states—their own lives were brutally ended. Some stay because they protect certain places or people who were special to them. I've seen some move on, too. When the time comes, when they're satisfied something has been solved or fixed or recti-fied—when justice has been done, or someone else is saved."

She was staring at him but he couldn't read her expression. The light changed to green and he turned his eyes to the road.

"There is an incredibly small percentage of the popula-tion with gifts," he continued. "Most keep quiet about it. Other people laugh at them or don't believe them, and yes, that makes life uncomfortable. Anyway, I'm grateful you're willing to work with me. I've personally felt protective about the Everglades most of my life. And I believe a heinous killer is using this land now as a dumping ground. I know this has been done far too often in the past. But I think this is a very particular killer. A calculating, organized killer—someone who is getting rid of people for a reason, and who believes the Everglades will hide the fact the murders are continuing."

He glanced at her quickly. She was looking at him and nodding gravely.

"Thank you," she said simply.

"You're okay with all this?" he asked.

He liked the wry smile that touched her face.

"Hell, no!" she told him. "But it's better to try to understand." She hesitated. "I've just never…well, I've never been to the morgue. But I did touch my grandfather when he died. And all I felt then was that he was gone. His body was cold. The man I loved was gone."

"I think it's always best when they just move on," he said. "And yet I'm grateful some remain behind." He glanced carefully at her again. "Real people perpetrate real crimes and murders. Not the dead. They…they're not to be feared. Not in my experience, and I work with that minuscule percentage of special people who see the dead or experience strange messages from them."

"Messages from the dead."

"Not like text messages," he said dryly. "But the dress, for example. You were touched by the dead through the dress. We don't know how this all works. But we don't close our minds to anything."

"Okay. But other people will be in the morgue, right? Or do you have the power to close the morgue?"

"The autopsy has been completed. Right before I called you."

"Did the autopsy help identify her?"

Axel shook his head. "No. Another clerk at the dress shop remembered who'd tried on the dress last. She helped with a description for our sketch artist. It showed on the news last night at eleven. The woman's name was Jennifer Lowry. She frequently worked up in Orlando and that's why there weren't any missing-persons reports that could help identify her."

"Oh!"

She fell silent, staring out the front window.

"Are you all right?"

"How did you explain how you came to find the dress shop?"

"I report to Jackson Crow. I didn't have to explain anything to anyone. Nigel Ferrer is the lead detective on the case locally. When someone questions me on that, I say I received an anonymous tip."

"But the cops know I called in the body. They brought me in for questioning."

"We'll work through that when the time comes. Sometimes, when you get started in the right direction, events and evidence along the way provide what you need."

She shook her head. "I still don't see how you manage all this. When the police were questioning me, I was getting a little crazed, but I really couldn't blame them."

"We'll just see how it all goes, hmm?"

Raina nodded.

"You can back out at any time."

"I don't back out when I've committed," she said quietly.

"That's admirable, but you can."

They arrived at the morgue near Jackson Memorial Hospital, and he quickly found parking. He'd arranged to bring Raina before he'd picked her up. It wasn't a place where visitors were expected or wanted. There were thirteen medical examiners and dozens of various forensic technicians and experts working at the morgue where nearly three thousand people a year were met with an autopsy to determine the causes of their deaths. Pictures were usually shown to loved ones.

There was an information desk complete with a panic button. A grieving family member had once leaped the desk and threatened a worker, so now they took precautions.

Grief could prompt all manner of unlikely behavior.

There were thirteen stations for the medical examiners and their crews. Room for the dead was finite. Miami-Dade was a big county.

Axel signed them in and, before he had completed his name, Dr. Warner arrived to greet them. He offered his hand and a warm smile as Axel introduced Raina; she seemed to feel better meeting him.

She glanced at Axel as if wondering if the medical examiner also saw the dead as they appeared in their spectral form.

He said simply, "Dr. Warner has sadly become accustomed to many a bizarre and sad circumstance. Shall we?"

They moved through the morgue. Raina looked straight ahead as they walked and focused on reaching the gurney where the body of Jennifer Lowry waited.

The autopsy had been completed just thirty minutes or so before they arrived. The Y incision had been sewn and a sheet had been drawn up respectfully to her shoulders.

She might have been asleep. Her body had been bathed at the morgue; all signs of her blood were gone. Most of the damage done to her remains on the embankment in the Everglades had been covered up.

Even along the line of her throat, the necklace of blood was down to just a line. Her lids now covered empty eye sockets.

All this, and yet Axel knew when she was touched her body would be cold. Ice cold. And even a brief touch would prove to the living she was gone. The body that remained had lost all essence and vitality—all that might be termed a soul.

Axel watched Raina as she gave her attention to the body on the gurney. Her eyes showed tremendous sadness, but not the fear or trepidation he had expected.

She glanced at him and he nodded slightly.

She set her hand lightly on the young woman's shoulder. He watched her intently.

Dr. Warner did the same.

When she touched the cold body, she did not recoil. She stood there silent and still for a long moment.

Then at last, she let her fingers fall from the dead woman's shoulders and she turned to him and Dr. Warner.

"Dr. Warner, thank you," she said. "Axel, I think we can go."

Warner nodded. "I believe she has friends making arrangements for her now," he said. "Sadly, no family. But good friends. All we take with us, really, is the love of those we leave behind."

Axel thanked him, as well, and quickly led Raina out. She didn't speak as they headed to the parking lot surrounded by the courthouse, the hospital, jail and other municipal buildings.

Finally, they were on the road, shooting south on Twelfth Avenue and then west once they'd reached Northwest Seventh Street.

She didn't speak until then, and when she did, she turned as best she could in her seat belt, looking at him with a mixture of awe and fear.

"She was there," she told him. "Right there."

He was silent a moment, but he knew she was reaching out to him—perhaps for help in accepting what couldn't be believed.

"You're truly gifted," he told her. "Did you learn anything?"

CHAPTER FIVE

Raina still didn't believe what she had seen and heard.

Had she really felt what she had experienced in reaching out to another person?

It was all far too strange.

He didn't press her until they were back at her house. Inside, she hugged Titan—a living creature who was always warm and loving and happy to see her. Then she went into motion, offering Axel coffee, getting it ready and then sitting with him in the living room at last, knowing she had to talk while the sensations were all still fresh in her head.

"When I touched her, I could have sworn I could see her, that she was standing near me. She was sad," Raina explained. "A presence in the air. And she was almost crying."

"Begging for your help," Axel said softly.

"Yes."

She was silent again for a minute and then she told him, "I don't really know how to describe this. It was as if she was next to me, as she had been in life, never really looking at herself on the gurney. She was distressed because she couldn't just tell me what had happened. She could only tell me about her last few minutes…and the terror she had felt. And the denial."

"What did she say?"

"First, she couldn't believe it had come to this. She was referring to herself in the morgue. She didn't know what she did. She said she had no enemies, no one who would do such a thing to her. She'd shared some beliefs on social media, but nothing like many of the hateful things that are said."

"How was she taken, when was she taken, did she see anything at all?" Axel asked intently.

"No, that was part of her pain and confusion. She was home. She went outside to get her mail. Her box is down in the front yard by the street. She had one of those mailboxes set on a pole, designed to look like a smiling dolphin. She opened the box and that was it. Someone was behind her and then threw a bag over her head. She tried to scream but she couldn't breathe. She was suffocating and it was fast—so fast. She was picked up and thrown into the back seat of a car. She remembers burlap or some kind of rough material. Her hands were quickly tied, and she was shoved downward. I guess so no one could see her. She believes the car was a sedan. She'd vaguely noted a dark car at the curb, but she hadn't paid any attention to it. She was just getting her mail."

Axel was thoughtful. "So that's it. Whatever is going on, the victims are taken entirely unaware, driven out somewhere and then executed. But I don't believe they're chosen randomly."

"She has no idea what she might have done to offend someone—much less to a point where someone would want to murder her."

"There has to be something that links the victims. Did anyone speak to her?"

"Yes. She was told that she needed to just stay down and keep quiet. The voice was almost gentle, assuring her it would all be over soon. She wanted help. She was lost and confused. Even when the bag was over her head and she felt the car moving, she never thought it would 'all be over soon' because she would be dead."

Titan had been sitting protectively at her feet. Axel leaned forward to answer her, and Titan moved over to him, certain the man had inched forward to pet him.

Axel responded, and despite the gravity of the situation and the strange cold shivers she was still feeling, she found herself liking him more.

Her father had always been convinced you could tell a lot about people by the way they treated animals. Some, of course, were allergic to dog and cat fur. But those who would boot a dog or cat out of the way might well treat people the same way.

Then again, she'd liked him when she'd first met him— that schoolgirl crush she'd felt for an older man. And when she'd seen him again, she'd felt an instant attraction. He'd simply matured into a wonderful man.

"We need to study the victims," he said. "We now know who she is. Need to figure out what ties her to the other victims."

"I remember growing up, we'd hear about bodies being found in the Everglades. It seems it's always been a problem."

"I'm afraid human beings have long committed murders, yes. But this, I believe, will be ongoing. I think it's become a method of work for someone—someone who is just ridding the world of people causing trouble to someone." He hesitated. He needed Raina to know the background of the ongoing cases.

"Years ago, in fact, the night that all of you were camping out there," Axel continued, "a young woman went missing. Her car was found by the casino. She disappeared. She has never been found despite multiple searches. The hope had been she went partying in someone else's car at first. But she never returned. And it's unlikely she just abandoned her car and decided to change her name and make a new life. Remotely possible, yes. But highly unlikely. Whoever this is has not tortured his victims. There have been no indicators of sexual assault, no marks on the body other than at the throat. These murders are executions, carried out by an executioner who's using the Everglades as a way to destroy evidence. Somewhere along the way, they will make a mistake. And evidence will win out, but that day could be a long time and many victims away."

"How does what I saw help?"

"It helps. We know she wasn't on a date and suddenly spirited away. We know our suspect attacks quickly. That means they watch their prey and strike when they know they have a clear field. Trust me, it will matter in the end."

She nodded. "I just wish I could do more."

"I'm sorry you're going through this."

"Trying on the dress and seeing the body in the mirror definitely freaked me out. Now, I feel a connection. I want to do more. If this is going to happen, I wish I could make better use of it." She frowned. "You didn't see anything... sense her...feel her?"

He was thoughtful before answering. "I had a sense of her, but not as you did. It's strange. We gravitate toward certain people, or perhaps feel that certain people will hear us more clearly. I felt her...there." He shrugged and offered Raina a slightly twisted smile. "It's something we try. Ghosts, remnants, spirits—whatever you call them—don't often hang out in the morgue. And only some hang out at a cemetery. They hover near those they mean to protect, or near places that mattered to them in life. But just as we never really understand one another in life, we never really understand or know what will happen with the dead. She could grow stronger. Eventually, several of us might see her. But for now, you became her link. And you've done beautifully."

"Oh, if you call screaming like a terrified banshee handling things well, then…"

He laughed. "Everyone deserves their chance to freak out. Not many would have done as well as you've done since." He stood. "I will see you tonight," he told her.

"Yes. I'm so glad you're coming."

"It sounds like it'll be a wonderful time. I'm grateful you've arranged for me to attend."

She stood, as well. For a moment, she felt like an awkward girl again. If he were just a friend, she would give him a hug or a kiss on the cheek and say, "Yes, see you later."

But she waited for him to start for the door and then followed.

Carefully.

At a distance.

Titan, however, barked and stayed with him. Axel paused to pet the dog while opening the door before leaving. "I suggest you lock this. Even with Titan, it can be a cold, cruel world."

She came to the door. But doing so, coming close to him, brought a flush to her cheeks and, she was sure, to the length of her. His magnetism now seemed to leap through the air. She stayed where she was, imagining a scene in which she just stepped forward, threw her arms around him and used her best husky voice to beg him to stay—she had a little time.

But he didn't. She knew that. And she had no idea if he felt any of that electric heat she was feeling.

"Tonight," she said, forcing a cheerful smile.

Titan barked and wagged his tail.

Axel waved, and he was gone.

Nigel Ferrer arrived at Andrew's house just minutes after Axel. They'd agreed to meet there. Though they were grateful for all the help they had from every quarter, it was good to meet and talk about what each had learned themselves.

Axel was first up, telling the other two about his experience at the morgue with Raina.

"Jennifer Lowry. We're finding out more about her," Nigel told them. "She was a dental assistant for Dr. Herbert Wong. He has his office in the Kendall area. Jennifer has worked for him for three years. She was certified to do cleanings and, according to Dr. Wong, his patients all loved her."

"Can't see it being a patient," Andrew said. "I've had a dentist or two I'd have loved to sock in the jaw, but not many people want to kill the assistant."

Axel looked over at him, arching a brow. Nigel continued. "Hey, I'm just saying. I can't see this as something being done as a statement against dental assistants." He grew serious. "We just had an ID confirmed on the last victim before her through dental charts—finally finding their way to the right place." He pulled out his phone to read notes he'd taken on it and continued. "Alina Fairchild. It took a long time for her to reach the ranks of 'missing person' because she traveled the state. She worked for what had been a boutique clothing firm now extending its reach not just through Florida but upward into Georgia and the Carolinas. Sounds like a good deal. She traveled all over, seeing what people were wearing, and what would be comfortable first for year-round heat, and then for changing temperatures. She was a designer, but also, so personable that she met with people to talk about clothing. Attractive clothing that wasn't torturous to wear. The company is called Sea Green Clothing. If you haven't heard of it, they started with women's clothing. Now, they're stretching out.

"Anyway, because she traveled so much—and met with so many people—she wasn't missed right away. But once we knew who she was, we managed to trace her last known meeting to South Florida. She had lunch with three women down at Bayside, talking about boating wear."

"And that's the last that anyone is known to have seen her?" Axel asked.

Nigel nodded gravely. "She was driving. She kept a condo here, but officers at her building say people weren't very helpful. Seems people just come and go—and don't really notice their neighbors. When shown her picture, most of them knew she lived there and had seen her around, but they had no idea when."

"Where was her home base?" Andrew asked.

"Orlando. Like I said, she was all over. An outgoing and friendly individual, full of spice when defending a friend, well-liked by everyone who knew her."

"Not everyone," Axel murmured. "Though..."

"What?" Nigel asked.

"I don't think it matters. I don't think these murders are personal. I think people are being executed for something they may have done, and whatever it is, it ties them all together. We really need to find whatever it is and fast."

"The murders were spread out," Andrew reminded him. "And who knows? There might be a copycat involved here, too."

"Maybe. And maybe there are more we don't know about yet."

"Let's hope not," Axel said.

They talked awhile longer, all agreeing they would have their agencies discover everything they could about all four victims. They'd dig deeper.

And they'd meet again the next day.

Axel rose, nodding, glancing at his watch.

"Hot date tonight?" Nigel asked him.

Axel looked at him with surprise. "A benefit for a children's facility—"

"Oh, yeah, I know about that. Jeremy is going," Andrew said.
"Oh?"

"Yeah, Jeremy Gray. He's a member of the council now and, of course, both the Seminole and Miccosukee tribes will be involved, but the land just about borders reservation land so he wanted to be there to represent what we can do." He shrugged. "You're aware there are areas of the country where the tribal police and the county police butt heads. So far, we're lucky out here. All going for the best possible outcome. But you never know, so it's always best to be represented."

"Yep," Axel agreed.

"Some ranking cops are going to be there, too," Nigel told them. "I take it you've received a special invitation? It wasn't closed to the public or anything. But tickets sold out long ago."

"I inveigled a special invitation," Axel said.

Andrew looked at Nigel. "Hot date!"

"It's not a date. We all know whoever is doing this knows the Everglades. And many of the attendees will be people who know the area well," Axel said.

Nigel looked at Andrew. "Hot date."

"Seriously, Raina Hamish has been incredibly helpful," Axel said.

"Seriously, the air drips with pheromones when you're together."

Axel merely arched a brow to the two of them. "Whoever is doing this has a plan and an agenda. And they know the Everglades. As you said, Jeremy Gray is going. Rangers will go, and rich people who like to play in the Everglades will go. It's a chance to see how people are reacting to what's going on."

"Sure," Andrew said.

Nigel shook his head, his smile fading. "And we could be barking up the wrong tree. God knows. These murders might have been committed by someone over in Naples or Fort Myers, someone we haven't even begun to suspect yet."

"Well, we haven't suspected anyone yet. It would be nice to have a roster of suspects," Axel said. "At worst, I'll go donate to a good cause."

"At worst," Nigel said, grinning at Andrew again.

"Hey, my friend," Andrew said to Axel, "what's wrong with that? Think of it. Which of us has much luck when it comes to relationships? We see too much—too much that's far too difficult to explain to others."

"It all comes from the pirate ship," Nigel said quietly. "We saw the damned pirate ship."

"We'll meet again tomorrow," Axel said, leaving the two of them at last.

Axel wasn't late to the fundraiser, but he was among the last to arrive. Raina had to admit to herself she'd been afraid he wouldn't come.

She wasn't sure why. He had asked her for the invitation.

And it was a little alarming, feeling that rush of fever that was becoming more and more prominent within her each time she saw him.

She had been talking about the proposed plans for the children's facility with her brother, Tate Fielding and Lucia when she saw him come into the country club.

He cleaned up very nicely. Dark hair combed back and shimmering from a shower, shoulders filling out the blue suit. She watched his face, loving the contours, as he looked around the room.

"Raina?"

Her brother was frowning. He'd apparently spoken to her. And she hadn't replied.

"Robert, Axel just got here," she said. "I guess I should greet him. I doubt if he knows many people here."

"Ah, sure. Yeah. Bring him over," Robert said.

As she headed toward the entry, she saw that Axel did know people there—Jeremy Gray, one of the Miccosukee council members attending, had greeted him. He turned to her as she reached them, smiling and asking her if she remembered Jeremy.

She assured him she did. "Mr. Gray, you are an incredible speaker and gave us all so much on the culture, history and geography of the area. I loved being out there. It's a pleasure to see you again. We did meet, but I imagine you've been through so many school groups that—"

"Miss Hamish, it's hard to forget a student truly interested in all that was said," he told her. "A pleasure to see you here—and a delight to know you're involved with helping."

"Thank you," she said. She smiled. "I think the lectures and walks and history and culture you bring to all young people are wonderful. I'm glad we're involved. I'm an animal trainer, but I must admit, I don't know much about alligators except to keep away during mating season!"

"And that's a good thing to know," he assured her.

"I see your brother," Axel said to Raina. "Jeremy, will you excuse us? We're going to head over and talk to Robert."

"Looking forward to your performance, Raina," Jeremy said.

Raina smiled. She was very aware Axel had taken her arm as they moved across the room. By the time they reached Robert, he was surrounded by her old friends.

"Hey, all," she said as they joined the group. "I don't know if you remember back when we all met—"

"Axel Tiger!" Tate said, reaching out a hand. Tate had grown into a good-looking man. He was a lawyer, already moving up in his father's firm. Sandy-haired and blue-eyed, he had a charming smile and an easy way about him. Lucia liked to tease that he made the perfect lawyer—he was snakelike. "Tate Fielding," Tate continued, offering his hand. "And yes, you told some damned good stories."

"I was there, too," Jordan Rivera said, offering his hand, as well. He and Tate had been friends through grade school, high school, and they'd gone off to Gainesville together for law school. Jordan also worked for Tate's father, specializing in civil suits.

"And my tent-mates that trip," Raina said, presenting Lucia, Mya and Elly.

They all greeted Axel, smiling like Cheshire cats.

"Oh, and this is my husband, Len Smith," Mya said quickly, introducing the man at her side. Len Smith was with the police department for Perrine, one of the many municipalities making up the county. He greeted Axel warmly, as well.

"Cop—and FBI," he said, explaining his position to Axel.

Since Len had grown up in Orlando, Raina assumed they'd been talking about Axel since she'd gone to greet him.

"It's so cool you're here," Lucia said.

"Very cool," Mya agreed, but then frowned. "But you're down from the DC area. We have FBI here, don't we? And cops." She paused, laughing softly. "We have lots of cops! City of Miami, City of Perrine, City of North Miami, Miami Beach, Coral Gables, Miami Springs and literally a few dozen more. But I guess it's good to have an agent come in from outside the area."

"He's here because he grew up in the area and knows the Everglades like few others, I'd imagine," Len said, smiling at Axel.

"Because of the recent murders?" Tate asked. "I'd have thought it would fall to the county or maybe even the Miccosukee police?"

"I just go where they send me," Axel told him.

"And Axel has come down before," Robert said. Her brother liked Axel. He respected him, Raina knew.

"Well, I can see where you'd be helpful," Tate said. "You know the terrain. Except the terrain may have nothing to do with it."

"A date gone bad?" Jordan suggested.

"Drugs?" Mya asked, wide-eyed.

"Still under investigation," Axel said easily. He looked around the group. "You all know just how hard it is. Especially with the terrain. Leave a body. If any of the bigger beasts don't get it, the little ones will. Flies, mosquitoes, you name it."

"Too true," Elly said. "I know you guys all love it out there, and the Miccosukee restaurant makes the most delicious pumpkin bread known to man, but for me, yuck! Too many mosquitoes. And in summer, the heat is drenching."

"The birds we saw were gorgeous," Mya said. "Herons, cranes, egrets—"

"There's an egret sitting on my car almost every morning when I head out to work," Elly said. "He's a cutie, but I can enjoy watching him from my window. In the air-conditioning."

"I guess you love it or hate it," Axel said lightly.

"Well, I suppose it's fun now and then to take the Trail across to Naples. You know, stop for pumpkin bread and maybe take a break at the ranger station. But now that Alligator Alley is part of I-75 and you have more than two lanes all the way. Oh! And you can stop at the Seminole village up there! That's fun!" Elly added, clearly excited.

"And there are the casinos, too," Tate mentioned. "Poker is just as good at either—Miccosukee or Seminole."

"Ah, but the Seminoles now have the Hard Rock with the giant guitar in the air," Mya said. "I mean—"

"Axel is part Seminole, too," Tate put in.

"A little bit of everything," Axel replied lightly.

"Oh!" Elly said suddenly. "I have to announce seating for dinner. Raina, where's Titan?"

"Titan is ready. He's in the lounge with Clive the Clown. The two of them bonded when they met. He told me he would stay with Titan. When we're seated and you've started speaking, I'll go back and get him ready to come out," Raina assured her.

"You left Titan?" her brother teased.

"I trained two of Clive's cats once," Raina told him. "Beautiful animals. He has the two cutest, furriest rescues you ever want to see. He's a great guy. Titan is in good hands. Trust me. Titan is a great judge of people."

"Dogs usually are," Axel said lightly.

A small podium had been set up in the ballroom where they were gathered. Elly gave them a brief and awkward smile and hurried toward it. A mic was already positioned for her, and she quickly welcomed everyone and thanked them for coming, for the purchase of their tickets and for their generous donations.

She announced dinner.

Raina took Axel's hand, doing it so quickly she didn't realize her own motion until it was completed. She flushed slightly.

"I have you up with us. I'm where I can head back to Titan in a second."

"Sounds great," he told her.

"I'm near your table," Tate Fielding said. "And I think one of our old chaperones is there, too. You might remember her, Axel. Loretta Oster. In fact, you might remember her way better than any of us. She and Frank Peters have chaperoned students for years and years."

"I do remember her," Axel said. "I believe those two still chaperone some of the school trips out into the Everglades."

He smiled at Raina, his hand now easily wrapped around hers. "I guess we should go in?"

They joined the throng entering the dining room. Raina noted Frank Peters and Loretta Oster entering together. They were old friends.

As they reached their table, Loretta was ahead of them. She turned and saw them both, looking at Axel with surprise and then pleasure. "Axel Tiger! How wonderful to see you!"

"Thank you, Loretta. Great to see you, too."

"What are you doing down here?" she asked. "Aren't you some federal bigwig now?"

"No bigwig. Just FBI."

"An FBI agent from Washington. You will have to tell me all about it!"

Raina found the chair with her name tag, speaking to Loretta as she took her seat. "He's down here working on the murders in the Everglades."

Raina was glad to see she was next to Elly, and Axel was next to her. There was an empty chair by Elly's seat, but it was filled when Robert came around, smiling at Raina as he did, almost as if assuring her they had the situation handled.

"He can't talk about active murder cases," he said cheerfully. "Come on, Loretta, you know that. And tonight is for happy thoughts. All good things to be done for children."

As he spoke, they were joined by Jeremy Gray, who introduced them to his companion, a striking older man with fine features and a very straight stance—Larry Stillwater, representing the Seminole Tribe of Florida.

Lucia suddenly slid into the seat next to him, casually introducing herself.

Raina smiled and arched a curious brow at the same time.

"They oversold my table and Elly was supposed to be here. She's just going to float." Lucia made a face. "Lawyers. Bigwigs. Big contributors!" she said. "I was happy to give up my seat and to get to be with you lovely people. It's so wonderful. Mr. Stillwater, maybe you can help me. I'm still trying to figure out how everyone was a Seminole, and now we have two tribes."

Loretta wagged a finger at her. "Young lady, you weren't listening at camp!"

Lucia laughed good-naturedly. "I was too busy chasing boys back then. And, of course, Axel. We all had this major crush on you!"

Robert piped in. "Hey, you were supposed to have crushes on me—your friend's sexy big brother."

"Oh, we had minor crushes on you, too. And Tate, and Jordan. We were teenage girls!" She laughed. "Please, let's move on. Let's talk about the present, what's going on with all of us. And can someone explain how the Seminole tribes work?"

"With the Seminole Tribe of Oklahoma and the Seminole Tribe of Florida, we are part of one of the officially recognized Seminole tribes. As the Miccosukee tribe, we were officially recognized in 1962," Jeremy said.

"We were recognized in 1957. When the Indians began fleeing south into Florida, they all became known as Seminole. During the Seminole Wars, white soldiers considered all Indians they were fighting to be Seminoles," Larry Stillwater explained. "At that time, most fleeing here were loose members of the Creek Confederation. But some spoke different variations of the Creek language and, eventually, through different families traveling in different directions, they became separate between those groups. Now, we all speak English, and we have to focus on our children learning our Native language. Some—today's Miccosukee—fled deep south into the Everglades. Some were established a bit farther north. We're proud to say those of us who remain here are the descendants of those who fought for our freedom and would not be removed. Naturally," he added with a smile, "we are close with our brethren in Oklahoma."

"I think I've got it now," Lucia said. "Thanks. I'm grateful for the little lesson!"

A waitress came around with salads.

Onstage, Elly started to make announcements. And it was time for Raina to move back to the "green room" since Titan would not like being alone once Clive the Clown came out.

She excused herself. "Time to check on Titan," she said.

"Break a leg!" Lucia told her, and then looked around the table. "I mean, not really, but you know what I mean."

Raina smiled. "I'll be careful."

She couldn't help but notice the light in Axel's eyes and the slight twist to his smile. He gave her a thumbs-up.

Break a leg...

Yes, that was the expression.

Lucia had said the words meaning the best. That night, they sat with her oddly. And she had the strangest feeling someone who might not wish her well was watching as she quickly slid around the side of the stage to reach the wings and the green room.

That was ridiculous.

Jennifer Lowry, the poor dead woman, certainly had no intention of causing her any harm. She...she just wanted a friend in her strange place in the world of the in between.

She had to forget it all. Titan sensed her moods. She wanted to be her best so that Titan would be his best.

And like it or not, she was nervous. She wanted to be entertaining.

She wanted to impress Axel.

Because he was such an impressive man.

She paused just before she curled around the stage to reach the wings and looked back. Her table seemed to be enjoying themselves. Each person was leaning forward in conversation. Only Jeremy Gray and Larry Stillwater seemed to sit straight with dignity bred into their every movement and nonmovement.

She glanced over to the next table where her friends were sitting—Tate, Jordan, Mya and her husband, Tate's father and mother, a middle-aged woman and Frank Peters.

They didn't seem as engaged with one another. But to be honest, Raina herself had always had trouble engaging with Tate's dad. Jefferson Fielding had a great reputation for maintaining a stellar law firm, but he'd always seemed overbearing to Raina. On the one hand, Tate—and Jordan—had risen like young skyrockets in the firm. On the other, Raina wondered just how resentful Tate might be—his dad seemed to call every shot.

Then again, while Helen Fielding had greeted her cordially that night, Jefferson Fielding had barely afforded her a nod. She didn't think he could dislike her because of her failed high school romance with Tate, especially since she and Tate were still friends.

She was suddenly grateful that Helen and Jefferson Fielding were not at her table.

She realized she had paused too long. Clive was about to come onstage. She gave herself a little shake—mentally and physically—and hurried back.

Clive and Titan seemed to be doing just fine. She thanked him, and talked to Titan, gaining the dog's attention as the clown left. She really wanted them both to be at their very best that night. And admittedly, she was getting to the point where she was suspicious of the sun just for shining.

But even as she kept talking to Titan, she realized why.

She couldn't forget being in the morgue. It hadn't been "creepy."

It had been sad.

And she'd had that strange sensation. As if the woman, a pale remnant of the dead woman, had stood just beside her, reaching out desperately, not knowing why someone had stolen her life and who that someone might have been.

As she and Titan headed out to the stage wing, the thought took precedence again.

A ghost was trying to reach her.

How? Why? The dress had done something to her. It seemed a woman she had never known in life had somehow really managed to touch her. And the sensation of her overwhelming sadness and the fear she had encountered suddenly seemed to rush through her again.

A thought occurred to her.

The murderer was in the room.

She almost groaned aloud—a big mistake when she was wearing a lavalier mic and any sound she made would be heard by the entire audience.

She managed to push the ridiculous thought aside, firmly tamping it down.

The murderer could be anywhere in the state.

Or across the country or even in a foreign country by now.

At her side, Titan gave out a low growl.

As if even he was afraid that someone dangerous was in the room, as well.

CHAPTER SIX

Clive the Clown was a good performer, playing with the front tables. Everyone went along with his sight gags and jokes, and he didn't seem to mind performing while the salad plates were taken away and the main course set down. He was a slim man. With his clown suit and clown makeup on, it was difficult to know what he really looked like. When he'd come out, Lucia had whispered that Clive was really a shy man, almost an introvert—unless he was being Clive the Clown.

Axel had met a few of the performers at Adam Harrison's rescued theater who were brilliant onstage and shy when off, so he wasn't surprised. Costumes and makeup could help a person change what they were—almost as if they were two different people.

Clive left the stage to a nice round of applause.

"So, you're in town because of a murder?" Loretta said, leaning forward, waiting for the last of their table's plates to be laid down.

"Mrs. Oster…" Robert began.

"I'm suddenly Mrs. Oster again, Robert?" she queried. "I

was Loretta before! You've been out of school a long time, young man."

"We're at a fundraiser. He doesn't want to talk shop," Robert said.

"Frank Peters and I still take kids out there once a year," Loretta said, looking back at Axel. "We need to know the dangers."

"The dangers are always there," Axel said. He shrugged. "Maybe now more than ever. The estimation is that we have about sixty thousand pythons and boas out there. Certainly dangerous to small pets and children."

"True, but we have guides that are extremely careful and who know all about snakes and gators and critters," Loretta said.

She sat back. She was a slightly chubby woman with a round face that fit her. She was, he imagined, a little too old to be termed cute, but she was. Short, puffy black hair, rosy cheeks and that comfortable...roundness about her.

Everyone and anyone was a suspect at the moment. And she was interested. That in itself meant nothing. People tended to be curious. They followed police and forensic shows. Sometimes a little knowledge was good, but sometimes a little knowledge without background and truth wasn't so good. But interest seemed to be universal.

"You've been going out there every year for years, right?" he asked her.

"Frank and I both. We volunteered about fifteen years ago and we've been chaperoning ever since. I love the Everglades. I go walking out at Shark Valley and I like stopping at the ranger stations. When it comes to critters, rangers and guides know all about them. People murdering people...that's scary."

"Yes, it is. It has been happening as long as anyone can remember," Jeremy said. "We've had a lot of killing out there. To this day, there are miles and miles of wetlands, hardwood hammocks, muck, grass and trees. All places where people might be alone with other people, and where they might commit unspeakable acts." He smiled again. They were all staring at him uncomfortably. "I'm sorry. I didn't mean anything by it. Just an observation."

Loretta frowned. "Well, we all sit with the notion that killing is wrong. But what about the justice system? Sometimes horrible people aren't punished, and then maybe a family member decides to punish them. Then, say, they committed murder. But is it murder if it's justice?"

"Loretta, I'm sworn to uphold the law," Axel said. "Vigilante justice and mob rule can be just as frightening. That's why we have laws."

"But the court system doesn't always work," Loretta argued.

"We still honor the law," Jeremy said. "And yes, sometimes the law fails. But the law hopefully protects us all, sees us all equally."

"If only!" Lucia said. "I've heard that punishments aren't exactly equal when it comes to many things."

"I work with competent people who see every man and woman as equal when it comes to justice. I vote like everyone else. I state my opinion. And I work with people who put their own lives on the line to find the truth. No, we aren't judge and jury."

"And this is supposed to be a lovely social occasion—not grill Special Agent Tiger night," Larry Stillwater said, speaking up again.

"We have an FBI guy at our table. I'm just asking. And you were curious, too," Loretta said.

"Anywhere you have a landscape where people can hide bodies, you have a problem. I know a Cheyenne up in Wyoming who is with the tribal police and on good terms with his county sheriff, too. They have acres of hills and cliffs and caves, and they wind up with bodies far too often, as well," Jeremy told them.

"I just wish I knew more," Loretta said.

"Everything we know now has been on the news," Axel told her. It wasn't far from the truth.

"But could we be more careful, or perhaps—"

"Hey!" Robert announced. "Raina is coming out."

Lucia turned her chair around to face the stage.

Axel watched as Raina walked out, accompanied by Titan. She introduced herself and the dog, asking Titan to say hello. The dog barked.

Typical.

But then the two of them together did much more. She'd give him a number, and he'd tap it out with a paw. She asked him if he was feeling relaxed, and he rolled onto his back. She reminded him they were in front of a large crowd, and he sat up straight. She told him they might need to search for a missing friend, and he lifted his ears and his tail and one paw, staring out at the audience.

She had people laughing and clapping. And then she told the dog they needed to do a duet.

Axel had never seen anything like it. A young man, perhaps seventeen or eighteen, came out with a guitar. Raina sang Neil Young's "Old King" with a beautiful, clear voice. That in itself was a talent, but the amazing part was the fact the dog managed to let out a howling sound for the last two lines of each verse that sounded as if it were in true harmony.

She ended by telling the dog she loved him.

Titan seemed to bark, howl or whine out the words, as well, even if it was a bit like, "I ruf you."

Raina and Titan were met with thunderous applause and a standing ovation. Axel applauded along with the others, wanting to go to her and tell her she was amazing—except she was swamped.

Titan might have been a fantastic performer, but he wasn't really welcome in the dining room. Raina disappeared backstage with him. Axel glanced at Robert.

Raina's brother smiled and said, "Raina will be back out in a minute. Clive is a good guy, and he'll let her have dinner with us. If we don't see her soon, I'll sneak back to Titan with some of my meat!"

A high school glee club came up next.

They left the stage, and Elly came on to thank people, to tell them to socialize and not to forget to purchase raffle tickets.

Then Raina emerged from backstage. He rose, thinking she'd join them quickly and get to have her main course.

But people were rising to greet her and talk.

He watched as the table next to him rose one by one, catching Raina on her way to the table.

Tate Fielding was up, catching her and pulling her to him, kissing her on the cheek and whispering something in her ear. She moved back from him a little awkwardly, but smiled and said something. Jordan gave her a hug, as did Mya and her husband and then Frank Peters.

The others at the table shook her hand and she finally begged away, but was stopped by a grade school girl who wanted to say something.

Raina stooped to talk to her for a minute, leaving the girl with a brilliant smile as she ran back to her table. Raina stood, glancing his way.

He noted she hadn't worn the dress that had been tried on by Jennifer Lowry, but the black cocktail gown she had chosen fit her just as well.

At last, she joined them at the table.

Naturally, everyone there applauded her.

"My darling," Lucia told her, "I know Titan is a special dog, but how the hell did you do that?"

"Oh, I didn't really do it," Raina said. "Some dogs are just naturals." She laughed. "Check out YouTube. You'll find dozens of dogs that sing, especially huskies. They should really come up with a husky choir somewhere along the line. Now, that would be cool!"

"Excuse me," Robert told them, pushing back from the table. "I see one of our police captains I work with. I'm going to say hello. And, my friends, you are not limited to socializing here. Go forth and buy raffle tickets."

"Raina is just getting to her chicken!" Lucia protested.

"It's not chicken! It's Cornish game hen!" Robert said.

"It's fancy chicken. For a great cause, though," Lucia returned.

They were comfortable together, Axel thought. Raina and Lucia, certainly, and Robert—and even Jeremy and Larry.

They'd drawn the better table. It seemed the one next to them had been a little stiff. Maybe not. Maybe he was feeling just a bit of a rise in the green eyes there. He wondered if anything had ever gone on between Tate Fielding and Raina or perhaps Jordan and Raina. Or maybe there had been some awkward dating while they'd matured from teens to adults.

And then he warned himself that it had nothing to do with the situation at hand.

Still...

"I'm happy sitting here with Raina," he said. "You all feel free to go get those raffle tickets."

"I think I'm done already," Raina said. "Not too hungry. We can all be good attendees. Socialize and buy raffle tickets."

She pushed her plate aside, having taken only a few bites.

"Kiddo, you're going to be hungry," Lucia warned.

"Adrenaline, or something," Raina said. "Really, all of you, you're being wonderfully polite, but it's not necessary. I haven't had a chance to look at the goods being raffled."

"Some fabulous spa gifts!" Lucia said.

"A trip to the Bahamas at Atlantis!" Robert said. "Okay, she's my sister. I don't have to be polite. Really, she bit me as a baby!" he teased.

"Atlantis?" Jeremy asked.

"Go buy tickets!" Raina said.

Finally, the others began to rise. Axel stayed.

"Finish your chicken."

"Cornish game hen."

"Whatever."

She smiled. "I'm telling the truth. I'm just not hungry." She hesitated. "Axel, is this normal? I feel as if, well, not as if she's still with me. She isn't. But somehow ridiculously suspicious. As if anyone I look at—right down to the waitstaff— might be a murderer."

He shrugged. "I'm suspicious by nature. Hard to say what is and isn't normal with a killer on the loose. But if you're really all set with your food, I think I will chat with a few people and see what I can find out."

"I am finished. I'm off to view the baskets and goods. Go mingle. I know you're here to meet the people involved in the project. People who know the Everglades," she told Axel. "Go do it. I do want to throw some tickets into that Atlantis/ Bahamas basket! Oh, and Clive is great with the dog and likes being back there, but I don't want to leave Titan forever. So, if you need me and can't find me, just cut through the wing, stage left, to get to the green room. That's where I'll be."

He smiled. "Sounds good."

She stood, allowing him to do so, too. They were alone there for a minute. The others had moved on to talk with friends or view the raffle goods.

She turned quickly, heading for the back of the room.

The woman selling the raffle tickets was an old friend of her mother's and she chatted with her for a few seconds before moving on so others could buy tickets. Then she walked along the length of the tables. She smiled, grateful her performance had gone so well. Her donation of five hours of in-home dog or cat training was doing well, too. The little basket with tickets was filled to the brim.

She wasn't sure she could teach another dog how to "harmonize" in five hours. And of course, during that kind of training, she'd really be training the pet owner—teaching him or her how to train their own pet. Animals responded best to positive reinforcement. Especially rescue pets; they just needed to be loved.

"Hey, Raina."

She felt someone close behind her as she was putting her tickets into the basket for the Atlantis trip and glanced around.

It was Tate Fielding.

"Hey!" she said. She hadn't felt uncomfortable around Tate before, even when they'd broken up after briefly dating. They'd stayed friends. But it felt like he'd made a little bit too much of an effort to kiss and hug her when she'd come offstage.

"Hey again," she said, smiling to take the slight reproach away.

He grinned at her. "You really want that Atlantis trip."

"I might as well put my tickets toward the prize I'd really like to win."

"We all offered free legal consultations," Tate said lightly. "People do love their dogs, though. Your donation is doing well."

"Yes, people have long had strong relationships with dogs," Raina replied, smiling. She had the odd feeling he had sought her out purposely.

"So, you're seeing the government guy now?" he asked her.

"I…we ran across one another."

"There's more to that last murder than they're telling everyone. And then there was that murder a few months back. I guess that's why he's here, not that Miami-Dade County doesn't have its fair share of murders. And the county has a damned good homicide department, too."

"You don't practice criminal law. You do civil cases," Raina reminded him.

"I do civil cases, but my firm has members who practice criminal law. Jordan is going in that direction."

She laughed. "Keeping the scum of the earth on the streets?" she asked.

"Ouch! Jordan would take offense at that. You know people are accused of crimes they didn't commit."

"Of course."

"And sometimes an attorney fights for the rights of his client. People who commit murders wind up out in a few years, and some silly white-collar crime can result in the same sentence. Jordan has gotten involved with several groups making sure innocent men and women aren't rotting in jail."

"That's great," Raina said. "The innocent shouldn't suffer."

"So, has he talked to you about the investigation?" Tate asked, giving her his signature charming grin.

She frowned, wondering why it seemed everyone wanted to know what Axel was doing. Was it natural human curiosity? Or something else?

Tate could be a jerk, but he wasn't a murderer.

"No, it's an ongoing investigation," she said. "You know there's only so much he can say."

She saw Jeremy Gray was next to them, studying the paper that explained the trip to Atlantis in the Bahamas, donated by one of the local travel agencies.

"Hey!" he said, as if just noticing she was there. "Great display of...stuff!" he said. He flashed Tate a smile, as well. "Raina, for that pet thing you've offered, I'm taking it you aren't into training alligators?"

She laughed. "Nope. I'm too much of a coward. I don't see how anyone manages that whole alligator wrestling thing. I've seen the size of Big Ole Mac out in the village."

"A little secret—we'd never wrestle anything as big as Big Ole Mac," he told her. "Like everything else, it's learned."

"I don't think I'd be into learning," Tate said, shaking his head.

"Well, when people ran south, they learned to live with alligators. And snakes and mosquitoes. That's why we have chickee huts to this day—usually built up, to keep creatures away. Make use of our natural wood, thatched roofs using our palm fronds—hey, we knew survival out here."

"You still have a chickee?" Tate asked him.

Jeremy laughed. "I have a nice little house made of concrete block and stucco that I sleep in at night. I do have a chickee in my yard. Nice to hang out in when you've been in the pool."

"Oh. On reservation land?"

Jeremy nodded. "We really are aware of modern standards of living. I've got cable, too."

Tate chuckled good-naturedly. "Of course, I wasn't implying you all were backward in any way. If I was offensive, I'm truly sorry. But I do have some friends up in Broward who practice the whole going back to culture and nature kind of thing."

Jeremy nodded an agreement. "I was not offended. I, too, have friends who embrace the old ways. Thankfully, they help keep our culture alive. But we bring down some of the biggest music acts in the country when we have powwows, and we don't care if they're Native, African American, white as the driven snow, yellow, red or pink."

Larry walked up, smiling. "And we do love our casinos. Talk about revenge on the white man!"

They all laughed. Raina looked past Tate as she did so.

Axel was in conversation with Tate's father, Jefferson Fielding, Jordan and Mya.

She excused herself, remembering she was supposed to throw twenty dollars' worth of raffle tickets in the Atlantis bowl for Clive the Clown. It took a few minutes to write his name on them. While they'd call out the numbers, the winners didn't have to be present to collect their rewards.

Elly was soon back onstage after that, telling them they were welcome to keep mingling, but the raffles were about to end and volunteers would be collecting all the bowls with the tickets. She'd soon be calling out the numbers, once everyone could get comfortable to see their tickets.

Raina smiled at her friends as she headed back to the table, texting Clive his numbers. As she was doing so, Axel joined her at the table.

"I guess this will be rather long," he said.

"Not so bad," she assured him. "Elly is quick and good at this."

And Elly was.

Raina hadn't seen Axel put tickets anywhere, but apparently he had done so and had given his tickets to Jeremy. She saw him smile as he pushed them over to Jeremy and a number came in. The ticket won a complete set of fishing gear. Jeremy appeared exceptionally pleased when he lifted his hand indicating he had the ticket. He stood and brought his number to Elly for verification. Everyone clapped and the night went on.

Her training session was won by a teenager who looked to be very excited, and Raina was definitely pleased.

Clive won a spa day.

She was amazed to discover she'd won the trip to Atlantis. Jokingly, all her friends turned to her, suggesting they should be her "plus one."

When she sat down, Axel was looking at her, grinning.

"Oh, I've always wanted to go but just never found the

time or the occasion. Now, I'll have to! Have you seen the pool? The dolphin encounters?"

He laughed and told her he'd piled the rest of his tickets into a day with a trainer at the Dolphin Research Organization down in Marathon. "There is nothing like a good animal encounter to shake it off after a difficult case," he told her.

Finally, everything began to wind down. Raina excused herself, walking to the back of the room where the ticket baskets had been set out on the tables with explanations of the donations. She'd seen the teenager who had won her services there, and she wanted to assure the girl they'd work it out on a timetable that fit both their needs.

The girl's name was Eva Herrera and she looked shy at first, and then threw her arms around Raina. Raina caught her, hugged her back and smiled, then gave her one of her cards. "Just call me. What kind of pup?"

"A rescue. He was at the pound. Sweetest thing you ever want to meet, but I think he's mainly pit bull, though you know our rescue guys. They called him a terrier mix. But he's huge and he jumps and because he's so big he can hurt people, but I love him and…"

"We can cure him of jumping. I look forward to meeting him."

The girl's parents were apparently ready to go; she saw the middle-aged couple waiting, smiling at their daughter and Raina, but ready.

Raina hugged the girl goodbye. As she watched her walk away, she leaned against the table.

That's when it hit her. An overwhelming sensation of fear. She felt as if something touched her throat. Something cold and hard. Then it felt as if a trickle of hot liquid slipped down her chest. She saw darkness, but felt sudden terror and realized she was feeling what Jennifer Lowry had been feeling in those seconds before she had died. She smelled the earth and blood as she stood there, a wave of dizziness almost claiming her. She felt herself falling on soft, damp grass.

"Raina?"

She blinked. Jordan Rivera was standing near her, frowning with concern.

"Are you all right?"

"Jordan!" she managed. "I'm, uh, fine. Excuse me!"

She fled. At first she wasn't sure where she was going. She couldn't see properly, and people were everywhere.

She hurried back toward the stage and then around it, rushing through the wings and back to the green room.

Clive was there with Titan. The clown was out of his makeup. In real life, he was Clive Bower, a sixty-year-old, semiretired entertainer from St. Pete. He was lean and silver-haired with a shy and sweet disposition and he stared at her, quickly rushing to her.

Titan, of course, did the same.

"Raina? Raina? What happened, what's the matter? You look as if you just discovered Mars was about to collide with Earth," Clive said, catching her arm and leading her to one of the sofas to sit. "Raina, please…?"

"I—I'm all right."

She was all right. She was away from the table.

"Can I get you something? Anything that will help? My goodness, what happened?"

"I—I don't know," she said quickly. She hadn't been able to think at first. Now, she managed a smile. "Exhausted, I guess, and I hadn't realized it. I'm fine. Honestly."

"There are no more bottles of water in here," Clive said. "I guess it was only you, me and Titan using this room tonight. I'll run and get you some."

He started to the door and turned back. "Are most of the people gone? Not that they'd recognize me, anyway, but you know me with crowds when the makeup is off."

"It's clearing out," she said.

Titan was by her side, his nose on her knee, his large dark eyes expressive as he stared up at her, mournful and anxious.

"Thank you, Clive."

He nodded and hurried out.

She stroked Titan's head. "It's okay, boy, it's really okay."

The door opened; she thought Clive was returning. Maybe he hadn't found any clean glasses or water carafes.

It wasn't Clive.

It was Axel.

She looked up at him and said, "He was here. You were right to want to come. The killer was here."

CHAPTER SEVEN

Axel didn't want to leave Raina that night, but he was worried her brother wouldn't take it well.

Robert liked him, but he wasn't sure just how much Robert would like him in the future if he thought he was making a move on his sister, especially while living and working in a different state.

Admittedly, he was fascinated by Raina. Attracted. Really attracted.

She had come to the function with her brother, so naturally Robert assumed he would drive her home.

Raina's brother had shown up in the green room soon after an older man Axel quickly recognized as the clown—sans his makeup and costume—came back in bearing a cup of water.

Now, he teased his sister.

"Hey, you okay? What's up? Is this just excitement over winning the Atlantis trip? You look pale," Robert had told her.

She had smiled. "Yeah, big night, I guess. I'm fine now."

"Great. Ready to head home?"

"I think a few of us were going to go for a nightcap," Axel said. "Do you want to join us?"

"Personally, I'm beat. And my work comes home with me. We have several major trials coming up. Forgive me. I'd like to be more fun, but duty calls," Robert said. He looked at his sister and seemed to frown slightly as he looked at Axel.

"I will give her a ride home," Axel said.

"You're taking the dog—to a bar?" he asked.

"There's a new pub with outdoor seating and dog bowls by the door. They're welcoming the canine crowd," Axel said.

"You could take him home for me," Raina said.

"Titan will be fine," Axel said, before Robert could answer. "I think he deserves a night out, too. What the hell other dog can harmonize?"

Axel still wasn't sure Robert looked happy, and he wanted to stay on the man's good side. They'd had a good working relationship.

"Robert, if Titan is with me, you really shouldn't worry," Raina said.

"True. No one messes with that dog. All right, then, I'll leave you guys. Have fun," Robert said. He walked over to give Raina a kiss on the cheek and frowned again. "You're as cold as ice," he told her.

Luckily, Clive chimed in then. "They have the air-conditioning back here down to about zero. We do too much of that around here, freezing everyone inside 'cause it's so darned hot outside."

"Didn't realize how cold it was!" Raina said lightly.

"All right, then," Robert said. "Don't forget the family thing. I'll be sleeping, but text me you're in safe, huh? If I wake up, I won't worry."

"Promise," Raina told him.

"I'm out of here. Great night, and thanks for getting me my raffle tickets," Clive said.

"My pleasure. It's always great to see you!" Raina said.

Then she was alone with Axel and Titan.

"What happened?" he asked her. "And it's nice you two keep tabs, by the way."

"We've always done it," Raina murmured. "When anyone is flying anywhere. We keep my parents in on those texts."

"What happened?"

"At the end there, I leaned on the raffle basket table or just touched it or something and I felt this sensation. I suddenly knew whoever was behind the murders was here! I can't explain it. I don't know who, just that whoever touched Jennifer Lowry also touched the table. I'm sure that sounds irrational—"

"Not to me," he said quietly.

"But how could it even help? There were hundreds of people here tonight, all of them supporting this project. Where would you even begin?"

"It's a better beginning than what we had," he told her. "Can you get me a list of the people who were here tonight?"

"Yes, Elly would have that. I'm not sure how to ask her for it, but there's a way, I'm certain."

"That will be helpful."

Titan let out a soft, warning growl.

There was a tap on the door and it opened; it was one of the workers for the country club. "Oh, sorry, just trying to get the place all closed up for the night. Hey, pup!" The man beamed at Raina. "Saw your act with him. Great dog!"

"Thank you," Raina said. "Say hi, Titan."

Titan obediently barked, staying close to Raina.

"And we're on our way out right now," Axel said. "Sorry to keep you."

"No problem," the man said.

Axel took Raina's hand. "You need anything else from here?"

She indicated a box that held some of Titan's counting toys.

Axel picked it up, and they smiled at the club employee and quickly left the room.

Raina made a point of brushing by him. She realized she was trying to see if she could get anything—any sense of anything—from touching him.

She did not.

She smiled and hurried out the door, Titan at her side. Axel followed with the box.

Mya and her husband and Lucia and Elly were standing in front of the stage when they emerged, as if waiting for her.

"There you are, Raina. And Axel!" Lucia said.

"Were you waiting for me?" Raina asked. "I'm sorry. I didn't realize."

"I begged these guys to get a drink with me," Elly said. "It's over! It was a success. And the raffles did exceptionally well, too. We raised a bundle. I am so happy, but keyed up. I've talked these guys into a drink. Or coffee. It's late for coffee, but I can consume a boatload of the stuff and sleep."

"Up to you, Raina," Axel said.

He couldn't suspect anyone in this group, she thought. But maybe he did. She was the one who had just told him the killer was in the room.

Elly wanted to go out. They would go.

"Sure, but we have to go somewhere we can bring Titan. Axel knows of a new place."

"For sure!" Elly said. "Titan, you were the best!" She stooped down to hug the dog. Titan easily accepted her touch. He knew Elly well.

"Lead the way, Axel. Oh, should we address you as Special Agent, Secret Agent Man or something else?" Elly asked.

"Axel works just fine," he told her, smiling good-naturedly.

"It was really cool to have you here," Elly told him. "Mrs. Gintry told me how many raffle tickets you bought. And they received a large donation from a man who said he learned about what we were doing from you."

Axel smiled. "Our titular director happens to be a wealthy man known to involve himself in many projects. That's how I met him years ago. Anyway, I'm glad. And it speaks well for the project. Adam Harrison investigates anything that warrants his attention."

"Well, thank you!"

"This is still my original home," he said. "Anyway, I'll text the address to you all so we can hit the road. They're trying to close down for the night."

They headed out. In the car, Axel glanced her way. "You okay with this?"

She looked at him. "You really think Elly could be a suspect? Or Mya? Or Lord, Lucia?"

"Nope."

"Okay. Then..."

"I thought you might want a little time with your friends. Time to wind down, as well."

She smiled. "And now I'm not a liar. I told my brother the truth."

The pub Axel had suggested was new. Raina hadn't even seen the sign for it before. It was a charming little place. The owner had used natural foliage to create a courtyard area surrounded by flowering shrubs. There were other patrons out there, but Axel found the perfect place for them, a little nook just a bit off from the other tables with flowering hibiscus bushes creating something of a little alcove for it.

A flip-page menu was on the table, offering drink specialties, nonalcoholic specialties, late-night food and a page for "Fidos."

She smiled. The "Fido" page offered bowls of water and a two-or three-biscuit choice. No charge.

"Okay, I like this place!" Elly said. "Cheese sticks! Chicken wings! I'm starving. Yes, we just left a dinner, but I didn't eat enough."

"And I'm sure Titan is ready for a biscuit," Lucia announced.

"Titan, you want a biscuit?" Raina asked.

He let out an agreeable woof.

"I think he'll take the three-biscuit option," Raina said.

"I'll take a craft beer," Len added.

A waitress came, and they ordered.

Axel and Raina sat next to one another on one side of the table; Len and Mya were together on the other. Elly and Lucia brought up the ends.

Raina casually touched Elly's hand as they sat.

Nothing. Then she reached across the table to tap Mya's hand and suggest she note the flowers around them.

Nothing.

It was going to be a bit harder to touch Len. And Lucia. For the moment at least.

"So! How long do you think you'll be down here, Axel?" Lucia asked.

"As long as I'm asked to be around, I guess."

"I'm not asking questions. I swear!" Elly said. "I know it's an 'ongoing' investigation. But how does it work? I never really got the whole thing. Sometimes it's local, sometimes it's federal…and we're glad you're here, of course, but…"

"Nigel Ferrer is lead on the case. He's working with Andrew Osceola, Miccosukee police. They asked for me to be sent down because I grew up in the area. I'm not in charge on this. I'm assisting," Axel explained.

"Ah," Lucia said.

"My beer!" Len said happily. The waitress was bringing their drink orders.

"Okay, so what's the story with this Adam Harrison?" Mya asked.

"I know!" Lucia said. They all glanced at her. "I googled

him. He's a special assistant director or something like that, and he's in charge of a unit called the Krewe of Hunters. Apparently, you all have one of the highest solve rates of any organization in the country."

"We work hard," Axel said.

They were all still staring at him.

He smiled. "Adam Harrison was down here, involved in another charity event, when I was about ten years old. I happened to be there and I spent some time with him. We talked about legends that have to do with the Everglades. We kept in contact now and then. I always knew I wanted to be in law enforcement. And by the time I finished with the military, I figured FBI, and by then, he had his unit going and he contacted me. I work with great people."

"How can your name be 'Tiger' when there are no tigers around here?" Len asked.

"Family name. It's just my name."

"Cool name," Elly said.

Axel shrugged, looking at Len. "And in a way, as common as Smith."

"Not that common," Len assured him.

"Maybe not quite as common," Axel agreed.

"And you're half white—and half Native American? Miccosukee or Seminole?"

"Technically, I guess. I'm a quarter Miccosukee, a quarter Seminole and a half mix-match of Northern Europeans through the centuries," Axel said. "No conflicts in my life. My mom's family loved my dad, and my dad's family loved my mom."

Mya laughed. "Well, that's great. My dad still isn't sure about Len!"

"Thinks I shouldn't be a hands-on man," Len said. Then he sighed. "That didn't come out right. I'm a contractor. I believe he thinks that Mya should have married an attorney or a doctor."

"He's coming around," Mya assured him. "I think he's actually glad you're a big, strong guy. Protect his little girl, you know."

"So, Axel, this latest murder...seems as if the news stations are saying it was just like one that occurred some months back," Len said, frowning. "Strange, because from what the news gathered, they were just kind of...killed. How does anyone get anyone else out to the Everglades to kill them and get away so easily?"

"That's what we're trying to find out," Axel said.

Len lifted his beer glass. "Well, it's good to have you with us."

"Thanks," Axel said.

"You think it's because you were dating Jordan Rivera before?" Lucia suddenly wondered, looking at Mya. "And he saw how quickly he was rising in Fielding's firm?"

"You mean my dad not being sure about Len yet?" Mya asked, frowning, having moved on from that area of their conversation.

"Yeah, sorry, I was thinking. I mean, we all love Len!" Lucia flashed him a smile. "But your dad always liked Jordan."

"We all like Jordan. He's a friend we grew up with," Elly said.

"I get along fine with the guy," Len said, shrugging. He smiled at his wife. "He was just a practice dude. I'm the real deal." He looked over at Raina. "You dated his buddy, Tate, right? And you're still friends."

"Yes, we agreed we were just friends. I think we both wanted to go to the prom with someone we knew since neither of us had a high school romance," Raina said. She was surprised to feel a slight flush.

It was so long ago.

It was also something she'd never mentioned to Axel. Of course, she and Axel weren't dating. And even if they were, they had surely each dated several different people by then, some relationships being closer than others. She still felt Axel by her side then, as if his heat had heightened or he had moved imperceptibly closer.

"Right," Mya said. "We all just played dating back then. Probably because we were all together so long. Long enough to know we had to grow up. It's not that big a deal."

"He's going to like me a lot once we have grandchildren," Len said. "Your dad, I mean."

"True. So there you have it!" Mya said.

"It was cool to see your friend tonight—Jeremy Gray," Lucia told Axel. "He's so interesting, like a walking, living, breathing description of dignity."

"He would like that. And he is an amazing man. Loves kids and thinks everyone has a story that should be shared," Axel answered.

"Did you know the other man? Larry Stillwater? He was nice, too. Had a great sense of humor," Mya said.

"I've known him. He's a council member for the Seminole tribe. He reminds me a lot of Jeremy. Same kind of easy manner, accepting of all, open to new ideas. He, like Jeremy, seems like an all-around good guy."

"And you, too!" Lucia said.

"Well, thank you, Lucia," Axel told her.

Titan barked. Axel laughed and patted the dog. "Thank you, too, Titan. I think?"

He looked at Raina questioningly.

"He approves of you. And he's picky, so you must be a good guy," Raina said, smiling.

"What does he do when he doesn't like someone?" Axel asked.

"He's never bitten anyone that I know of," Lucia said.

"But we met him when he was young, when Raina had just got him," Elly said. "He thinks we're relatives."

"He loves you, and as I said, he's a good judge of character. No, he hasn't bitten anyone, but he has warned a few people away from the door. When we're out, if he doesn't like someone, he stares at them and stays right by my side," Raina explained.

The waiter arrived with food. Even those who'd eaten earlier seemed to enjoy the wings, mozzarella sticks and nachos they'd ordered. Finally, the evening came to an end, and they all bid one another good-night.

And as they did, Raina got her chance to hug Mya, Len and Lucia as they said good-night.

She didn't speak her thoughts aloud until she, Axel and Titan were alone in the car.

"Nothing," she told him. "Nothing at all. And I'm not sure that means anything. I might have convinced myself in some secret chamber of my mind that I see or feel things."

"Don't discount yourself," Axel told her. "And thank you," he added.

"I'm not at all sure of what I can do," she told him. "But this matters so much to me. I mean, any murder is horrible, heinous, but Jennifer... I don't know. I can't help but take it personally."

"I'm going to be talking to people tomorrow morning, and meeting up with Andrew and Nigel in the afternoon at Andrew's place. It's our easiest venue for saying things we don't say in front of others. You're welcome to come. Titan, too."

"Thank you."

"That's a yes?"

"Definitely."

They arrived at her house. She started to open the car door when Axel stopped her. "Wait. I'm not risking getting into any trouble with your brother. I'll walk you to the door and make sure everything is okay," he told her.

She waited while he walked around. Together, they walked to the front door and she unlocked it. Titan bounded inside.

Raina lingered on the porch next to Axel. They stood almost touching.

This was the moment, she thought. They were growing closer. Not just by the bizarre circumstances. She was extremely attracted to him, so much so she wanted to run her fingers down the front of his dress shirt.

But she didn't move. And neither did he. She could swear fire or electricity or something snapped and crackled between them. But he didn't move and she couldn't allow herself to, either.

At last, he smiled and stepped back.

"You're not going to check under the beds?" she asked, smiling wryly.

"The way Titan rushed in? You have an amazing alarm system right there. But please, make sure I'm on speed dial, okay?"

She nodded.

"I'm not sure of the time for tomorrow. It'll be sometime after noon—"

"I'll be ready whenever," she told him.

He lowered his head, smiled and nodded, then turned to walk away. Raina watched him go, closed and locked the door and looked at Titan, who was wagging his tail, awaiting her next move.

"You were a very good boy. And now, it's time for bed!" she told him. "Just a second. I have to text Robert." She pet Titan with one hand and, with the other, sent a quick message to her brother, letting him know she was home safely.

The events of the day seemed abruptly to wrap around her and sap her of all energy. In her room, she didn't bother to change.

She fell back on her bed. Her eyes closed. She wasn't sure if she drifted or not.

She jerked up as Titan suddenly began barking, the sound of it ferocious and insistent.

Bolting out of bed, she ran to the living room. She'd left a night-light on in the kitchen, but the house was otherwise dark and in shadow.

Titan came tearing around from the back to the front, continuing his tirade.

Raina hurried to the back door. Both locks were in place. She ran back to the front just in time to hear a car revving up in the distance.

Had someone been there? Sneaking around her house?

Why? That was ridiculous. Who could possibly know she was seeing things? And if they did, why on earth would they believe it?

She stood in the living room, shaking and afraid. She ran into her room for her purse and her phone, ready to call Axel.

But she didn't. She couldn't call him every time her dog barked.

She sat there, holding the phone, awake and frightened for a long time.

She turned on the television for the company, not even aware of what was on. Then she walked through the house, grateful all the glass was stormproof and secure, and that her two doors were also double-bolted.

No one was in the house. If someone had been outside, they were gone now.

But she stayed awake until nearly dawn.

Because she couldn't shake the feeling.

The feeling a killer somehow knew who she was. That a killer had underestimated her home and her canine alarm system.

That a killer might now be plotting a way to find her away from home, away from Titan and away from Axel Tiger.

CHAPTER EIGHT

It didn't take long for Axel to be thoroughly convinced Dr. Herbert Wong was entirely innocent when it came to the death of Jennifer Lowry.

It was a Saturday morning when Dr. Wong usually had office hours, but he'd closed for that morning. He wasn't taking patients, but he had called his staff in so that Axel and Nigel could question him and his staff.

"I don't know what, but maybe someone knows something that will help," Wong told him.

The dentist was about five-ten and lean with dark hair and eyes that watered whenever Jennifer's name was spoken.

Axel wondered if they'd been having an affair.

But he doubted it. Wong was just extremely shaken.

Jennifer had come to work the day before she'd disappeared. They and other staff members had joked with her about a date she had planned for the following weekend. "It was supposed to be tonight," Wong said, shaking, tears burning his eyes again. "She left as she always did, smiling and waving. I think it was close to seven. We try to close earlier, but things back up sometimes. She never minded. Never once complained. I pay overtime, of course, but she was just cheerful no matter what. A wonderful person. Then she just didn't show up for work. We have no clue as to what might have happened. She just left work as usual. I don't know if she got home. We all left her saying, 'See you tomorrow.'"

Wong paused, his eyes once again burning with tears. "She was just a beautiful young woman, shy, stayed home. Oh! She did sometimes write opinion pieces. She was a big believer in equality, that kind of thing. Passionate."

"So she might have had enemies?" Axel asked.

The dentist shrugged. "She never insulted anyone. She didn't get political. She just wrote about the wonder of people—all people—citing good things. I can't imagine she acquired any enemies that way."

"Thank you," Axel told him. He hesitated. He and Nigel had decided they would both question everyone in the office separately just in case something was said to one of them that wasn't said to the other.

Wong hadn't been offended by that; he had thought it a good idea.

"Please. I wish I could think of something, or someone…"

"Who was she going on a date with?" Axel asked.

"Oh, I don't know. But I figure you might find out through her cell phone or her computer, maybe."

"Techs are working on her home computer."

"You're welcome to the work computer system, too. Anything and everything on the system could be read by anyone here. The system was to keep up with patients and treatments, but my employees could do personal business from work during their breaks," he said, giving his head a little shake. "My people are good. When they need to do something and they have the time to do it, I have no problem with them doing it at work, or as I said, through the computers."

"Thank you. I will get that work computer to the right people. They'll find something, if it's there."

"No texts on her cell phone?" Dr. Wong asked.

"We haven't found her cell phone."

"It's probably at the bottom of a canal somewhere," Wong noted.

"Quite possibly. What about her other relationships? Dates, friends or anyone out there you know about?"

"She spent a lot of time here. She was dedicated to the job. Jennifer was an introvert, great on paper when blogging about the downtrodden, but an introvert. The date was a big deal because she didn't go on dates. If she had a boyfriend, it was before she worked for me."

"I guess we'll switch around, then, Dr. Wong. Thank you for your help, and for going out of your way to accommodate us."

"I want to know who did this," Wong said. "She was a lovely young woman with so much to live for. This was too horrible."

Axel nodded and left him, passing Nigel in the hall.

They looked at each other and shook their heads. "Dr. Wong?" Nigel asked.

"Ready for you. And you—?"

"One at a time. Marci Alonso, Roger Martinez and Belinda Douglas. Coworkers. All loved her. Or so they say. They come off as sincere."

Nigel passed Axel and went on in with Dr. Wong. Axel entered the staff office.

Marci was a dark-haired woman who was surely once beautiful; she was aging now, but doing so with a subtle finesse. Roger was young. Medium in height and build with close-cropped hair and a serious expression marring what was probably a decent face. Belinda Douglas was small and thin, a tiny blonde with big blue eyes, which were red and bloodshot now.

They all looked at him without guilt.

Then he'd never thought her coworkers were guilty. He had just hoped they might somehow point him in the right direction.

"Are we all right here? Detective Ferrer talked to us one by one. We just gathered…instinctively, I guess," Roger said.

"Then maybe it's good we all talk together," Axel said. "Why don't you just talk? Draw me a picture of Jennifer. Let me see her through your eyes."

"Kind," Marci said.

"Never a complainer," Belinda offered.

"No, not at all!" Roger said.

"She'd cover for any of us," Belinda said. "She gave up one of her vacation days when I called in because my daughter was sick. I mean, Dr. Wong is a decent man, but I knew the schedule that day. And Jennifer was supposed to be off, but she covered for me without blinking an eye."

"Did you guys ever hang out?" Axel asked.

"Sure," Roger said.

"When we could," Marci added. "Belinda and I have kids and husbands and babysitters. But every other Friday night we would hang out. Went to a little place down the street that's quiet. The kind of place Jennifer liked. She'd only gone to a club once, when she'd gotten out of high school. Or anyway, that's what she told us, and I never knew her to lie. She hated crowded places, so…"

"She really didn't have much of a life. No family here," Roger said.

"None anywhere. Her parents were killed in a car accident years ago," Belinda told him.

"We were her family," Marci added.

"What did you talk about when you were out? Did she tell you all anything about a date she had planned for tonight?" Axel asked.

"She did talk about going out with someone," Belinda said.

"Do you know where she met him?"

"I wish I did," Marci said. "But they were definitely going to meet somewhere. She said she didn't give her home address to anyone."

"Where were they going to meet?"

Marci looked at him. "Um, I think the same place we go as a group. Maybe. I mean, she didn't tell me, but it's a place she would trust. It's called Sunshine and Moonlight. It's quiet, just a softly playing jukebox or sometimes a couple of musicians. And there are only about ten tables there. Still, safe and public, you know. We told her she had to be careful about people she just met."

"Yeah, well, at least she met him in person. You never know with people you meet online," Roger said.

"I guess she won't have to worry about him being different than what he wrote," Belinda said, sobbing softly again.

"Were you aware of her being upset with anyone, or anyone being upset with her?" Axel asked.

"When she got angry—patients can be jerks—she never let it show. The patients here loved her," Marci told him.

"Did she mention any problems with anyone else? Anyone outside of work?"

The three looked around at one another.

"She was such a pretty girl and so sweet, but—"

"She was one of those people who was always careful. She didn't believe in online dating. Said she had read too much about bad things happening. I tried to convince her otherwise," Belinda said. "I met my husband online!"

"But she must have had other friends," Axel suggested.

"Not even a cat," Roger said. "She loved working here. I mean, of course, you never really know someone, but she was just shy. We were her friends and family."

Belinda sobbed softly.

"And you don't know anything more about the man she was supposed meet tonight?" Axel asked.

They all shook their heads again, looking at one another.

"Did she say anything to you at all?" Roger asked Belinda. "You two shared a job, more or less."

"Oh! At first, I teased her. I'd suggested she'd broken down and finally looked into online dating. She said no, they'd met in the coffee shop across the street, definitely not online," Belinda said. "But she wouldn't even tell me his name."

"But they definitely met across the street?"

"Well, down the street, really. It's across from that dress shop. She loved that shop! She was going to buy something there for her date. They're pricey, though, so she wanted to be sure," Belinda said.

"When? Do you know."

Belinda was thoughtful a moment. "Monday, yes. It had to have been Monday. She came in here whistling and happy and that's when I started wanting to know what was going on with her. Yes, she'd just come from the coffee shop!"

He knew the coffee shop. He'd been there.

Now, though, he had a valid reason for investigating further—without having to say that a "witness" had seen her dead after she'd tried on a dress worn by the victim.

He thanked them all and met Nigel back in the hallway.

When they left, Dr. Wong, Roger, Belinda and Marci all stood in the hall, looking stricken, swearing they'd call if they thought of anything at all.

Outside, Nigel looked at Axel and said, "Everything we touch seems to make this all the sadder—young girl, hard worker, her whole life ahead of her."

"Want some coffee from the shop down the street?" Axel suggested.

"Sure. You know I tried to order a cup of coffee there once."

"And?"

"I finally got coffee. After saying I didn't want a mocha, cappuccino or latte—flavored or non."

"I'll do the ordering," Axel told him.

"You have a picture of our victim? Her name was never released to the media."

"You bet."

"They have some kind of food, too. Pastries. But I'll eat anything right now. If we want all the receipts, we'll have to get a subpoena."

"Maybe the owner will just be nice," Axel said.

"And maybe this dude pays with cash," Nigel said wearily.

"Maybe there's some kind of security camera on the place or at least nearby," Axel suggested. "Let's go. And yes, I'll do the ordering."

Knowing Axel wouldn't be coming until the afternoon, Raina agreed to accept a new client at her house in the morning. The request came through a phone call, and she accepted.

It was with a woman named Sara Moore who had a Pekingese who wouldn't listen to anything.

When the woman arrived, she did so with Jordan Rivera.

Raina smiled curiously as he introduced her to Sara. "Hey, I recommended you," Jordan whispered to her. "I mean, you are good, and you're a friend!"

"Thanks," she whispered back.

Inside, the little Peke began growling at Titan, who simply stared at him as a judo master might stare at an ant.

Sara apologized, but yelled at the dog, giving Raina a great place to start, explaining positive reinforcement.

"But do you have to give an animal food every time?" Sara asked, confused.

She was a pretty woman and Raina grinned at Jordan, who was just sitting on her couch silently, watching what was going on.

She assumed Sara might be Jordan's latest love or tentative latest love.

"No. Dogs respond to affection as well as food," Raina explained. And she began working with the Peke, gaining the pup's trust. First, she resorted to bribery, and then put him through his paces by rewarding him with pets and hugs. Her method had to do with training people to train their dogs themselves. The Peke was a smart little thing and quickly seemed to get the concept.

An hour and a half after they arrived, Raina had the Peke sitting on command and coming to her as well as Sara.

Sara was pleased but uncertain, anxious to come back.

Raina wasn't sure about making more appointments. She was working with the family of a man killed in the service but determined they would, at least, care for the dog who had been with him and had survived. The poor shepherd was badly damaged. She also had a few appointments with service dogs and their owners and an ex–K9 pooch who was a little too aggressive.

And she wanted to be available for Axel.

When she hesitated, saying she had to check her calendar, Jordan came in on the conversation. "Aw, come on, Raina. Sara rescued this little guy. Someone dumped him dirty and matted in a field by her house. You love to help rescues. Please?"

"If you call on Monday morning, I'll figure out how to get you in," Raina promised Sara.

Sara smiled and thanked her and headed toward the door. Jordan followed, but when she was outside, setting the Peke down on the grass for a chance to relieve himself before getting in the car, Jordan hung back.

"What? Getting cozy with the FBI guy?" he teased.

"I do like him," Raina said.

"Yeah. He seems like a good character. I know you all

liked him way back when, too. I can't help but be curious
about this whole thing, though. Bodies do show up in the
Everglades. We do have good cops. This guy isn't even as-
signed down here."

"I don't even begin to understand the legal machinations,"
Raina said.

"Well, I'm an attorney. I do," Jordan said.

"He knows the Everglades."

"Yeah, that's why Miami-Dade cops should be working
with the Miccosukee police. Or even local FBI. Anyway, I'm
just watching out for you. Don't fall head over heels for a guy
bound to take off."

"I'm not head over heels. It's nothing like that."

"Then why so much time?"

"Why not?"

"Do you know something about his investigation?"

"No," she said, and smiled, lying with, "His friend has a
horse I'm in love with and an animal that needs some work."

"Ah," Jordan said, his dark gaze searching her face.

She smiled.

"Well, anyway, thank you for helping Sara."

"You two hot and heavy?"

He laughed. "Trying, at any rate. Okay, kid, see you later,"
he told her.

"See you later. And thanks."

"You are the best animal trainer I know," Jordan said, sliding his fingers over his dark hair and grinning. "Wait, you're
the only animal trainer. No, teasing, kid. You're the best."

"I hear you're pretty good at what you do, too," she said.

"The best! Well, almost. Getting there," he assured her. He
grinned. Then they both realized Sara was watching them—
her expression a little worried and confused.

"Whoops, I'm out of here!" he said.

Raina watched as Jordan hurried to the woman, gave her
a kiss on the cheek and then opened the car door for her.

She waved.

Jordan looked at her for a moment, then lifted his hand
in a wave.

They left.

And it was only when they were gone that Raina realized
she had never touched him.

And she should have.

The whole thing might be futile, but she'd never really
know unless she tried.

The clock was edging past noon.

She wished Axel would arrive soon.

"Titan, this has turned me into a mess!" she told the dog,
sighing and plopping down on her couch.

Where Jordan had been sitting.

She didn't feel the same rush of fear; she didn't feel as if she
could see and touch a knife or death.

But something was wrong. It was a strange cloud of darkness.

She cried out loud, frustrated.

Just what the hell did it mean?

The owner of the coffee shop was in. His name was To-
maso Gregorio. He was a big, cheerful, white-haired man in
a white cap and apron. He was working behind the counter
that day with two girls. Saturday mornings were apparently
hopping.

He took one look at Axel and accepted an order for two
cups of black coffee without suggesting anything else, even
as Axel quietly explained who they were and why they were
there.

He called to the girls, telling them he needed to step out
for a moment.

Before he did, Nigel slipped in to order a ham, egg and cheese croissant, as well.

Gregorio got the orders himself and then suggested they sit at a table near the front window.

They could see the dress shop from there.

"I will do anything I can to help you. I saw the sketch on the news, and it could have only been Jennifer. She was lovely." He cast his head at an odd angle. "Well, the news never confirmed it *was* Jennifer Lowry, but I knew. Always tipped my help and had a kind word to say. Never complained. Always complimented people. She was like they say, a ray of sunshine. What happened to her is beyond despicable. If I knew who did it…"

"We're incredibly grateful for your assistance," Axel told him.

"And we think you might be able to help us," Nigel added.

Gregorio looked at them both, waiting.

"According to her coworker, she met a man here, one she was going to go on a date with. Now this poor guy may know nothing, but we'd like to find out who he is," Nigel said.

Gregorio frowned. "I don't know anything about her meeting anyone here. I mean, she often talked to other customers. She'd get out of line if she knew someone was distressed and needed to place an order quickly. She loved kids. Always had a friendly word or two to say. You know, we've gotten rude and kind of cruel in this world. Jennifer was something wonderful against that. Gave you hope for humanity, you know?" He paused, thinking. Finally he shook his head. "I didn't see her with anyone in particular. Maybe one of the girls did."

He looked back at the counter. One employee was at the cash register taking orders. The other was running behind the counter, grabbing a plate from the microwave with one hand while managing the espresso machine with the other.

"It's not a good time," Nigel suggested.

"Yeah, well, there's no right time for a murder," Gregorio said.

"Do you have any video surveillance in the shop?" Axel asked.

"I'm sorry, we don't," Gregorio said. "I had a camera installed a few years ago, but it went on the fritz and I never bothered to have it fixed."

"We can use whatever you and your staff remember," Nigel told him.

Gregorio stood and walked back to the counter, telling the girls to both go and talk to Axel and Nigel.

"Hey," the first said nervously, once they were settled. "I'm Beth."

"Suzie," the other introduced herself.

Both appeared to be in their twenties: young and energetic. Beth was cute with freckles and reddish hair. Suzie was tall and skinny with dark hair.

"We're here about Jennifer Lowry," Axel said.

"Yeah, she was so nice," Beth said. "So nice. Any of us here would help if we could."

"She was supposed to be going out on a date tonight, as a matter of fact, with a man she met here. Did either of you see her with anyone?"

"She was a morning person. She came in before she headed to her job," Suzie said.

"She would talk to others in line, but I never saw her sit with anyone," Beth told them.

"No, I didn't ever see her sit with anyone, either. But there was this one guy I saw her with. Last Monday morning, I think. I don't know—the days get mixed up. Beth, remember I pointed at them? We were both giggling, thinking, wow, hmm, maybe?" Suzie said, frowning as she looked at Beth. "Remember?"

"Yeah...kind of," Beth said slowly. "He had dark hair?"

"Light hair, I thought. But with the sun and all, it was hard to see," Suzie said.

"I'm sure his hair was dark."

"Not that dark."

"But you did both see her with a man?" Axel asked.

"Yes," they chimed in.

"Has he been in here since?" Nigel asked.

They looked at each other. Then Suzie winced sorrowfully. "I—I don't know. He might have been in here before or after, but I didn't see his face."

"I didn't, either."

"Was he tall or short?" Axel asked.

"Tall," they said in unison.

"Wearing?" Nigel asked.

"A suit," Suzie said.

"Business suit. Blue or black, I'm not sure," Beth said.

"Blue or black," Suzie agreed. "I mean…the way the sun hits the glass in the morning, it's hard to see much with any definition."

They looked at each other. Both nodded.

"But we're in a sales and business area. Do you know how many tall men in suits come here on any given morning?" Suzie asked.

"Do most customers pay with credit or debit cards?" Axel asked.

"Some. Some pay cash."

"I'm sure Mr. Gregorio will gladly let you see Monday's receipts or the week's receipts. He's a superdecent guy," Beth said. "I mean, we'd help more. Honestly."

"Yes, thank you," Axel said.

The line at the cash register was growing longer.

"We'll ask Mr. Gregorio. Thank you."

They scurried back to work. Nigel ate his croissant sandwich while they waited for Gregorio to come back and talk to them.

"Thank you—sincerely, thank you—for letting us disrupt your morning," Axel told him.

"I'm a small-business owner. I may never get rich, but I manage it all my way. Getting the receipts together may take me a bit. Can I get the week's paperwork together for you to pick up this afternoon?"

"That would be a tremendous help," Nigel assured him. "And truly appreciated."

Gregorio nodded and looked back to his counter.

"Right. Thank you. We're leaving, and one of us will stop back by around five. Would that be good?"

"Six. I close at five. Takes a few minutes to get customers out," Gregorio said.

"Six, it is," Axel said.

They turned to leave. On the way out, Nigel turned back. "Great coffee—and great sandwich!" he told him.

Gregorio nodded his thanks and watched them head out, hurrying back behind his counter before the door could close on the two of them.

Axel glanced at his watch. He looked at Nigel.

"We need to find out if there are any security cameras in the area."

"All right. I'm on that. And you?"

"I'm going to get Raina. And bring her back to Andrew's. You'll meet us there?"

"I will meet you there. You know..."

"Yeah?"

"We would have gotten this—Jennifer's workplace, the coffee shop, the unknown date—once Jennifer Lowry's picture was posted and she was identified. But hell, we wouldn't have had the sketch if it hadn't been for Raina. We might not have even found the body. We've worked with things a bit different many a time, but this..."

"This?"

"This is something special. She's something special."

Axel nodded. "I know," he said. "Trust me, I know."

He left Nigel and headed for his car in the municipal garage.

Raina was indeed special.

He found himself worrying, hoping no one else—such as the killer—would realize just how special she was.

He was letting himself step out of the logical, and logical was the first keystone for the Krewe of Hunters. Accept all possibilities, but look to the logical.

Logically they were whistling in the wind, having no idea...

Dozens of groups were involved with the Everglades— engineers, hunters, horticulturists, Miccosukee, Seminole, campers, tourism providers, the stray innocent having no idea what they were doing, the odd hiker who loved Shark Valley. Many law enforcement groups looked after the Everglades, too. Cops, marshals, deputies, FBI—even the coast guard— worked murders in the great sea of grass.

The list of possibilities could go on forever.

But logic could take years.

And they had Raina Hamish.

Logic was good.

And someone like Raina Hamish could be so much more.

He needed her help.

But he admitted, more than that, he needed to be with her. Just in case.

Maybe.

Or maybe he just needed to be with her regardless.

CHAPTER NINE

When Axel arrived, Raina was ready. Titan at her side, she headed out of the house before he came to the door.

He barely had a chance to stop the car before she hopped in.

Titan obediently jumped into the back seat while Raina slid into the front.

"Hey," he said.

She smiled. "I've been restless."

"Because?"

She turned to him as he slid the car onto the street. "Jordan."

"Jordan?"

"Jordan Rivera came over with a young woman who needed her dog trained. And I don't know what I felt. I mean, I meant to actually touch him and I didn't! I forgot, but when he was gone, I sat on the couch where he'd been sitting. And it wasn't like last night—that horrible feeling. It was just a little dark. Uncomfortable. I've known Jordan most of my life. He's always been brilliant in school, but nice. Fun, but never obnoxious. I don't understand why I had that feeling."

Axel had briefly touched her life and then come back into

it. She had no right or reason to suspect Jordan of anything. It had just been that strange feeling.

He was quiet for a minute and then said, "You'll figure it out eventually. I know that's not particularly comforting, but you will." He glanced her way. "And you don't need to worry. We only proceed against people with real evidence. We just use feelings sometimes to point in a direction. And honestly, I've known a lot of cops who don't see ghosts or have sensations, but have a hunch, an instinct, but no one can prosecute anyone on a hunch. We're different, and we're the same." He flashed her a smile. "You trying on that dress led us to the dress shop. The police sketch led us to an identification. Now, we're looking into Jennifer Lowry's life and going from there. We might have a lead. Someone she was supposed to have a date with. We think we know where. We think she met this man at the coffee shop by the dress shop where she tried on the dress. It's all threads. We follow the threads. And trust me, we'll be looking into Jordan Rivera, too."

She let out a little sigh.

"I don't think I can give you more than I've given you."

"Nigel was checking to see if he can find any cameras that might give us an image of the man Jennifer met. He'll be meeting up with us at Andrew's house."

Raina leaned back. She really wasn't going to be any help that day. But she hadn't wanted to be home. She loved her work, but she hadn't wanted to work. Restless, she needed to be with Axel. She needed to be busy. Or something.

"Maybe I can spend some time with that horse of his."

"I'm sure that will be fine."

He glanced her way again, seeming to be worried about her. "I shouldn't have involved you so deeply," he said quietly.

"You didn't involve me. The dress did." She shook her head. "Last night..."

"Last night?"

"I think the whole thing is making me a little crazy. I kept thinking someone was by my place in the night."

"And you didn't call me?"

"I was afraid I was being paranoid."

"Paranoid or not—promise you'll call me in the future if something worrisome happens, no matter what."

"Okay. I will."

She closed her eyes. Her lack of sleep through the night must have gotten to her; when she opened her eyes, Axel was touching her shoulder gently and looking into her face. He was smiling.

"Sorry. You were resting. But we're here. Don't want to just leave you sitting in the car."

"Oh!" She sat up straight, almost smacking into his face. His reflexes were good and he moved back quickly, still smiling. "Sorry! I'm so sorry," she murmured.

"Don't be sorry. You evidently needed sleep."

She saw Andrew was outside, waiting for them. Titan bounded out of the car and raced happily to see him.

Andrew ducked down with the dog. "I love this mutt!" he called to Raina.

Then he straightened. "Nigel called. He should be here in thirty minutes to an hour."

"Raina wants to see Wild Thing," Axel said.

"Come on, then," Andrew told her. "I've been busy. He needs much more attention than he's gotten from me. Jacob is in there, too. You said you work with horses, as well, right?"

"On occasion," she said.

"You ride, don't you?"

"I do."

"Want to take him around the paddock?"

"Love to. And I'll talk to him first, bridle him myself, if that's all right?" she asked.

"I heard about Titan harmonizing. If you can pull that off,

I'm sure you're going to be okay with Wild Thing. He may try to throw you, though."

"He may try."

Andrew smiled. "Go on, then. He's in the stables."

Raina hurried along, Titan following.

She passed Jacob's stall. The old quarter horse was munching on some hay. He seemed to say hello with a soft whinny and then returned to his munching.

Wild Thing was in his stall, snorting, pawing and kicking his door. Raina hurried to him and began speaking in a soft tone. She saw his bridle on a hook and took it down, telling him she was coming in. The horse looked at her mistrustfully. She just continued talking and stroking his nose.

Andrew didn't come in and she noted that Axel had shifted his position. He was still outside the stables with Andrew, but he could see her.

She smiled. He was worried. That was nice.

She wondered what might have happened if they'd met under different circumstances. Not at a police station where she was trying to defend herself because she knew where a body could be found.

Wild Thing snorted; she gave her full attention to the horse and bridled him without incident.

Titan was a help. She always wondered about the way different animals seemed to communicate. Titan met Wild Thing's nose with his own, wagging his tail. They were introduced. They seemed to like one another.

Opening the gate, she led Wild Thing out of his stall and, while still inside, asked him politely if she could ride him, then caught up the reins and leaped onto his back. When he started to shy backward, she leaned forward, stroking his long soft neck and whispering her thanks again.

She was able to lead him calmly out of the stables.

"Told you," Andrew said to Axel.

She grinned at Axel. "Nice. You doubted me."

"Not for a minute," he said, and then shrugged. "Okay, maybe I worried. Just a little."

Smiling, she led him toward the paddock and then paused, looking back at Andrew.

"There's a path. Where does it lead?"

"Through reservation land. You take it far enough, you reach the village," Andrew told her.

"Could we ride the trail for a bit?"

Andrew shrugged. "As long as you don't come along any snakes on the way. Wild Thing is not fond of snakes. He's big for a mustang, and any alligators in the ponds will just stare at you. And Titan—he won't go after a snake or a gator or anything, right?"

"He will not."

"Sure, take the path a bit. Don't go too far, though, okay? We've been having torrential thunderstorms out here lately. The landscape is always changing," Andrew warned.

"I won't go far, and I'll be careful."

"And if anything—"

"Trust me. I can scream like a banshee."

Andrew grinned. Axel still looked worried.

"Wonderful!" Raina said. "I'll just go for a bit. Wild Thing and I can get to know one another."

"Wait—" Axel began.

But she smiled and trotted on before he could stop her. Titan followed.

Axle might know criminals, but she knew animals. And she loved horses. Wild Thing had personality, and it could be a sweet one.

And riding away—from people, murder and bodies. That *was* wonderful.

Axel watched Raina go, and while he didn't possess her ability to touch things and feel anything from them, he did have an inner warning system. Intuition? He didn't know. He couldn't stop her from moving. She clearly loved horses. This property was off any known byway unless you were a member of Andrew's family, his circle of friends or among those living in the village.

She wasn't stupid enough to want a picture of an alligator, and she would avoid any snakes. She might get some mosquito bites.

"That path is pretty safe," Andrew reminded Axel. "She's okay."

"I know."

"She's an adult, a talented one. An unusual one," Andrew added softly, and then he turned, hearing tires on the track leading to his house.

"Nigel is here," he said.

Nigel pulled in and exited his car, frowning at the two of them.

"What are you doing out here? Did something happen?"

"Nope. We're just waiting for you. Raina took Wild Thing for a ride," Andrew said.

"Oh," Nigel said simply, looking at Axel. "So, I have officers asking all the local businesses for any security footage they might have. I'll be able to see whatever they get in a few hours. Then, I assume you're going to a pub with me tonight to see if anyone is hanging around looking for his date?"

Axel nodded.

"Do you have anything else?" Nigel asked him.

"Let's go in," Andrew suggested. "You have a lot to say, Axel, don't you?"

"Well, we should have kept Raina here. I can only tell you what I know, but I'll try to do so. And who knows if it will really get us anywhere or not?"

"You can't keep staring down that path," Andrew said.

"Yeah, I can," Axel said.

Both men were silent.

Axel looked at them and spoke quickly, telling them everything he could regarding the fundraiser, his take on the interviews they had done that morning at Dr. Wong's and then what Raina had said about her longtime friend Jordan Rivera that morning.

Then he said, "Excuse me. Jacob could use a little attention, too, you know."

He headed straight to the stables and bridled Jacob.

Then he started down the path Raina had taken.

There was no safe place along the trail to allow Wild Thing to break into a good run. But she let him canter and trot, loving the feel of the air, the redolent smell of the earth and the feel of the animal beneath her.

Titan was happy, too, running ahead of her, then running behind.

She saw a few alligators drifting just off the embankment when she crossed a pond; they didn't move. She hadn't expected them to. They weren't beasts she felt particularly warm and cuddly about, but they were creatures of the Everglades and she was on their land.

It was a good ride and she was about to head back—she didn't want to worry Axel—when Titan suddenly ran ahead, barking vociferously.

"Hey, Titan!" she called.

He was by a mangrove tree with deep roots that stretched out into one of the narrow, grassy waterways.

"Titan!" she called, but he barked again and then looked back at her, whining.

Almost as if he were afraid but insistent.

She paused, thinking she just needed to head back. But Titan, always obedient, ignored her call.

She wasn't leaving her dog.

Sliding from Wild Thing's back but keeping her grip firmly on the reins, she moved forward.

There was something just under one of the thick mangrove roots. Something that appeared to be white and shiny beneath the afternoon sun.

Wild Thing didn't want to come forward. She held on the very tip of the reins and bent to stoop down and see what was making Titan act up.

She stretched out her free hand, dusting a splash of mud from the large root.

The object became clearer. For a moment, she froze.

It was as if she were in a theme park, one with a section in the deep, dank swamp. Because she was certain the thing she was seeing was a skull.

A human skull.

She stared, blinked and looked up. She wasn't alone. A man stood there, and yet he didn't. He wasn't real. Couldn't be real.

He had long gray hair and a grizzly beard to match. He was bowlegged and wearing breeches, a puffy-sleeved shirt and a worn vest.

"You're all right, lass. There's no one out here now. This I've never seen before. Time and nature…they hide sins, and sometimes reveal them."

She stared; she wasn't seeing the man. She couldn't be seeing the man. It was just that there was a skull in the earth, and she'd heard all the tales about the pirate ship.

She'd seen the pirate ship on a foggy night. Seen it in her mind's eye, at any rate.

Titan whined. She looked quickly at the dog.

Titan, too, was staring at the pirate. He was seated right by her side. Her protector, no matter what his own fear.

"Dear lass, it's all right. I'm trying to help, to watch over you!"

The pirate came over and knelt down before her. He

seemed so real. "I know they come, those who do evil. We try to watch. We try to atone. We can't see all. We can't stop all. Maybe not any. We try," he said.

She stared back at him, still silent. Astounded.

Maybe she shouldn't have been so eager to ride off alone.

"You have to tell them. They have to know," the pirate said. "Lass, there's a body here. Bones, but once a living and breathing human being. Lass, come now. You know you're all right, that you see me because you have the power, because I choose to be seen. Please. You mustn't be weak and afraid—"

"I am not weak!" she said. Yes, she was. "Or afraid!" She was terrified.

But then she wasn't. As she kept staring at him, it slowly became okay. She wasn't at all sure she was happy about this, but after everything else...

Why the hell not see the ghost of a long-dead pirate, roaming the Everglades, praying that one day he might atone for his sins?

"What is going on out here?" she asked him.

Her ghost was truly distressed.

"I don't know. These bones, this death, it was long ago and time has taken its toll. But this was someone's beloved son or daughter, father or mother. Justice, as well we've learned, can be slow and hard. And yet it's never out of order. You must bring them out here."

"Raina!"

She heard her name and she realized that Axel was calling to her.

Wild Thing grew skittish, fighting her hold.

"It's all right," she said, soothing the horse. She stood again. Titan ran back along the trail, ready to greet Axel, to bring him to her.

She waited. The pirate waited. And to Raina's surprise, she was calm.

Titan came running back, Axel, on old Jacob, right behind

him. He stopped a few feet away, dismounting, and raising a hand gently as Wild Thing pranced and pawed the ground.

"Raina—" he began.

"Hey, glad you're here. Your pirate friend and I have found the remains of someone. I'm thinking that we're going to need to call this in."

He frowned and turned to look at the pirate. The pirate shrugged.

He looked back at Raina.

"Raina, I see you've met Peg-legged Pete. Pete, Miss Raina Hamish."

Raina smiled at the pirate. "Peg-legged Pete? For real?"

"Aye, lass. Peter MacIver in full dress, but as you might note, I managed to get my leg mangled taking a galleon in the gulf. Therefore, Peg-legged Pete."

"Nice to meet you, Pete," Raina said, looking at Axel, glad he hadn't been there to see her when she'd been frozen with fear. "Axel, I'm glad you're here. I think maybe Pete was worried I couldn't get this information to you, or that I might forget exactly where I'd been." She hesitated. "There are bones here, Axel. Or, at least, a skull."

"A skull?" he said, frowning.

"Yes, a human skull. I haven't touched it, though I imagine it's been here a long time."

"Rain might have hidden it years ago. Rain might have dredged it up now," Pete said.

There was something odd in Axel's expression. He wasn't worried about Jacob taking off on him; he let the horse's reins dangle as he stepped forward, past her and Pete, hunching down to look at the object.

He still looked a little off as he rose.

"All right. Let's get back. We'll have to get a coroner out here. And maybe some experts from the university."

"Axel?" Raina said softly.

"Pete, keep an eye out, huh?"

"Sure," Pete said. "But no one is coming back on this one. This happened long ago. A decade or more, I'd say. Maybe longer."

Axel was already heading back to Jacob and leaping up on his back.

"Raina?" he said softly. "Please. Let's get someone out here. Quickly."

She nodded, turned to smile at Pete and was grateful that Wild Thing stood like a lamb for her to swing up on his back.

They rode back in silence.

Raina seemed to be fine. Absolutely fine.

Maybe having seen the body of a woman so recently killed had inured her.

Maybe it had been the trip to the morgue.

She had discovered a skull, and taken it in stride.

When they returned to Andrew's, they unbridled the horses and left them in their stalls. Raina promised to return with apples or carrots. Titan was quiet but trotted along close beside Raina.

Striding into Andrew's, he told them what Raina had discovered, letting Nigel get busy bringing out the proper authorities and experts to unearth the skull and hopefully discover the bones that went with it.

He excused himself, then went to make a phone call.

"Andrew, do you have any apples or carrots?" Raina asked. She shrugged a little awkwardly. "I promised the horses. I mean, I know we're dealing with an urgent situation here, but I don't think I can help and I did promise treats."

Andrew was watching Nigel, who was already on the phone, but he told Raina, "Sure. Help yourself to anything in the kitchen."

Raina headed to the kitchen with a quick, "Thanks."

Axel stepped into Andrew's bedroom to make his call; he wasn't worried about Nigel or Andrew hearing him. He just didn't want him and Nigel talking over one another.

He was glad he was able to reach Angela Hawkins quickly. He'd already reported the unusual abilities of Raina Hamish; but he hadn't had a chance to speak with Angela or Jackson Crow since the fundraiser, so he went through the evening before telling her, "And thirty minutes back, Raina went out riding. She stumbled upon an old friend, Peg-legged Pete—"

"Living or dead?" Angela asked.

He glanced at the phone, remembering why it was so good to be a member of the Krewe of Hunters.

"Dead. But she actually ran into him as she made a discovery—a skull."

"I see. Not a recent victim?"

"Angela, I really don't think so. We've had some major league storms down here, but the skull was edging out of a mangrove root. I'm assuming it was part of a body buried there some years back, and who knows what has gone on over the years? Where it is, it's pretty deep in the Everglades. Land that's along a private road. Anyway, Nigel has a medical examiner and a couple of anthropologists from the university coming out."

"Will you be there when they come?"

"Probably not. We have a lead on someone the last victim might have met. She was supposed to have had a date with him tonight, so we're going to try to ID him from local surveillance cameras and possibly find him." He hesitated. "Andrew knows what he's doing, and there are a few cops who want this stopped as much as he does."

"I know. Don't worry. Andrew Osceola and Nigel Ferrer wrote to us here, asking for you and our help."

"They saw the pirate ship," he said. "I can say anything in front of them."

"Right." On the other end, Angela hesitated. "You think this is the young woman who went missing when you were eighteen?"

"It's possible," he told her.

"I started on the names you gave me. I'm checking out social media, legal records, all else. If anything is more definite—"

"Jordan Rivera," he said.

"I have that name. So far, nothing criminal or suspicious. A stellar performance through law school, and an instant job with his best friend's father. So far, he's proving to be an asset. And he doesn't even have any parking tickets. But I'll keep at it."

"Anything you do have?" Axel asked.

"Your friend Jeremy Gray had an assault charge against him. Did you know that?"

"No."

"Eight years ago—you were still in the military. He got into a fight in the village. Apparently, someone was teasing 'Big Ole Mac.' That was his explanation to the police—the Miccosukee police. The charges were dropped so I don't have much. Who is Big Ole Mac?"

"Big Ole Mac is an alligator. They do alligator shows, but the tourists aren't usually dumb enough to tease the alligators."

She was quiet.

"What?" Axel asked.

"Bear in mind, your suspect pool is largely compromised of the white and Hispanic population down there. You can't be afraid to accept it if it proves to be a Native American. Good and bad come in all ethnicities, you know," Angela explained.

"I'm not afraid to accept anything. I want this ended. Yes, I think it's very possible we found the girl who disappeared when I was a kid. We'll see what the medical examiner has to say. And find out what the anthropologists have to say, if he defers to them."

"All right. I don't have much else, but I'll give you the tidbits I have," Angela told him.

"Thank you. You got time?"

"I'll email, too, but here goes," Angela said.

Raina sat at the table with Andrew and Nigel.

Andrew reached for the pot, poured her a cup of coffee and pushed it toward her.

"He's calling in to his headquarters. His field director's wife, part of his unit, is brilliant when it comes to online research," Andrew said.

"She'll get background info and other basics on dozens of people in a matter of hours," Nigel assured her.

"I see," Raina murmured.

Andrew leaned forward. "A girl went missing years back," he told her. "Her car was found by the casino. There was an investigation. Friends, family and neighbors were questioned. There was an intense search. Everyone was in on it. FBI, Florida Law Enforcement, Miccosukee, Seminole officers—everyone searched for a long while."

"She was never found," Nigel said.

"You think...this might be her?" Raina asked.

"I believe that's what Axel is thinking. We were still kids back then, just finishing high school, getting ready to move on. But we were part of the search teams, too," Nigel said, glancing over at Andrew. "I was with a young service group, earning extra credit heading into college. The service group came out to search, too. We had the area near the casino."

"One of the school groups was out here then...might have been the group you were with," Andrew told her.

"And that was years ago?" Raina asked.

"I think we all wanted to believe she'd just disappeared on

purpose," Nigel said. "No one wants to give up, and no one wants to believe something awful befell a young woman."

"But you know better than that," Andrew said.

"So it haunts you. Not every waking minute, but it's always there, somewhere, in the back of your mind," Nigel finished. He sighed. "Trust me, we've all seen very bad stuff since. Sometimes, though, you remember what happened when you were young and still innocent."

Axel returned. "Nigel?"

"Proper people on the way—medical examiner and his crew and two anthropology specialists from the university," Nigel assured him.

"Andrew?"

"I'll get them out there. You two best get in and see the security tapes and get out on your 'date night,'" Andrew suggested. "I will keep you apprised of what's going on every step of the way, I promise."

"Good. Thank you. Raina, let me get you and Titan home."

She stood, awkwardly thanking Andrew for her ride with Wild Thing. He thanked her gravely in return for all her help.

When they were in the car, she asked Axel about his date night. "Are you and Nigel pretending to go on a date together?" she asked. "Oh!" she said. "I mean, if it's for real, it would be fine, of course. I just didn't—"

"It's not for real," he told her, smiling, but still wearing that slightly distant, distracted look. "We're looking for the guy who might have had a date with Jennifer Lowry. Raina, you've been phenomenal. Frankly, you've been a phenomena. I can't keep dragging you along on all these things. It isn't right—"

"It won't be right for you to just drop me off and leave me, either," she said.

He frowned, looking at her. "I think I'll tell Nigel we need a patrol to watch your place. I feel good with Titan, that dog is amazing. But if you're worried—"

"I am worried, and I don't want a patrol car watching my place. I want to go with you."

He glanced her way again. "Raina, it's not fair to you."

"It's not fair for you to leave me. Besides, you need me. I brought the authorities to Jennifer Lowry's body. And I just found an old victim," she added softly. "I'm an asset on this case, and I'd rather be with you than alone."

"Titan can't go tonight."

"Titan knows he needs to guard the house sometimes. He's had a good day running with Wild Thing. Titan is going to be fine."

He was quiet a minute.

"Please. I want to be with you."

He nodded slowly. "All right. We need to get to Nigel's station. His people were working on the cameras. Then we'll head to the night spot. Maybe we'll even have an idea of who we're looking for."

"Do I have two minutes to change?" she asked him.

"I'll give you five," he told her.

At her house, she refreshed the dog's food and water bowls and ran in for a fast shower.

She wondered if he might be thinking about her, naked and under the warm flow of the shower, the way she was thinking about him. Her skin tingled, and she couldn't help wonder if he didn't feel just a little of what she was feeling. But she knew he would be far too circumspect to make any kind of move. He would never make that kind of assumption.

Not to mention he was more intent on the case at hand than ever.

She was true to her word. She didn't make her five-minute limit, but she was ready to go in ten, clad in a casual dress, heeled sandals and a jacket in case the night—or air-conditioning—grew too chilly.

"You're quick!" he told her. "I'll be quicker. We'll drop by my hotel for just a minute, and then head out."

He was staying just a few miles from her house at one of the chain hotels. He left her in the lobby with coffee and brochures that advertised airboat rides and the wonders of the park.

He was equally fast, and in a matter of minutes had returned. He was quiet as they headed for Nigel's station.

At last she said, "Andrew and Nigel were telling me about a young woman who disappeared years ago. You were all in on the search."

He nodded. "We were young then—too young to be much good, but we did know the area where we were searching. Everyone came out. You haven't been to the village yet, but believe me, we're all the same beneath our skin. We all care when a young woman disappears. We never found her, though." He looked over at her.

"And you think that maybe...?"

"I'm not an expert on bones, I'm afraid. That could have been a man or a woman, dead a few years or maybe a hundred, though I sincerely doubt that. That environment can be harsh and brutal even on bone."

Raina shook her head. "That was...thirteen years ago. Almost fourteen. Could the same person have abducted her... and still be killing people now?"

"I don't know. I hope not. If so, there may be more bodies out there. More people who've disappeared." He was quiet a minute and then he turned to her. "Here's what scares me— that the murderer isn't just one person. But maybe, just maybe, the murders are being perpetrated for one reason—and perhaps orchestrated by one person. Or one group."

"Like an order of assassins?" she asked, frowning.

"Or, more likely, a murder association. Murder for a reason. Maybe even for hire. I don't know. I have my own sense of intuition, you know, but nothing as good as the magic in your touch. I truly believe these people are being killed for a reason. We just have to find out what that reason might be." He was quiet a minute. "There's something. Something these victims have in common. I can't help but believe if we find out what it is, we'll understand what's going on."

"But what might thirteen years ago have to do with today?"

He shrugged. "I don't know. And maybe it doesn't." He glanced her way. "But my intuition tells me they're all connected."

CHAPTER TEN

"We have some footage from a bank security camera and a traffic cam," Nigel's tech, Jeff Gamble, told them. He was a serious young tech at Nigel's station. "I've gone over them, and looked for our girl. And this is what I've found. Bank camera first."

There was Jennifer, a cup of coffee in her hands. She was greeting a patron in a dark suit. Somehow, though, the man had managed to approach the coffee shop with his back to the camera, talk to Jennifer with his back to the camera, enter the coffee shop and leave backward, ostensibly opening the door with his back to carry out a cardboard tray with several cups of coffee in it.

Axel asked him to run it several times. He studied the way the man moved. Studied his height, and everything he could.

"Thanks," he said. "Anything better from the traffic cam? Was it at a different angle?"

"Oh, yes, but you'll see why that didn't go so well, either," Gamble said, shaking his head. "I've enlarged the best I can, but see for yourself. It's as if this guy knew where the cameras were. The traffic cam has only his back, too."

Jeff Gamble was telling them the absolute truth. He slowed down the footage, froze it, went over and over it, but it was true.

Jennifer Lowry's possible date for the evening never once showed his face.

"Well, he's tall, right? Six or six-one?" Nigel said.

"Dark-haired, so it appears," Axel said.

"I'm sorry, guys—uh, sirs. Detective, Special Agent," Gamble said, stuttering and looking at them both.

Axel smiled. "You can only show us what's there, and we sincerely appreciate your efforts," he assured him.

He and Nigel left the conference room where Gamble had allowed them to see the footage on a large screen.

The size of the screen hadn't helped when it came to seeing the man's face.

They had seen Jennifer Lowry's face. Seen her smile, even seen her giddy, happy little laugh when she'd moved away, heading back to Dr. Wong's office.

"How can anyone know to avoid a camera like that?" Nigel asked with disgust.

"We're looking for a tall man with dark hair," Axel said. "That's something."

"What do you want to bet there are several tall men with dark hair at this place?" Nigel asked him. He shook his head, looking at Axel with his eyes narrowing.

"Yeah, I know. What if we find the dark-haired six-foot-plus man at the club? If he's there waiting for her, it means he didn't kill her," Axel said.

"True. He wouldn't be waiting for her if he knew she was dead." Nigel shrugged. "Then again, he might not be waiting for her simply because he saw the police likeness on the news."

"He might know something."

"They talked for two minutes in front of a coffee shop. And she made a date."

"Unless she saw him before or again somewhere else we know nothing about. She only talked to him briefly at the coffee shop, but surely she didn't get to know him through that two minutes. That can't have been their only meeting. If he's there, he just might be able to tell us something," Axel said. They stepped out into the reception room. Raina was there, chatting with the desk sergeant.

Apparently, he'd known who she was and what she did. He was telling her about his problem with his blue heeler puppy.

"Remember, they were bred as herding dogs. They nip at the heels of sheep or cattle to keep them in a herd. But you have to let him know he shouldn't use that behavior with people. Don't swat him. Be consistent. A firm 'no' is most important. The more consistent you are, the better he'll understand what you mean. And remember, treats are good in training, and so is a show of affection."

The sergeant nodded enthusiastically.

"Another fan?" Axel teased.

"Another dog-lover," she said. She glanced at Nigel, smiling a little grimly. "So, we're off, right? Clubbing? Did the cameras pick up a likeness of the man?"

"We have the back of his head down pat," Nigel assured her.

"Ah." She cast her head slightly to the side, looking back and forth between them. "Her picture was on the news. If this man saw it..."

"We're taking a stab in the dark. If nothing else, we've already worked long hours and we'll hear some music," Axel said.

"Music is good," Raina assured them.

"And they have food," Nigel said. When both Axel and Raina looked at him, he returned their stares with exasperation. "Hey, food is good, too. Keeps us going and we have to go for hours on end without it sometimes."

"Often," Axel teased.

Nigel waved a hand in the air. "Okay, you two just sit there. I'll order food."

Axel drove with Raina beside him while Nigel took the back.

When they arrived at their destination, Axel quickly knew why the staff at the dentist's office had been so impressed.

While a lot of clubs kept loud dance music going, this one catered to good but quiet performers. No DJs were spinning. There was a hostess at the door who led them to a far back table where they had a great view not just of the duo onstage, but of anyone entering or leaving the club, and those seated at the tables, as well. The couple performing were doing a Simon and Garfunkel number as they headed for their table. Once they were seated and ordering, the duo switched into Lady Gaga and Bradley Cooper, and then a Stevie Nicks/Don Henley number, "Leather and Lace."

"They're good, really good," Raina commented. "And we can still hear each other."

"And order food," Nigel said. "Sorry—starving."

"He's always starving," Axel said.

"Listen, I'm one of the top homicide detectives in the county. That requires nourishment," Nigel protested.

Raina smiled at them both.

"Bring on the food," she said.

They ordered. The club offered an eclectic collection of options from sushi to Latin American.

Axel might've teased Nigel about food, but he gave his own order in seconds flat.

Nigel did the same.

The duo on stage continued, switching from country to pop and rock, jazz and soul. Axel could see Raina liked the musicians. There were moments when she just watched them without looking anxious at all, then her gaze would turn back to the door.

He thought that she was exceptionally beautiful as she watched and listened. There was an incredible vibrancy and life in her eyes, in her very being.

There was just so much about her that appealed to so much within him.

She glanced his way. "They're very good. Music like this makes you want to…move," she said.

"Ah, yeah. Move," he murmured. Well, the music was good, she was beautiful and…yeah. It all made him want to move.

Their food came. As their friendly waiter served them, he obstructed their view slightly.

They'd just started eating when he noticed Raina had paused, her forkful of food halfway to her mouth.

She was staring.

"What? A tall man with dark hair?" Nigel asked.

She nodded, still for a moment, staring.

Axel followed the line of her vision.

"A tall dark-haired man I know," she said softly.

Raina stood automatically, surprised to see the man she had known most her life and had seen at her home so recently.

Jordan Rivera was there alone, it appeared.

He chatted with the hostess; Raina thought he was asking her about someone. The girl shook her head, and Jordan smiled and spoke softly again.

The hostess led him toward a table.

She thought Axel was saying something to her, but somehow it only registered on a back burner in her mind.

She saw where Jordan was being seated and started to walk in that direction.

She was surprised when Axel took her arm.

She looked at him blankly for a minute.

"Wait," he told her softly. "Let's see if he's meeting someone."

"He was at my house earlier. With a woman. And her dog."

"So, let's give it a minute. You've barely touched your food."

She hesitated, but then relented.

The performers had taken a bit of a break, but they came back onstage, chatting for a minute, then moving into a Sonny and Cher number.

Raina turned to Axel and Nigel.

"How long do I have to wait?" she asked.

"A few minutes," Axel said, glancing over at Nigel.

"He is waiting, it seems. I catch him looking at the door every few minutes, then at the time on his phone," Nigel said.

"Yeah, he keeps looking at his wrist, too. He must have recently worn a watch," Axel noted.

No one came.

Raina tried to be patient, but it wasn't working well.

"No one is coming to meet him," she said after a moment. She winced. "Sorry, guys, but at this point it doesn't take a crack investigator to figure that out. He's already downed one drink. He's not a guzzler. Soon?" she asked.

"Now," Axel said softly.

"You two go. I'll observe," Nigel said.

"Remember, it's date night," Axel said quietly next to her ear.

He took her arm as they wound their way to Jordan's table. He'd been watching the door, then the duo onstage, and he jerked a little with surprise when he saw Axel and Raina appear in front of him.

"Oh, hey!" he said. Then he smiled and stood and indicated the extra chairs at his table. "Please sit. What are you two doing here? I just found out about the place a few months back. Please, join me. I think I've been stood up."

"Are you waiting for Sara?" Raina asked him.

He flushed, looking away. "Um, no. A new friend. Met

her here a few weeks ago, then ran into her again. We were supposed to meet tonight."

"Oh, nice," Raina murmured. "This afternoon I thought you and Sara…"

"Yes. Kind of. But we're not at that stage yet," Jordan said. "I'd made this date and, well, looks like my bad. I have been stood up. So. Cool. The two of you out together. I guess everyone needs a break from a long day. Are things moving forward for you at all, Axel?" he asked as if the question were a polite one, and he wasn't really all that interested.

"Baby steps," Axel said.

Raina looked at him.

He gave her a slight nod.

"Jordan, were you supposed to meet a girl named Jennifer?"

He'd been looking at the stage again. He jerked hard to stare at her.

"How did you know that?"

She glanced at Axel again. He was staring intently at Jordan.

"Jordan, I'm so very sorry to tell you this, but Jennifer—the girl you were to meet—is dead."

Raina had seen Jordan's performances in a few plays throughout their school years. He just wasn't that good an actor. His look of surprise, quickly turning to one of sick denial, was real.

"Dead? No." He shook his head. "No, I just saw her the other day. We agreed to meet here. You have to be wrong. I mean…it can't be."

"I'm afraid it's true," Axel said. "We're so sorry."

Staring at Axel, Jordan slowly swallowed and his face wrinkled into a bewildered frown, as if he still wasn't quite comprehending, but should be grasping at something.

"That's why you're here," he said sickly.

Axel nodded.

"The woman found in the Everglades."

"I'm sorry," Axel said again. He let that sink in. Then he leaned forward. "Jordan, maybe you can help us. You were meeting her. How well did you know her?"

"I knew her from here. She was sweet, bubbly, and she loved the music. She came with friends, and said it was because they could hear one another. She was nice. Always up. I never saw her in a bad mood. I never saw her do anything other than smile and..." He broke off.

He didn't quite sob, but he looked as if he might cry any minute.

Raina wasn't sure she'd ever seen Jordan appear quite so lost or bereft.

"I, uh..." He broke off. He shook his head again. "Oh, God! She's the one you found in the Everglades! How could anyone...?" He stared at the two of them. "Her coworkers? Did you talk to them? They all worked somewhere near here. And they knew her at the coffee shop. I just saw her there."

Again, he stopped speaking.

Raina wasn't sure what, but she thought something in him changed slightly. She thought there was a growing anger in him.

"What is it?" she asked. "Jordan, do you know something?"

He shook his head. His jaw looked to be locked.

"I don't know how anyone could have done something like that to her. It would be like killing a kitten. If I knew who did it..."

"Okay," Axel said. "Tell us about meeting her. Everything. Anything you can think of."

Jordan started to talk. He described Jennifer much as they had already heard her described. Raina realized she was watching the crowd again.

The front, the players on the stage.

Then she noted someone else coming in who she knew.

"Excuse me. It seems we have other friends here tonight. Well, old teachers, anyway. I suppose we're friends now."

Jordan looked across the room. "Yeah, Frank Peters and Loretta Oster. They come here all the time. Well, I assume. I've seen them a few times. I come maybe once a week, depending on work." He shrugged.

"Do you talk to them?" Raina asked.

Jordan shrugged. He had grown into a handsome man with his dark good looks, and that night he'd dressed in jeans and a casual jacket that added to his appeal. But at the moment, he was sunk down into the chair and his face appeared drawn and sallow.

He didn't seem interested in the newcomers.

"Jennifer," he said softly.

"You didn't see her likeness on the news?" Raina asked.

"What?"

"We had a sketch of her on the news. That's how she was identified," Axel said.

He shook his head. "We've been busy at work. I wasn't all that concerned to tell you the truth, sad though that might be. I mean, it's terrible. It is sad, when we hear someone has been killed. But this is Miami. We're not a particularly bad big city, but we're a big city." He looked at Axel and then at Raina. "I didn't know I knew the victim in the Everglades."

Raina couldn't help herself; he'd been her friend forever. She stood and reached out to him. He stood, as well, and she hugged him, and to her surprise, he started to cry. "I didn't know... I just didn't know," he said.

"I'm so sorry, Jordan. I'm so sorry."

After a moment, he regained control. He nodded, wiping his face. An old-football-player-turned-attorney shouldn't cry, she thought.

He sat. She had one eye on him, another on Loretta Oster and Frank Peters.

They'd chaperoned in the Everglades together a long time apparently. And now here they were together for a night out.

Were they a couple?

"Excuse me. I'll be right back," Axel said.

He stood and walked over to Frank and Loretta, leaving her with Jordan.

Jordan didn't notice him go.

He opened his mouth to speak, but then paused, staring downward, looking for words, and then looked up again. "We'd never been alone. I mean, nothing had gotten serious. I just knew her. I was seeing Sara, but that wasn't a serious thing yet, either, you know? And maybe I shouldn't be taking this the way I am. Maybe I appear ridiculous to you. But Jennifer didn't deserve to die. She deserved the best. She was a rare kind of person, just a really good human being wanting the very best for others. Does that make sense to you?"

"Absolutely," Raina assured him. "I didn't know her, but I've learned a lot about her. Everyone loved her. She was a good person. It's okay to be upset, Jordan. It's really okay."

He was silent a minute and then he stared at her, shaking his head. "It's not okay," he told her.

To her surprise, he stood and started to walk away from her, heading toward the door. He stopped halfway there and came back.

"I'm sorry," he said again. "I can't stay here. I didn't mean to be so rude. Good night."

"Jordan," she said, standing, as well.

But he was moving fast then, heading out of the club as quickly as he could go. She stared after him, remembering the strange feeling she'd had after touching the couch where he had been sitting at her house that day. Was it because Jordan had known Jennifer Lowry? Perhaps because he had cared about her so much? They had only seen each other here and never really had a date.

And he'd been with another woman that afternoon.

Raina heard a voice behind her.

"Well?"

It was Nigel, certainly weary of holding down the table himself.

"He didn't kill her," she said with certainty.

"But?"

She shook her head. "I don't know what it is. He had no idea she was even dead. I guess he never saw that likeness in the news, and Jennifer's name hasn't been released to the media yet. But his behavior was so strange." She turned to look at Nigel. "It seemed as if he was really and deeply involved with her, but he'd only seen her a few times."

"We should join Axel," Nigel said, pointing closer to the stage where Axel was now at a table with Frank Peters and Loretta Oster.

They were both dressed for a night out. Not an elegant night out, but a casual Miami night out. Loretta was wearing a flowery maxi dress with little studded sandals.

Frank was in a light denim jacket and an open-neck blue shirt, hair freshly washed and slicked back.

Raina realized she had always thought of the two as teachers. Not that she had seen much of them since she'd left middle school.

But she had come across them now and then. Especially after they had become involved with the fundraising event.

"Hi!" Loretta said. For the first time, Raina found herself wondering about Loretta's and Frank's ages. When she'd been thirteen, anyone over twenty had seemed ancient. Now she realized when she'd been thirteen, the two had probably been in their mid-to late twenties. They were still young.

And involved? If so, for how long?

"Hey!" she said, forcing a smile.

"Take a chair," Frank told her. "It's nice to see you out. You are one hardworking young lady. Your act was wonderful."

"I'm not really an act. I was just showing a training technique. I'm hoping they'll have children working with animals. It's amazing how therapeutic animals can be."

"Pit Bulls and Parolees," Frank said.

"Something like that, yes. Dogs are incredibly loyal creatures and working with them can be good for children and adults," she said. She glanced at Axel, who'd pulled out a chair for her.

How had the conversation been going thus far?

"We didn't get to meet," Nigel told them.

"You're Detective Nigel Ferrer, a very old friend of Axel, and a county detective. Axel has been telling us all about you."

"Oh, good things, I hope." He frowned teasingly at Axel. "Did he tell you that I'm always hungry, or something like that?"

"Hungry—for information," Axel protested.

Raina smiled and hoped her smile wasn't too plastic.

Frank leaned forward and said, "You're all just out for the night? The three of you?" He leaned back. "Strange date," he said, eyeing them one by one.

Loretta giggled. "Frank! Please. They're all grown-ups…"

"They are not on a three-way date, Loretta," Frank said. "I saw that sketch on the news. It's online, too. I think I saw that young lady in here a few times. I'm betting that's why the three of them are here. Raina, are you giving up dog training to join law enforcement?"

"No, not at all," Raina said quickly.

Loretta giggled. "Then there is something going on between the two of you!"

"The two of them?" Frank said. "There's three of them."

"Well, she was with Axel last night," Loretta said. "Such lovely young people—it's a delight. Okay, well, perhaps the reason you've met again is not the best, but fate will have its way. Lovely, lovely, lovely!"

Frank didn't seem to think anything was too lovely. He might not have heard a thing Loretta had said.

He stared from Axel to Nigel.

"You're here because that girl in the sketch came here, and she's the victim you found in the Everglades," he said.

"Yes," Axel said. It was his turn to lean forward. "So, you knew her from the sketch? You knew you'd seen her and she came here?"

Frank waved a hand in the air. "It was a sketch. A good one. But no one knows anything from a sketch. And I can't say I knew her. I believe we've seen her. But tons of people come here, young and old."

"Did you ever see her with anyone?" Axel asked.

"With anyone? What a question. Of course I saw her with someone. She came in with lots of people. Well, several people. She seemed to talk to a lot of people. Did I know them? No, I can't say I did."

"But you noticed her," Raina said softly.

Frank shrugged. "She was a pretty girl. Of course I noticed her, anyone around her noticed her."

"She wasn't that pretty," Loretta said.

Frank shrugged again. "She had a light about her. She was always smiling. I guess that made her pretty. Hey, if this is an interrogation, you'd better drag us down to the station. But there's no more I can tell you."

"We're looking for help," Axel said quietly.

"We would love to help," Loretta said. "I just can't think of anything more to add. Frank?"

"Sorry, I'm not trying to be a jerk. We saw her, yes. We didn't know her. She liked to sit close to the stage and watch the entertainment. She did seem to come with the same group of friends, but she was friendly to everyone." He finished speaking and rose. "Sorry, my evening is shot for me. I didn't want to believe that pretty girl is dead, but now I guess we have to. Loretta, come on. Let me take you home."

"Is it all right?" Loretta asked anxiously, looking from Raina to Nigel and then Axel.

"Of course, and thank you," Axel said, rising, as well, bringing Nigel and Raina to their feet.

"If we think of anything, we'll call you. I wish there was something more we could offer," Frank said. "Anyway, good night."

He took Loretta by the arm and they headed out.

"And he's such a great guy, chaperoning kids," Nigel said.

"He has been a chaperone on field trips for years," Raina said. "He would be in charge of the guys, always respected and liked."

"He was weird," Nigel said.

"Yes, but not as strange as Jordan," Raina muttered.

Both of them looked at her. "Oh, no," she clarified. "I believe with my whole heart that Jordan was stunned, that he knew nothing about Jennifer being dead, and he did care about her. He cried. The Jordan I've always known is not a crier. No, Jordan didn't kill her. He was just weird. But it's true, I mean, most of us are decent human beings, and it's horrible and painful to hear about any murder, but when someone you cared about is murdered, it becomes more."

"Think we're done here?" Nigel asked Axel.

Axel was quiet a minute. Then he shook his head. "Bartenders. They know everything."

CHAPTER ELEVEN

They split up.

There were three bars spread out along the three walls that surrounded the opening, one of them a distance from the musicians.

Nigel walked across the far wall; Axel and Raina started at the stretch down from the stage.

They ordered. He'd been drinking soda with lime all night and had noticed Raina was opting to do the same. He told her she was welcome to something stronger but she shook her head.

"Whatever these strange 'touch' intuitions are, I don't want to mess with them in any way," she told him.

"Have you gotten anything in here?" he asked her.

She shook her head. "Nothing. I still can't figure out Jordan or Frank Peters. Jordan was broken, and then angry. And Frank was strangely callous for a man who has dealt well with young people all his life. That's why he and Loretta are still at it, I imagine. Never anything improper in any way. They can both discipline and gain respect at the same time. Good people, one would think."

"And did you know they were a pair?"

She shook her head. "I don't think they were back when I was in school. You have to remember, I was thirteen at the time and I haven't been involved with alumni groups or anything like that. We're still looking for a needle in a haystack."

Axel nodded, but he wasn't so sure. For the moment, he said, "You know, you're not a bad partner."

"Partner?" she queried, smiling.

"You're helping as much as a partner," he said. "Not to mention you're much better looking than most."

"You're not too bad, yourself," she said lightly. "Always thought so."

"Pardon?"

"Oh, you know, years ago… Anyway, never mind, the bartender is coming."

"Hey!" Axel said, smiling at the bartender, a man of about forty with an easy manner, able to chat a bit with his customers without being too intrusive.

"You ready for another? You've got to watch it with those wicked drinks," he teased.

Axel had his picture of Jennifer Lowry out.

"You've seen her here?"

The man—whose name tag identified him as Gregory—nodded grimly. "Jennifer. She was in here about once a week with that crew from the dentist's office."

"You knew them all?"

"Nice group and great dentist. I go to him."

"Good to know."

"You some kind of cop?" Gregory asked.

Axel nodded.

"You're looking for her killer? Man, talk about an injustice! I don't get it. She didn't lead men on, she was never nasty, she always had something good to say. We saw the picture, but no one wants to believe from a sketch that it's really a person they know. I thought about calling in, but didn't think I could really help in any way."

"Can you tell us anything about her? People she hung out with outside her coworkers? Did you ever see her with anyone who came on to her, or…?"

"Sure. She liked the guy you were with earlier," he said to Raina.

"Jordan," she supplied.

"She was excited about him. She came up to me one night for her order and she asked me what I thought. Said he was an attorney, a solid guy, and he wasn't touchy-feely, if you know what I mean."

Axel smiled. "I can tell that you see the whole room. You're good at what you do. I'm betting you know what the cocktail waitress and waiters are getting from you at the service bar and where they're going with their orders most of the time."

Gregory grinned. "Someone who has also bartended."

"All through college."

"And now? Cop?"

"FBI," Axel said.

"Oh, you're with the local office?"

"No, I came down. But I'm from here."

"Oh, well, good. Hey, maybe you can arrest whoever dumped their so-called pet pythons in the Everglades!" He shuddered. "Now they're making TV shows about it, making us all look like we're toothless yokels, like they did with the gator people thing in the Louisiana shows. Ugh."

"If they get more of the big snakes out of the Everglades, it's a good thing," Axel said.

"I suppose. Here's my fear—don't tell me snakes don't swim or hitchhike. They'll be making it down to the Florida Keys, and if so, they'll start munching on our key deer, and that will be just horrible. I take it you've seen a key deer? Cutest little things you ever want to see."

"They are adorable, aren't they?" Raina said, smiling politely. "Gregory, can you help us in any way? Did anyone try to buy a drink for Jennifer? Did you ever see her leave with anyone, or perhaps see someone try to persuade her to leave the club?"

He was thoughtful and shook his head slowly. Then he seemed to remember something, arching a brow. "Yes!"

"Yes?"

"Well, you were with that guy, too, the guy with the pretty, curvy lady. That couple you and your buddy over there were with." He pointed to Nigel over at the other bar.

"Really?" Axel said.

"Were they together that night? That couple?" Raina asked.

Gregory shook his head, a little smile on his lips. "Not sure. I was close to the entertainers. Jennifer had been talking to me about making sure I made an appointment because Wong is one popular dentist. Anyway, the guy came up to the bar and talked to Jennifer. He wanted to buy her a drink. She smiled and said no, said she didn't drink much, and besides, she was here with friends."

"And then?" Axel asked.

"That was it. She smiled and walked back to her table and friends, and he shrugged, bought two beers and headed back to his table." Gregory paused to grin. "He probably thought he got away with it because his lady had been busy watching the stage the entire time. But I saw her look around. She knew what he was up to."

"Oh, did you talk to her?" Axel asked. "Was she the jealous type?"

"You didn't see her react at all. Maybe they're not really a twosome. That I can't tell you. But they do come here together often enough. Then again, so do a lot of people. Owners here are nice and had a dream for a cool place to just hang out. There's not a bad night during the week here. We even fill in on Mondays. Not as late a crowd as we get on the weekends, of course. Doesn't hurt that the massive parking garage is near, right?"

"Parking always helps," Axel said. He produced one of his cards to pass to Gregory. "This is my information, if anything else occurs to you."

"I'll ask around. If anyone knows anything, we'll get it to you. Everyone here liked that girl. She tipped—not ridiculously, but consistently—and better than that, she had a smile for everyone," Gregory assured him.

Axel thanked him and paid for the drinks. He and Raina left the bar, and he looked across the room for Nigel, who was heading toward them.

"Anything?" Axel asked.

"Yes. Everyone loves Wong. He must be the best dentist in town. I think I'm going to make an appointment for myself," Nigel said, letting out a weary sigh. "You?"

"Maybe. Our boy Gregory over there says Jennifer was here often, repeats she was about the nicest human being walking the earth. And she did see Jordan Rivera while she was here, and our kindly chaperon, Frank Peters, tried to buy her a drink. An offer she rejected. Oh, and Frank was here with the other kindly chaperone, Loretta Oster, when he did so, and Loretta pretended not to see the exchange, but she did."

"So Loretta Oster has spent the last thirteen years or so killing people and dumping them in the Everglades?" Nigel asked skeptically.

"I came to no such conclusion. But I did decide she and Frank are worth more of our time," Axel said.

Raina was shaking her head. "If you're putting everything together, it would have been impossible for Loretta or Frank to have taken the victim thirteen years ago. They were with us that night. The night she disappeared. It's hard to chaperone forty-something young teens and escape for even ten minutes alone," she said.

"They were with you all day and all night?" Axel asked her.

"Well, no. Not all day. We were in school and had an orientation there at 3:00 p.m., and then the buses came at about four or four-thirty. When we arrived, we received another orientation and culture lesson from your friend Jeremy and then we had our campfire meal. Then you started with the pirate ship story, Axel."

Axel glanced at Nigel. "We need to go back and look at the old records. See what time people discovered the victim's car and found it abandoned."

"That's a long shot, isn't it?" Raina asked.

"It's all a long shot," Nigel told her, smiling ruefully. "All we've got is long shots. Anyway, I'm going to keel over. Tomorrow is another day. Axel, I'll get my people on records first thing in the morning," he said.

They all headed out together. Raina was silent as they walked to the car.

"What's wrong?" Axel asked her.

She shook her head. "It's just so insidious. Sometimes you can almost understand murder. Someone kills someone who has hurt someone else. A domestic situation out of hand. Greed, jealousy, but just killing time after time for no apparent reason?"

"We don't know if that's the case yet," he said quietly. "We're going on theory now, not facts."

She nodded. "But it is going to turn out to be the girl who disappeared all those years ago," she said.

"You touched the skull, and you know that?"

She shook her head. "I just know it. Your way. Intuition."

He was driving, but he reached out to set his hand on her shoulder. "Hey. I'm sorry. You shouldn't have been dragged in on this."

"No. I'm glad I was. But I need you to do me a favor."

"What's that?"

She turned to look at him. "I want you to stay with me tonight." She winced. "At my house, I mean. Not *with* me. You don't have to sleep with me."

The intense look he gave her had her rambling further. "Unless you want to. But you don't have to. It's a big house."

He smiled. "I don't have to?"

"No. That was terrible of me. I mean, people keep assuming we're together, and I'm hearing it so much—"

"Does it sound bad?"

"No, not at all. I just…"

"Does that mean I can sleep with you if I want to? It's not the criteria for me staying. I've got a hotel room. It's no problem."

She wasn't sure how serious he was being. "Is there anything wrong with me?" she asked anxiously.

He looked at the young woman he'd first met so many years before. And he remembered his first impression when they'd met again. She'd grown into a stunning young woman. She had confidence, but no idea of just how attractive she was, not just in her looks, but in her manner, her way of looking after others, being firm and assertive without aggression, and charming those around her with a smile. Those amber eyes of hers seemed to have a touch of gold from the sun in them, dazzling even in the shadows of the car.

She might train dogs, but she smelled as sweet and evocative as a jungle garden.

"Not a thing in the world," he said. He smiled, then. "And what about me?"

"What about you?"

"Is there anything wrong with me?"

"With you?" she asked.

"I mean, you're beautiful. Perfect. Awesome. Strange. Delightfully weird."

She was silent for a minute, looking downward, a smile creeping into her lips. She looked at him again.

"Tall, dark, handsome and extremely weird. I didn't know how weird. I'm not at all sure that either of us is delightfully weird, so I'm going to go with usefully weird on that one. But as to the other...you're beautiful. Perfect. Awesome."

"Wow," he said.

"Oh, please! You must get that often enough."

He fell silent himself. He wondered if there was a way to make her understand. Relationships in his life didn't last. The phone would ring and he would have to go; and far too often, he was distracted and even impatient. And, of course, there were the dead. Hard to explain to most others.

He didn't live as a monk in any way, but he seldom really connected. You met someone, there was an attraction, you slept together and then you tried to talk, get to know one another and...

Usually it fell apart.

This time...

They talked. And oddly, in little time, they knew one another.

They'd reached her house. She hurried out of the car before he could get the door. Running up the steps, she opened the door, greeting the dog, who boisterously greeted her in return.

"Special Agent Tiger is going to be staying with us tonight, watching over us," she told Titan. "You do a wonderful job of that, of course, but tonight..."

Her voice trailed. Axel was right behind her. He hunkered down to greet Titan, who seemed happy to see him.

He looked up at Raina. "Curious. What about you? Dating, I mean. Me, easy. Too much job. Too much weirdness in my life. But you dated handsome attorney Tate Fielding, right?"

"We just had different values," she said. "The breakup was mutual."

"Surely there were others."

"Well, of course I've dated!"

"And?"

She winced. "Well a lot of the time I was reminded of why I like dogs more than people."

"Hard to argue with that," he teased, rising.

He loved dogs, too. But he was suddenly awkward with himself, Raina and Titan.

"Think he's going to mind if we get close?" he asked Raina.

"I think he likes you," Raina told him. "I think he'll approve."

"Shall we test that out?"

She smiled, walking closer. He pulled her into his arms. She was warm and vital, her skin soft, her wiry frame strong in his hold. He found her lips and they were as sweet as he had expected, her mouth parting to his kiss, a passion building with the plunge and play of their tongues as they locked in an embrace, holding tightly, hands moving and bodies melding ever closer, till it seemed they were one being, burning together.

He broke away, heart thundering, breath coming fast. There were things to do.

"Doors locked?" he asked.

"Front and back."

"Window?"

"Hurricane code, all locked."

"Well, then…"

"Titan, guard the hallway!" Raina said.

The dog barked, and hurried ahead of them, ready to be obedient to his master.

Raina caught Axel's hand, drawing him down the hall and into her bedroom, leaning against the door to close it as they entered.

A night-light burned from the bathroom. It was enough. She was caught in a yellow-gold shadow, watching him as she slid from her shoes and started to disrobe. He watched as fabric fell from her body to the floor and felt his own body respond to the beauty of her form. He sprang to life, aware he wouldn't feel the fire and lightning fully from her body if his own remained clad.

But there was the one thing he never forgot—his Glock and the small holster at his back. He ripped himself away to set those on the nightstand within easy reach, then tore off his jacket and shirt and found her in his arms again, her lips on his, her fingers at his belt. In a matter of minutes, his pants were gone, even as he used every resolve of equilibrium to maintain his contact with her while not tripping out of his socks and shoes.

It didn't fully serve him. They fell together on her bed, laughing and pausing as she wound up on top, looking down at him, and then locking again in an embrace that brought them rolling and more fully into the center of the bed. It was more than his imagination had given him, the full touch of flesh against flesh, the vibrance and feel of her, the intoxication of her scent and her lips and the lightest brush of her fingers.

They scrambled to kiss and touch and tease. They rolled to one side and the next and twisted and turned in eagerness. He found her breasts and collarbone and ribs and worked his way down. Her fingers teased liquid fire into his shoulders and neck, grasping at his hair as whispers escaped her lips and she arched beneath him. The length of him seemed to be composed of lava then, hotter than melting steel, and the world became nothing but urgency. He came to her at last, for a second, just feeling that melding as if their flesh became one, frantic and eager, and longing still for the ecstasy and even agony to go on, rising like the sound of thunder crashing closer and encompassing all.

It was perhaps the best sex he'd ever had, a thought that shifted through his mind as they reached a shattering climax and slipped into the sweet and incredible afterglow that came as their hearts slowed and their bodies cooled.

They were both silent, just holding tight.

She lay curled against him, and he closed his eyes, savoring the silken feel of her hair against his chest.

And he wondered if it was true, if there was one person out there destined to be everything—lover, friend and all else.

She shifted, hands on his chest, rising against him, a sweet and slightly wicked smile on her face. She was about to speak.

But suddenly Titan began to bark, ferociously, frantically.

They both jumped out of bed as if a train were about to come crashing through the walls.

He was good at stumbling into his pants, grabbing the Glock and shouting at the same time.

"Stay here—leave this one to me and Titan!"

Stay here!

Weren't those the words used in dozens of horror movies? Kids messing around in the woods, the guy telling the girl to stay in the car while he checks out the situation.

Then the killer with a giant knife or hook sweeps in, skewers the guy and comes for the idiot girl who is just screaming in the car.

They weren't in a car. This was her home.

And Axel wasn't an idiot guy; he was a trained agent. Not to mention Titan. The dog would die before allowing anyone without permission into the sanctuary of his home.

But be that as it may, she couldn't just "stay."

She raced to the closet for a dress and threw it on. She

didn't rush out; she hesitated at the front door, listening. She could hear Titan barking.

And she could hear Axel speaking to him. "Good boy. It's all right now. Whatever it was, it's gone now. Good boy, you were great. Come on back in."

Raina ventured into the hallway, waiting. Titan came rushing in first, down the hall and straight to her, for once almost knocking her over in his eagerness to reach her and assure himself that she was okay.

She patted her dog, waiting for Axel.

She heard him relock the front door and saw him as he came back down the hallway, frowning.

"I didn't catch it," he told her.

"Catch it?" she asked.

He nodded, brows still tightly drawn. "I think someone stopped a car in front of your house. I don't know if they did or didn't get out, but it was blocks down the street by the time Titan and I got out there. I couldn't see the license plate." He shrugged lightly and offered her a half smile. "I could have chased the car down the road, but he took off. It was probably nothing. Animals are instinctive, and Titan probably knows he needs to be on high alert all the time. The car might've just belonged to a neighbor or someone visiting nearby. Anyway, doors are locked again."

"Why do you look worried?" she asked him.

He shook his head. "I'm not worried. I'm good friends with my Glock, and we have Titan."

"Do you think someone might really try to get to me? Why?" Raina asked. "I'm not a cop. I don't know anything."

"There's no reason. Unless someone else somehow knows you tried on a dress and found the body of a murder victim."

"Only my brother and the cops I saw that morning. None of whom seemed to believe me."

"You don't think Robert would have talked about it, do you?"

"My brother? No, that man is careful when he talks about the weather. He's an attorney to the nth letter of the law. Not to mention the fact most people would feel the way the cops did that morning. That I either killed poor Jennifer or know who did."

"Okay, then."

He walked toward her and took her into his arms.

"Where were we?"

She smiled as he kissed her, pulling back a little. "Well, I like where we were, and we'll get back to it. But let me reward Titan."

"Good plan. That is one great dog."

She stepped past him, hurrying to the kitchen to get one of Titan's favorite biscuits from a cupboard. She brought it back to the hallway and got him settled again.

Then she returned to the bedroom.

Axel was stretched back out on the bed, naked. His flesh was bronze against the pale blue of her sheets, caught in just a hint of the moonlight filtering in the edges of the drapes.

He leaned on an elbow, grinning as he waited for her.

"Well, that's cheesecake if I've ever seen it!" she told him.

"What!"

She lifted the ribbons on her dress, letting it drift to the floor.

"Well, now. That's straight out of a James Bond movie or the like," he told her.

"And your problem is? I like cheesecake."

"And I've been fond of every Bond girl. You getting back in here?"

"Of course. I'd never waste all that cheesecake!"

She made a flying leap for the bed and landed in his arms. They rolled, laughing, and then the laughter faded as he looked into her eyes, and his next kiss was very passionate, leading to much, much more.

She slept in his arms, and she thought she slept deeply. When she awoke, he was awake, and she felt he had slept, too.

But maybe not quite so deeply. He had been listening. Listening all through the night.

"Do you have work today?" he asked her.

"I do, but my schedule is easy, and I can switch anything around if necessary," Raina told him.

"Switch things around. Come with me to Andrew's."

"Okay. Is there a reason I shouldn't work?"

"No. I'm just happier if you're with me. And I want to chat with Jeremy. Maybe we'll take the horses over to the tourist area. It will be fun. Andrew will appreciate it."

"Okay."

"You can see Big Ole Mac."

"Okay. Alligator wrestling," she said. "Are you going to wrestle Big Ole Mac?"

"Not in this lifetime. Wait till you see him."

She smiled. "I have seen him. I've gone out there many times during the years."

"Good. You enjoy it?"

"I do."

"We'll stop by the hotel on the way. I can shower there."

"You can shower here."

"That might take too long."

"What's the difference?"

"You'd be too tempted. You'd come in."

"Wow. What humility!"

He glanced at his watch. "Okay, why not."

He headed for the shower. For a minute, she had decided not to follow him, but then she grinned and did so, pushing him aside as she entered.

"I told you," he said.

"Don't be ridiculous. I'm just trying to save time."

"I see."

"Want your back washed?"

"Are you trying to wash it?"

"I really can't stand a dirty back."

He turned. She used liquid soap on his back, caressing it as she did. She smiled as he turned around, slick and clean, and drew her into his arms.

"I didn't mean to be so time-consuming," she whispered.

He laughed softly.

"Time is what we make of it," he assured her.

Moments later, she thought he had a talent for making really good use of time.

"It's her," Andrew said, quiet and thoughtful as he shook his head.

Raina and Titan were out with the horses. She couldn't resist seeing them first. Either Axel would head out soon or she'd come in. One way or the other, he did want to ride out to the village. He was pretty sure he'd find Jeremy out there, and Jeremy might remember what had gone on in the past better than he did, if nothing else.

"They're still out there looking for more pieces. But thankfully, with the skull, they were able to match dental records through the cold-case department almost immediately," Andrew said.

"But still no cause of death, right?"

Andrew shook his head. "You think it will be the same, though, don't you. Okay, I understand, but it's crazy. I mean, just taking people and quickly severing their throats? That doesn't sound like any serial killer I've ever heard of. I know you're FBI and went through all kinds of classes, but I've been to a few myself even if I am just tribal police."

"There's no 'just,' Andrew, and you know it," Axel said, shaking his head. "Seriously, think about it. Serial killers—drawn by sex. Or Dahmer—a cannibal. John Wayne Gacy—

sexual assault, torture and murder. Son of Sam—told to shoot people by a dog. These killings have nothing in common. The victims have nothing in common and most likely never saw one another or frequented the same place."

"Well, Fran Castle didn't frequent the club we went to last night. It didn't exist back when she was murdered."

"No. Oh, and I got a call from Larry Stillwater. Don't know who he talked to at the fundraiser, but he said there had been some incidents up in their area you should know about."

"Oh?"

"No skulls, nothing so telling. But a few years back, some tourists found a bone. Everyone up there was in on it, but they never found anything other than the one bone. Two years before that, a necropsy was done on an old alligator that bit the dust."

"And?"

"They found human remains. Too digested for DNA or anything, really. But Larry thinks someone has used the Everglades—and Seminole tribal land—for some dumping, too."

Andrew had sheets out on the table. Axel looked at them, feeling his frustration grow.

"Five—counting Fran Castle way back. More with the bones. But then we have Hermione Shore, a young widow. Rich, but from all accounts kind and generous and well-liked. Peter Scarborough, separated, but his wife was in another state and he was a working stiff, a carpenter. No reason to hire a killer to get rid of him that we know of. We have Alina Fairchild, early thirties. Four women, one man. And as best we can tell, they were all killed quickly and cleanly and dumped."

"We don't know yet about Fran Castle," Andrew reminded him.

"I'm willing to bet we find out she died by having her

throat slit. With any luck, the crew out there will find more bones."

Andrew was silent. "You seem to suspect some of Raina's friends."

"I'm not sure how they could be involved. When Fran Castle was killed, you and I were barely eighteen and Raina couldn't have been more than thirteen or fourteen at the time. That means her friends were all kids back then, too. But..."

His voice trailed.

"Yeah?"

"The chaperones. Frank Peters and Loretta Oster. They were here then, and they're still around now."

"They were at the campsite the night Fran Castle disappeared."

"We don't know when she disappeared. We just know when it was reported she'd disappeared. Vinnie Magruder might know more."

"He was first on call. The detective on the case was a man named Hank Upton. He died of cancer about three years ago. Until he got sick, he'd come out now and then. The case frustrated the hell out of him."

"Maybe Vinnie remembers something. I'm going to talk to him, see if he can give me anything at all. Anyway, I'm off to see Jeremy. I want to know what he remembers."

"You driving over?"

"Taking your horses, if that's okay."

"Yeah, sure. The horses will be happy. I'll head back out on patrol for a while and meet you over there. You'll ride by the area where they're still digging. Maybe they've found something more."

"Maybe." Axel hesitated and pulled out his phone and called Angela.

"There's must be something," he told her, looking at Andrew as he spoke. "Something in common between these people, our victims. Hermione Shore, Peter Scarborough, Alina Fairchild and Fran Castle, and Jennifer Lowry. Angela, please, pull up everything. Reports from friends, social media, phone records—anything at all you can get. I can't help feeling if I could find the common ground, I'd find the killer."

Andrew nodded as he watched the call. Angela assured Axel she hadn't stopped searching and their best techs were on it.

When he hung up, he frowned.

"What?" Andrew asked.

"Scarborough's wife."

"Yeah, no money involved. They'd been split up."

"I still want to know more about her."

"You're thinking murder for hire again?"

"Well, why else would victims be so random, and it's as if they're being executed. As you said, these killings aren't typical serial killer. So random—so quick. Kidnapping. No ransom asked ever. Just a swift death."

He pulled out his phone again and put another call through to Angela. Scarborough's wife had been eliminated because she had an alibi.

In most murder cases, the wife, husband or lover fell under immediate scrutiny. And the police had looked at her first. Witnesses verified the fact she'd never left her state.

But you didn't need to be in the same state to hire a killer.

"Angela," he said when she answered. She amazed him; there were so many agents in the field, all needing her help. But she could switch cases at the speed of lightning. She was extraordinary.

"Yes? I don't have anything new yet. You've only given me four minutes."

"I know. I'm sorry. But what do we have on Peter Scarborough's wife? Of all the victims, he was the only one married, though separated."

Angela swiftly drew up her information on the woman.

"Scarborough's wife—Melissa, forty-eight, works at a pack-and-ship place. Two grown children living in California. Her children were from a previous marriage. Peter had no heirs other than Melissa, but he left nothing. She ordered his apartment cleared out with everything being given to the Salvation Army. His bank accounts covered a cremation for him."

"Well, no one killed him for his money. See if you can find out how and why they split up, huh?"

"I will."

"Thank you."

He hung up again.

"Maybe, just maybe, Jeremy knows something I can pull from him." He hesitated, thinking of the strange way Jordan Rivera had behaved the night before.

Stricken.

Not like a killer.

And still, so strange.

"Jeremy was setting up camp for the schoolkids and at the camp all day, from what I remember. I wasn't there, but—" Andrew stopped.

"I was. And yes, he was there all day."

"Then?"

"Gotta do something. Keep people talking." Axel stood, ready to join Raina outside.

"If nothing else…"

"If nothing else?"

"You can pay your respects to Big Ole Mac."

CHAPTER TWELVE

The head of the team digging and searching the area for more bones was Dr. Jinny Carlysle. She was about fifty with gray hair that curled tightly to her head. She had the look of someone who was both competent and determined.

Even as Raina and Axel approached the site on horseback, she was out in the road, waving at them, warning them to stay off the path and the area where she had set stakes out for her digging purposes.

She introduced herself quickly. She was working with a team of five—two people from the county forensics lab and two grad students from the University of Miami—and she introduced them all in a whirl, explaining she was both a medical examiner and an anthropologist, and thus had been put in charge.

She nodded gravely at Raina, hearing she had been the one to happen upon the skull.

And though Axel had used his first name with her, she preferred to keep referring to him as "Special Agent Tiger."

"Anything else?" Axel asked.

She nodded grimly. "So far? Three rib bones. I'm afraid the

skeleton was compromised by scavengers and whatever else. I believe we'll find most of the bones, though. Other than those bones that might have been picked up by birds and scattered. I understand we have an ID on our victim from dental records, a poor young woman who went missing a little over thirteen years ago."

"Yes," Axel said. "Is there damage to the bones you've discovered so far?"

"Sure," Dr. Carlysle said. "You don't stay out here for thirteen years without damage being done. Predators of all kinds, scavengers..."

"I'm looking for possible cause of death," Axel said.

But Dr. Carlysle shook her head. "I don't know yet. I haven't found anything that resembles a knife wound. Most of the damage I've found so far has come from a predatory cat and insects and worms. But we have a long way to go."

Axel thanked her.

Dr. Carlysle looked at Raina. She nodded her approval. "You found a skull and you're back out here. Good for you."

Raina gave her a grim smile. "When you find a skull, Dr. Carlysle, you want the truth."

Carlysle nodded her approval again. "We'll be doing our best to give you the truth." She looked at Axel. "And we hope you, sir, can find the truth." She was quiet a minute. "I know I can't ask you about the ongoing investigation, but it's hard not to wonder about the murders in the Everglades over the last few years, and now this."

"Of course," Axel said.

"Are you getting anywhere? At least the last victim was found right away."

"We like to believe we are." Raina watched as his head cast at a slight angle as he looked at the older woman.

"Dr. Carlysle, did you know any of the victims?"

"I did," she said quietly. "A man named Peter Scarborough. We were often in the same coffee shop."

"In South Miami?" Axel asked her a little sharply.

But she shook her head. "No, down by the Jackson hospital. He was doing some work there. My lab is there. And the morgue."

"I would like to speak with you about him, if I may?"

"It will be my pleasure," she assured him. She lifted gloved hands covered in mud and muck. "Later? Officer Osceola has offered us his home as a rest stop. I'm assuming you came from his house?"

"We did. We'll see you there later, then," Axel told her.

They skirted the area, riding on by. The workers all stopped for a minute to wave them on. When they were past them, Raina asked, "If she was a friend of Peter Scarborough's, wouldn't the police have interviewed her already?"

"They might have. But there wouldn't be much. Not if you just talked to a casual friend. She wouldn't have appeared on any kind of a 'person of interest' list, I don't believe. Think about it—the number of people the average person might see on any given day. In a big city at least. You might see the same clerk at a grocery store and chat with them often or the same folks in line at a coffee shop. Questioning anyone and everyone a person might see is exhausting and never complete. I don't know if she can help us or not. The first hours when a person is discovered missing or dead are always the most important. But when that fails, you have to dig a lot further. On this, following the trail of Jennifer Lowry was most important. Now, we have to look more fully at all of the victims," Axel said.

"And we're going to the village because…?"

"Because I haven't been there yet, and I want to talk to Jeremy."

"You don't think that Jeremy—"

"No. I don't," he said.

She fell silent for a minute, aware he thought someone they knew was involved in some way. But she couldn't believe her friends were involved.

"My group—we were all just kids when Fran Castle disappeared."

"I know."

"Jordan behaved strangely, but he was truly stricken when he learned Jennifer Lowry had been killed."

"I know."

She fell silent again; he didn't appear to be in the mood to talk.

The trail, she thought as they rode, was beautiful. In a strange way, of course. The trail itself followed spits of hardwood plateaus, while around them there was water, the eternally moving "river of grass" that made up the Everglades. There were birds in every color as they moved along—cranes, egrets, owls, hawks, and they came across one great blue heron, dead still and standing on one leg in the water as he eyed his terrain, awaiting a meal.

At one point, they passed a few adolescent alligators basking on the embankment.

Axel started to warn her to keep a wide berth, though it was unlikely they would attack something as large as the horses.

She knew to keep her distance. They rode by without the alligators so much as moving.

They had taken a different route to the village. The customary entrance was off the Tamiami Trail, and there was an outpost where a lone Miccosukee man of an indeterminate age sat in the middle of a chickee playing a game on his smartphone. He obviously knew Axel; he said hello and assured them it was a fine place to leave the horses.

As they arrived via a back road, they came upon a man

seated by a small pool with exotic birds. He raised a hand in greeting to Axel, and Axel waved back. They moved on to a large pool where a man in a typically colorful Miccosukee shirt was on a podium, talking about alligators while a second man was in a paddock with an adolescent alligator of about six feet.

The village also offered several "chickee" type structures occupied by men and women all dressed in the multicolored shirts and skirts that were typical to South Florida Native Americans.

But the pen where the man was working with the alligator had drawn most everyone's attention.

"We don't wrestle alligators, though that's what most say. We love our alligators here, and we demonstrate what they're capable of," he was telling a crowd of onlookers. "They have always been an essential part of the ecology here in the Everglades. But people enjoy a look at the giant mouths of our native creatures."

A cry of awe went up in the crowd as the man in the paddock opened the alligator's jaw with both hands, and demonstrated his ability to put his own head within the creature's mouth and then safely withdraw it.

"I think Jeremy might be in one of the little chickee kiosks," Axel said. "They've opened a nice air-conditioned shop at the entry where they sell tickets, but there are still men and women working some of the little hut areas. A friend of his is a wonderful seamstress, makes some amazing shirts. I love her use of color."

As they moved away from the show toward an area with several little shops, Raina could hear a strange grunting sound and she smiled. Alligators out in the canal.

"They sound like pigs," she said.

"Yeah?"

"Don't you think so?"

He grinned, looking at her. "I suppose. I just always knew what they were. Maybe pigs sound like alligators."

She laughed. "Maybe."

"Hey, chat Linda up when we're in there, okay?" he asked.

"Uh, sure," Raina told him. "You know Jeremy so well, you know that he'll be there?"

"I know Jeremy well enough to suspect he'll be there," he told her, a small smile curving his lips as he shrugged. "I called him on my way out to you and the horses to make sure he'd be here."

They reached the chickee. Most of the visitors to the village were watching the show; the kiosks were quiet.

Jeremy was at the back of the little kiosk, sitting on a folding wooden stool next to a woman Raina presumed to be Linda. She was dressed in a long, colorful skirt and a blouse with an incredible array of colors with different bands of color offering different designs. Her hair was long and straight, a beautiful pitch-black. She stood, seeing Axel, crying his name out softly and rising quickly to come and greet him with a hug. Stepping back, she looked at Raina, waiting for an introduction. Jeremy was already up and on his way over. He quickly welcomed Raina and introduced her to Linda, whose last name was Cypress.

"Common enough among Miccosukees and Seminoles," Linda explained. "We all have a 'clan' name, Axel is Tiger, and I'm Cypress…and Andrew is Osceola. Of course, Osceola is a hero to all of us, a truly great man!"

"Captured under a white flag of truce, to the discredit of the US military at the time," Raina said.

Linda nodded. "You know some history, huh?"

"Always fascinated me. And I was appalled once, up in St. Augustine, by the castillo, when a guide—a guide!—said he'd been executed. I mean, the way he was captured—dreadful. But the US didn't kill him. He died of disease."

"Yes," Linda said, "and his doctor was his friend, but the silly man took Osceola's head to study and use it to scare his children into good behavior by sticking it on their bedposts!"

"His son-in-law did the same," Raina said.

"And then the man's office burned, and Osceola's head was lost. I mean, I don't think he was using it anymore at that point, anyway."

"True, but historians and anthropologists believe they could better understand him—and his heritage—if they just had his head!"

Linda turned to Axel. "I like this girl!"

"I love the culture," Raina said. "And your clothing, your shirts and blouses and skirts—these are beautiful," Raina said.

"Well, thank you," she said.

Axel spoke up then. "Jeremy, you got a minute? I want to take you down memory lane."

"Sure," Jeremy said.

As they walked away, a pair of tourists sauntered up to the kiosk.

"You speak English?" the man asked Linda.

Linda smiled. "Why, yes, I do."

"Oh, great! Can you give me the price on a few of these shirts? So unusual. I mean, we're used to leather and big feather headdresses!" the woman said.

"The clothing you see here really didn't become popular until the early twentieth century," Linda told them pleasantly. "Before then, we dressed a great deal like your basic Eastern woodland tribe. But we do love beads and colors, and I do love my work."

"Lovely. Do you cook traditional food? I mean, what do you do for dinner?"

Linda kept smiling. "Frankly, on many a night, I order out for pizza."

"Oh!"

"You might really enjoy a visit to the museum," Linda said politely. "We Miccosukee—and our fellows, the Seminole—adapted to hiding in the Everglades, going deeper and deeper to avoid deportation and death. It's interesting to see all the different ways people came. We welcomed many a runaway slave back then, too, so you'll find many dark Miccosukee and Seminole Indians. And yes, we do have some traditional foods—we used *kontí* root and other food sources we found here—but we are certainly aware of most of the conveniences of the twenty-first century."

She hadn't stopped smiling.

When the couple had paid for a shirt and a blouse and moved on hopefully to the museum, Linda lost her smile at last.

"I think I was supposed to greet them with 'How!'" she said.

"Well, at least they're out here, and maybe they'll learn something," Raina said.

"They're probably on their way to the casino." She grinned. "Too bad they aren't up in Hollywood. Have you seen the guitar-shaped hall up at the Seminole Hard Rock?"

"I have. It's fantastic."

"Seminole revenge!" Linda said, laughing. "They are making money hand over fist. Of course, we make money at our casino, too. Still, I love going up to the 'guitar'!"

"Seriously, want to know one of the things I love best?" Raina asked.

"And what's that?"

"The pumpkin bread over at the restaurant. I don't even like pumpkin. But that bread is absolutely delicious."

"It is, isn't it? So, how long have you been seeing Axel? Are you up in the DC area now?"

Raina's eyebrows shot up at the sudden change of topic. "I, uh, no. I'm here—South Miami."

"Oh, you're the dog trainer! How silly of me. I didn't get to go to that fundraiser, but Jeremy was telling me that you were amazing."

"Do you have a dog?"

"I do. I'll introduce you some day," Linda said happily. "He's a big guy—a Dane. Doesn't pay to have anything too little around here." She sighed softly. "You can't blame an alligator for being an alligator. They really aren't vicious monsters. Little guys—and unfortunately little people—look like dinner to them. It's just what they are. And there are idiots who aren't savvy about them who think it's fun to feed them. To an alligator, an arm might just be an extension of the piece of chicken being offered up. I'm not really defending them, but this was their home before we came here. Most of us who live out here know what we're doing. That includes all kinds of park rangers, people who own airboat companies, even people who do a lot of fishing in the canals. But when you see people driving down trails that are truly off the beaten track and they look like they walked out of a department store's 'outdoorsy' display, you have to wonder."

"Have you seen a lot of that?"

"Only now and then. I fear we'll get another horror story about someone being bitten by an Eastern diamondback or the like. Chewed up by a gator. I'm rambling now. I'm sorry."

"No, I think it's important. Do you remember any specific time?" Raina asked her. "The recent bodies, they've gotten out here somehow."

Linda nodded worriedly. "That's true. I should tell Axel. I just never thought anything of it other than being annoyed."

"It's understandable. And you have a customer," Raina said, noting a young woman who had walked up to the booth.

"Viv!" Linda said, greeting the newcomer.

"Linda, I need two more blouses," the young woman said.

"My sister saw mine and adores it, and she wants one for a friend, too."

"Sure, and thank you. What's your pick?" Linda asked her. She hugged the young woman over the table that displayed some of her wares. Obviously a friend.

Raina slipped out of the booth area and returned to the common ground. She waved to Linda. She could see Axel and Jeremy were a distance from the booth near another displaying pottery.

A group was oohing and ahhing over one of the paddock areas. She smiled and walked to the fence to join them.

They were listening to a lecture on Big Ole Mac.

Big Ole Mac was seventeen feet long and would be eighty years old on his next birthday. He'd been born right there in the village and he'd spent his life there. In the wild, the American alligators usually lived between thirty and fifty years, with an average weight of about five hundred pounds. The females were smaller than males and very protective of their young.

"That's the one thing we're always trying to warn hunters. We do have an alligator hatching season. There's also a mating season. Alligators are territorial and are more dangerous during mating season when other males might try to intrude on their turf. It's never a good time to tempt an alligator, but many of you who play golf know they can show up on golf courses even in busy areas of our neighboring cities. Yes, they have gotten into residential pools upon occasion and they swim the canals. Never mess with an alligator—especially during mating season."

Big Ole Mac was oblivious to anything being said. He was just lying on the embankment of his little pool area, looking like something giant and prehistoric.

Which, of course, he was.

"An alligator is a crocodilian—a creature that was alive and well at the time of the dinosaurs," the lecturer said. "Now, we have crocodiles in Florida, too, in brackish water down at the tip of the peninsula. Note the difference in the snouts on the creatures, and remember crocodiles are still endangered here while alligators are not."

The lecture was ongoing, but Raina didn't pay attention any longer. She saw Axel was thanking Jeremy and saying goodbye to him.

She waited a few minutes and then made her way back toward Linda's chickee kiosk.

Linda was talking earnestly to Axel when she reached the booth again. He was looking at her with a question in his eyes.

"A paying customer walked up. I didn't want to intrude," Raina said.

Linda looked a little confused, oblivious to the fact Axel had asked Raina to stay with her.

"I had to pay my respects to Big Ole Mac," she said.

"Ah, yes, of course!" Axel said.

"I told him what I told you—about seeing strange cars on off-beat roads," Linda said. "I hope it was helpful in some way."

"Yes, it is," Axel told her.

"Well, I guess we should get Andrew's horses back," Axel said. He smiled at Raina.

"I guess we should," she agreed.

"Speaking of Andrew, he's right over there," Linda said.

Andrew was in uniform, talking casually to people as he made his way over to join them.

"I'm returning the horses, Officer, I swear," Axel said lightly.

"Good to hear!" Andrew said. "Just thought I'd check on you all. We've got a wild one here," he teased, looking at Raina.

"Her horse is the wild thing," Linda said. "Speaking of

which, isn't there another one of those school camp-out-in-
the-Everglades thing coming up? I'd be happy to lecture on
differences in Eastern woodland tribes and Western tribes,
cultures and history. I've meant to volunteer."

"I'm the one you volunteer with!" Jeremy said as he walked
up to the group. "You can let me know anytime."

"Axel and Raina made me think of it," Linda said.

"There's a group this weekend. And you're more than welcome to lecture," Jeremy said.

"A school group this week?" Axel asked.

"Yes, this is the weekend three of the middle schools
come—packs of eighth-graders. Maybe at some time someone thought it was a good rite of passage into high school or
something like that," Jeremy told them. "You're welcome to
come out, you know. I have plenty of little pop-up tents!"

"Maybe we'll do that," Axel told him. "You're going to be
there, Andrew, right?"

"I will be there," Andrew said.

Jeremy was regarding Axel steadily. "Because you're worried?" he asked.

Axel shrugged. "Back to basics, maybe. Fran Castle disappeared on a night like that about thirteen years ago. I don't
know. I guess it would be good to be there. Of course, I'd
be an idiot to think I could really watch the Everglades—an
army can barely do that. But yeah, I'm here—and not getting very far."

"We'll all make it safer for the kids, at any rate," Andrew
said, shrugging.

"How is Nigel doing with the investigation? I'm assuming
he has something like an army behind him. I mean, checking with witnesses, and all that?"

"We have people from all kinds of agencies working it,"
Axel said. "But the Everglades, as you know, can be brutal.
Finding leads is…"

"Needle in a haystack," Jeremy said. "Pin in a sawgrass swamp."

"Something like that," Axel agreed. "Anyway, we'll see you this weekend."

"Perfect," Jeremy agreed.

"Andrew, we'll take the horses back," Axel told him. He frowned. "Titan is...?"

"A very happy dog. I had a big steak bone. The place isn't locked. I figured if that dog was on guard, I didn't need to worry too much about leaving the place unlocked!"

They exchanged goodbyes, Linda giving Raina a big hug and a smile, Jeremy doing the same. "Hey, even if that lug goes back to Washington, you're welcome out here anytime," Linda told Raina.

"Technically, the big lug goes back to Virginia!" Axel teased. At last, he and Raina left them and headed back to retrieve the horses.

When they were mounted and back on the trail, Raina asked him, "Do you think you learned anything?"

"I don't know." He glanced her way. "Jeremy couldn't vouch for anything before you and your group and the chaperones arrived that afternoon. There had been a report earlier—around two in the afternoon. Vinnie Magruder—Miami-Dade back then—didn't arrive at the campsite until about 8:00 p.m. So, I don't know. I don't think I like your old chaperones very much. Frank Peters doesn't seem to be very true blue, but worse, I think Loretta Oster is conniving. According to the bartender, she saw what went on, but she didn't confront Frank about trying to buy Jennifer Lowry a drink. She swept it under the carpet."

"Maybe she's just trying to hang on to her man."

"Maybe. As I said, I don't much like either of them. That doesn't mean they're killers."

Raina's phone was buzzing in her pocket. She drew it out,

expecting Elly or Lucia or even Mya, curious as to what was going on with her and Axel.

It was Jordan. He was probably trying to see about her schedule for Sara and her little pup.

But he wasn't calling about training.

"Raina, I need to talk to you," he said.

"Okay. Sure, Jordan. Go ahead."

"No, in person. Where are you now?"

"Oh, I'm sorry, I'm not home. I'm out in the Everglades."

"You're out in the Everglades?"

"Yes, I—"

"Raina, be careful out there. You have to be careful."

"I'm with Axel. We were visiting some of his friends."

"Good." He was silent a second. "Stay with Axel. Call me when you're home. When I can talk to you."

"Sure. I can come right back in—"

The phone went dead in her hands and she looked at Axel.

"Jordan," she said. "He wants to see me. I'm supposed to call him when I get back home."

"Let's head back then. I don't think Jordan is a killer. I do think he might know who is."

As they were returning to Andrew's house, they reached the site where the crew was digging for bones.

Dr. Carlysle was in the path, waving them down as they reached the area.

"Special Agent Tiger!" she called.

Axel reined in and dismounted.

"Yes, Dr. Carlysle, you have something?" he asked her.

She nodded and produced a tiny object.

He realized it was a bone. "It's amazing we found this! Oh, we have a femur, too, and a few more ribs, and Katie and Jorge over there have just discovered a partial on the pelvis. But this! This is amazing. Maria from the forensics lab discovered it."

Raina had dismounted, as well. They both looked at the tiny object in Dr. Carlysle's hand.

"A hyoid!" Dr. Carlysle said.

The bone at the back of the throat.

"And can you tell anything...?" Axel began.

"Oh, yes! Definitely and unbelievably with the size of the bone and the amount of time it's been in the elements. But see this, right here? Thank goodness the sun is bright and your eyes are good, right? You can see this tiny scratch here, but it's deep, really, not just from a brush with a rock or something like that. No, sir, I believe this proves these bones belong to someone who was murdered. Murdered by having her throat slit. Most likely, from ear to ear." She wasn't being dramatic. The look in her eyes was one of horror. "Didn't that happen recently?" she asked. "Just days ago. That poor girl they found..."

"Thank you," Axel told her. "Did you share your findings with Detective Ferrer yet?" he asked.

"I called him just moments ago," she said.

"Good," Axel said. He looked over to Raina, his eyes signaling to mount up. She wasn't surprised and neither was he. It was as he had expected.

"Thank you. This is important to know," he said, as he looked down at Dr. Carlysle from the saddle. He glanced at Raina. She was stoic, looking back at him.

He lifted a hand to Dr. Carlysle and they started off again.

"You already knew," she reminded him.

"I did. And if you don't mind, it's given me an idea." He hesitated. "To use you."

She arched a brow his way. She didn't appear to be upset or afraid.

"How?"

"I need to call a friend. A coworker. And his girlfriend."

"And?"

"She has some unusual talents, too."

"She tried on a dress and saw a body?"

"No. I've mentioned them to you before. Past life regression—that brought her to the moment of what was happening."

"We need to see Jordan."

"I know. And to the best of my knowledge, my friends are in Virginia. Even if the jet is available, it will take them time to get here."

She looked at him steadily. "I'm willing to try anything you think might help."

"Thank you."

He looked back. Beneath the flickering afternoon sunlight, he saw someone else among the workers. Peg-legged Pete, and there, behind one of the big old cypress trees, another of his ragtag crew. Pete was trying to point something out to one of the workers. She didn't see him, but she must have sensed him.

She was looking where Pete was directing her attention.

Pete looked up and saw Axel. Grimly, he lifted a hand in acknowledgment.

Axel lowered his head, indicating his thanks.

CHAPTER THIRTEEN

Titan was apparently happy enough chewing on his bone at Andrew's house. He was equally happy they returned, greeting Raina with an affection that almost knocked her over.

She was glad to see Titan appeared almost as happy to see Axel, especially since Titan was a good judge of people.

"So now what?" she asked Axel.

"We'll get back to your place and get ahold of Jordan."

"What he wants to say—it may not have anything to do with any of this."

"But it does."

Raina was thoughtful. "It wasn't Jordan. You saw him. He was bereft. I don't remember his exact words, but he insisted Jennifer Lowry hadn't deserved it. He cared for her, and he was stunned and angry. Besides, Titan wouldn't like him if he was a murderer."

"I have a lot of faith in the dog, Raina, but even you said there was something off with Jordan. You knew it from when he was at your house, and you knew it after we saw him."

"I can't believe he'd be a party to this."

"Maybe he's not. Maybe he's seen or heard something that can help."

"That has to be it," Raina said. "I'll call him while we're on the way back to my place."

As they tended to the horses, Andrew returned. He found them in the stables.

"Well, this could be a total waste of time," Andrew said, "but I suggest we hang out at that camping trip coming up. Your couple-not-official-couple, Loretta Oster and Frank Peters, will definitely be there. They bring the kids in Wednesday night and the bus picks them all back up on Sunday around noon. Campfire tales Wednesday night—you do the pirate ship story best, Axel, as I recall—and then on Thursday they're doing Shark Valley and the Miccosukee restaurant. On Friday it's airboat tours, and Saturday the village and their final campfire. Now, here's the thing. The groups are a bit larger these days, so there are two additional chaperones. But all four of them are supposed to be with the kids from start to finish. I'm not sure what we can get." He hesitated. "If those two have somehow figured out how to murder people, I don't know how they can get away with it with sixty pre–high school kids in their care."

"And," Axel said, "if this is something organized or for some bizarre special purpose, there's no reason they'd be at it again so quickly. Still, I do think we should be there. I'll talk to Nigel and make sure he's in accord with us. And find out if he has gotten anything else."

Andrew nodded gravely, looking at Raina. "Wild Thing really likes you. That horse has never been so well behaved. Well, I like to think he likes me, too, but…"

Raina smiled. "I like Wild Thing. Great horse. I hope you'll… I hope you'll keep letting me come see him."

"Of course!"

They headed out a few minutes later. Raina tried to reach Jordan. His phone went straight to voice mail.

Axel had greater success in calling his headquarters. Raina wasn't sure what was said exactly, but another Krewe agent was coming down with his "unusually gifted" girlfriend.

"Jordan isn't answering," she said.

"We'll just keep trying every fifteen minutes or so until we get him," Axel said.

When they reached the house, Titan went bounding out the car door. Raina thought he was racing for the house, but he wasn't.

He was making a beeline for the bushes by the house.

"Titan!" she called, rushing after him. "What is it, boy?"

Axel followed her as she hurried toward the dog. Titan wasn't upset or growling at anything; he had something between his teeth and he was wagging his tail wildly.

"What the heck?" Raina said.

"Get it from him!" Axel said.

"What?"

"Get it from him—quickly."

"He doesn't kill squirrels or lizards or iguanas or birds—he knows better. He's just found—"

"Whatever he's found, get it from him."

He stepped by her. Titan might like Axel, but not well enough to allow him to take some treasure out of his mouth.

She hurried forward herself.

"Titan, drop it!"

For a moment, the dog stared at her.

"Titan, you heard me. Drop it!"

The dog did so, staring at her belligerently.

"What is it?" Axel asked, moving forward to take the mass the animal had dropped.

Titan let out a growl. Raina chastised him.

"I've got it!" she said.

She picked up the mystery pile the dog had dropped. It looked like a piece of charred meat.

"It's someone's leftovers, I guess," Raina said.

"On the side of your yard, in the bushes, next to your window?" Axel asked, his voice hard.

He dug in his pocket, producing a plastic baggie with a sealed closure.

"That's an evidence bag."

"Yes."

"You just walk around with evidence bags?"

"Always. Think we should give Titan some kind of reward for spitting out his find?"

"Right, yes, of course."

Raina unlocked her door. No one had tried to jimmy it. She wondered if Axel's work hadn't made him eternally suspicious.

"You know, a bird might have dropped that piece of meat," she said.

"What bird do you know that's big enough to carry that? No hawk out there is going to drop a morsel like that and leave it. No vulture or anything else I can think of. Anyway, better safe than sorry," Axel said.

"Yes, of course, better safe than sorry, always," she admitted.

"I need to get this to the local lab. Let's give Titan a treat and head that way. You can keep trying Jordan while we go. We can swing by his place and see if he's there, if you think it will help."

She was quiet a minute. "He might talk to me, but not you. I don't know."

"He knows you're with me."

"I guess. Anyway, we'll keep trying him."

She checked Titan's water bowl and gave him several of his favorite treats, then told him to stand guard.

Then they left again.

It was growing late. The Miami sun was going down.

But Axel apparently knew he would find someone at work at his local offices and he did. He left Raina in the reception area while he spoke with the local field director.

While he was gone, she tried Jordan again.

He still wasn't answering his phone.

In the middle of her dialing, a phone call came through and she answered it quickly, thinking Jordan was calling her back.

It wasn't Jordan. It was Lucia.

"Hey, I know this is late and you might be busy, but Mya and I were having pedicures this afternoon, and talked about doing something this evening. We called Elly and she was free, and Elly called Tate Fielding and he's free, and, oh, Mya's husband is free, and we thought, hey, Tall, Dark and Good-looking is still here, maybe we should have an impromptu dinner. All we need to get the gang back together is you and Jordan."

"Have you reached Jordan?"

"No, but Elly talked to him earlier. He won something or another at the fundraiser and she needed to see about getting it to him. Something big. A piece of exercise equipment, I think. Anyway, he said to let him know if anything was going on and he'd show up. Text him a time and a place, you know? So, how about it? You in?"

"Um, I'm not sure yet. Do the same with me, okay? Just text me the details, and if we can, we'll be there."

"Cool. We, huh? So, you are together, then?"

Raina hesitated. "Well, for now. We went riding today. Out to the village."

"You always did love all that nature and culture. But remember—your dude is an FBI agent. He'll go back to big-time civilization when this is over."

"Lucia, we live in big-time civilization. We don't spend our days in the Everglades."

Lucia laughed. "True. But it's there, you know. Reachable, easily. But you went riding? In the muck and the swamp and the snakes and the gators?"

"There's, like, a trail back there. I'm not into slushing through sawgrass, snakes and swamp."

"I guess no one is these days. Except maybe the python hunters. Hey, they're going to make a show about it, you know."

"So I've heard," Raina said.

She looked up. Axel was returning. "I have to go, Lucia. Just text me where you all are going and when."

"Well, it will be soon. And nowhere fancy. Maybe Sergio's—we all love that, right on Coral Way. Somewhere casual!"

"Text!"

"I will."

She hung up, standing.

"Did you get Jordan?"

She shook her head. "But I was just talking to Lucia. She wants to get together for dinner, and Elly told her she'd talked to Jordan earlier, and he'd said if they texted a time and a place, he'd try to be there."

He shrugged. "Sure, we'll go. Where does Jordan live? We can drive by and just see if he's home."

"He lives in Coconut Grove. At this time, it might be easiest to shoot straight down US 1."

"That's fine. Keep calling."

She did. She tried his number as they got to the car. Once again, it went straight to his voice mail.

"That's his cell. Does he have a house line?"

She looked at him, arching a brow.

"Hey. There are people who still have house lines. And is it a house? Or is he in a condo or apartment?"

"No, a house. He inherited it from an aunt he'd been good to all his life. His grandparents on his dad's side came over from Cuba and the family was close and very tight." She hesitated. "Jordan is a good guy, Axel. He really is."

"You never dated him?"

She shook her head. "We were always just good friends."

"But you did date Tate Fielding."

"He's not a bad person, either. Just a little full of himself."

"You said you stayed friends when you split up."

"It was never much of a romance. We were just together. I don't think he was ever particularly into just one person. Tate likes being adored. It's just the way he is. And he was cool in middle school and high school and college, and he stepped right into his father's firm. That might make him an ass. It doesn't mean he's evil."

"I'm just asking."

"And now you're going to want to know about Lucia, Elly and Mya?"

He looked at her. "You think women can't be evil?" he queried, a slight curl to his lips.

"No. Of course not. Anyone can be evil," she said. "But again, when Fran Castle disappeared, we were kids. Thirteen and fourteen years old."

He nodded. "Yes."

"What does that mean? Hey, I was on the bus with those guys. And through every lecture. Plus, we were at school all day before we got on the bus. In the same class. I saw all of them."

"Right."

"What does that mean?"

"Sorry—nothing. It doesn't mean anything."

"Yes, it does!"

"I need the address."

"What?"

"Jordan's address."

"Oh!" She gave him the address, watching him suspiciously.

"What are you getting at?" she demanded.

"I think I've told you. Angela is checking, a zillion techs are checking, looking for something that might in any way connect our victims. We're not finding anything that matches up, anything all of them might have been doing, or that they might have been associated with. All we have is they were killed in the exact same way."

"And?"

"That suggests they were murdered by a hired killer."

She was quiet a minute. "And you think one of my friends might have been a hired killer—thirteen years ago?"

"Not then. No."

"Okay, so one of them might be a hired killer now? But somehow, they're killing in the same way someone did years ago?"

"It's a quick and easy method," Axel said.

They turned off US 1 on Twenty-seventh Avenue and headed down to Tigertail. Raina told Axel where to turn.

Jordan's house was a pretty Mediterranean, built in the late 1930s. It was two stories, and maybe about twenty-five hundred square feet. Not massive, but nice for a single man.

"His car is here," Raina said, surprised.

"Maybe he fell asleep and just hasn't been answering his phone," Axel suggested.

"Let me try him again."

Raina did and, yet again, her call went straight to his voice mail.

"So, we try the door," Axel said.

They did. They rang the bell, then pounded on the door, and there was no answer.

"You don't know of any secret way in there, do you?" Axel asked.

"Uh, maybe."

"Don't tell me there's a key under the mat."

She shook her head. "Nothing so obvious. But his aunt always left a key in the flowerpot by the porch that opened the back door. But...is it legal?"

"No. But do you want to check on your friend? Would Jordan have you arrested?"

"I sincerely doubt it. I don't know if he still keeps a key there."

"We won't know unless we try."

They walked around the house. A flowerpot was next to a little cement porch at the back. Raina felt around in the dirt.

And found the key to the back door.

They went in.

"Jordan!" she called as they entered.

Axel quickly went through the downstairs rooms—kitchen, dining, living room and office. He headed for the stairs.

"Stay down here!" he warned Raina.

She did.

Jordan's home was nice, but not ostentatious. He had a large leather couch and wide-screen TV in the living room, and his kitchen held good modern appliances. His dining table had been his aunt's and it was a handsome, carved piece with chairs to match.

She wandered into the office.

"Anything?" she called up to Axel. "You know if he's just out, and he left his phone in the car or something, he's going to be pretty ticked at me for searching his house."

"He's not in his room, the guest room or bathroom," Axel called down.

Raina wandered over behind his desk.

She wasn't sure why—maybe curiosity. They had come this far; they were in the man's house.

She hit a key to bring his computer to life.

And a picture showed up on the screen.

It was a picture of Jordan and Jennifer Lowry, lovely, happy and smiling with all the life and vitality within her that had been so cruelly cut short.

CHAPTER FOURTEEN

Conveniently, the address of the restaurant where the group was meeting was also in Coconut Grove, in walking distance from Jordan's house.

Axel knew Raina was growing anxious. She was hoping against hope they would get there and Jordan would be there, and she'd be tripping over herself, admitting she'd been worried sick and they'd gone in his house.

He wasn't expecting to see Jordan.

The man had wanted to talk to Raina.

Then he had stopped answering his phone.

He didn't try the local office for help; he'd be told Jordan Rivera was an adult, more than welcome to not answer his phone for an afternoon if he so chose not to answer it. He wasn't gone anywhere near long enough for a missing-persons report.

But he was missing, and Axel knew it. So he called Angela and gave her Jordan Rivera's phone number, and asked her to somehow get a trace on it.

It might have been left in the house, but he doubted it. And the only neighbor he'd been able to find had said, oh yeah, someone had come to Jordan's house earlier—maybe he'd left with whomever that had been.

The neighbor knew someone had visited because she'd been watering her hibiscus plants on the side of the house and she'd heard voices.

"Male or female?" Axel had asked.

"Frankly, I don't know. And what business is it of yours? What are you? FBI or something?"

And so he had produced his credentials, but the woman still hadn't known. She just hadn't been paying attention and she'd only really known someone had been there because her earphones had fallen out. She'd been listening to music, and happily, that drowned out the rest of the world.

"I'm really worried," Raina said.

"Maybe he'll be at dinner."

"I don't think so," she said.

When they arrived, Mya and Elly were already there, along with Tate Fielding. The three stood as Axel and Raina arrived and they hugged all around.

Raina's group was out on the patio area of the restaurant. It was a great spot, covered but open, with fans to keep the heat at bay. The night was beautiful, the place right on the water.

"So, heavy on the trail?" Tate Fielding said, looking at them both. He grinned at Raina. "You're becoming a bloodhound yourself?"

"Pardon?" Raina said.

Tate laughed. "Well, Axel is down here on a case. And you're always with Axel, so…"

"Oh! His friend Andrew, with the Miccosukee police, has the most amazing horse! I've been working with him," Raina said.

"Out in the Everglades!" Mya said, and shivered. "I don't like to admit it, but I hated that camping trip we went on.

Snakes, mosquitoes…alligators. Mosquitoes! It just isn't me, I'm afraid."

"There are mosquitoes everywhere," Elly said.

"True," Mya said. "But more out there! Anyway, we should sit. My husband should be here any minute, and Lucia just went out to put another few hours on her parking. You know Lucia. She lost her ticket so she has to do the whole thing over again. Otherwise, the silly girl could have called it right in!"

"We haven't heard back from Jordan, but we have a seat for him if he's able to get here. He's been a bit secretive lately. Maybe it's a girl," Elly said.

"Jordan always has a girl. He brings a new one every time we get together," Tate said.

"Hey! Don't pick on Jordan. You have a new girl every five minutes, too," Elly said.

"That's because he doesn't want one for real," Mya said, shaking her head sadly.

"They're all real girls. Women, that is!" Tate said. He shrugged. "Give me a break—I'm young. And I'm looking for the best." He glanced over at Raina and said lightly, "Had a good one once, but she slipped away. Ah, well."

"You're such a liar, Tate," Raina said, laughing. "You love the law and moving forward, and that's okay. We are still young."

Axel noted she was truly amused. There was nothing bitter in her words, and Tate grinned, as well. It was all in good humor.

Or so it would appear.

"There, you see," Tate told Mya and Elly.

"Oh, your love life—or lack thereof—is your problem, my friend. One of us is always around when you need sisterly advice. Hey! There's Lucia," Mya said. "And cool! Len is right behind her."

The other two joined them, with greetings all around.

"No Jordan?" Len Smith asked, taking a seat by his wife.

"No, I guess he got busy. He had said he'd try to come, and we texted him the information. His loss, I say," Lucia told him. She sat at Axel's other side, happy to see him. "So, are you really relaxing for the evening? I guess no one can work twenty-four hours a day."

He didn't answer for a moment; their waitress appeared with the drink orders she'd evidently received from the first arrivals. Friendly and smiling, she asked the others for their preferences and suggested a few appetizers.

They ordered.

"So, you guys getting anywhere?" Tate asked him.

"One step at a time. Strange, though," he told the group. "A girl disappeared years ago—the night of your camping trip in the Everglades. Her body was just found. Or her bones, I should say."

"Where?" Len asked.

"In the Everglades."

"Near where that poor other girl was just found?"

"Different area—deeper into the Everglades, or more off the beaten path, really, between the Tamiami Trail and the tip of the peninsula."

"That's so sad!" Lucia said.

"Terrible," Mya said. "I told you—scary place." She shuddered. "And the fact that we were out there! Now that's truly scary. You're going to catch this guy, right?"

"Statistically, there are twenty-five to fifty active serial killers on the loose at any time in the United States," Tate said, shaking his head and looking at Axel. "Sorry, I went to law school—spent some time in the prosecutor's office. I looked you up, too. You're something special." He laughed. "More than being a 'special' agent. Your unit has its own offices, special assistant director, special field director—you guys are elite."

"Yes, I have a great unit. Actually, I think we've been promoted to 'branch,'" Axel said, shrugging pleasantly at Tate.

Tate Fielding had been a kid when the murders had started. But his apparently casual interest here seemed to be a bit too...casual.

And he'd looked up the Krewe of Hunters.

"And you go all over," Tate said. It wasn't a question.

"We handle special cases."

"A very special agent on very special cases. We're lucky we rate down here," Tate said, lifting his glass of beer to Axel. As he did so, their waitress returned.

"Soda with lime," Tate said as Axel's glass was delivered. "I guess you don't ever consider yourself to be off duty."

"Oh, sometimes I do. Not tonight," Axel said pleasantly.

"You're going to work again after dinner?" Elly asked him. "Your life must be exhausting!"

Axel smiled. He leaned forward. "That's why we're considered to be so elite. We don't stop, you see, until we get answers to all the questions we have."

He heard the sound of a chair scraping back. It was Raina. She stood. "Excuse me, guys. Trip to the ladies' room."

"Right inside," Lucia told her. "To the left!"

"Thanks!" Raina called to her.

"Still nothing from Jordan?" Len asked Lucia as Raina walked away.

Lucia shook her head. "Tate, he really didn't call you with any kind of an excuse or anything? It's not like him not to answer me at all."

Axel stood. He didn't know what they were going to find when the lab came back with a report on the hunk of meat he'd taken from Raina's yard. But anyone who knew her or knew about her knew full well a very big and potentially lethal dog would happily die before allowing anything to happen to her.

Now, Raina was away from her dog.

"Excuse me, phone call," he said.

He stood. As if on cue, his phone started ringing.

He walked away from the table, surprised to see by his caller ID that it was Raina calling him.

"You're all right?" he said quickly. "I was just heading in to check on you."

"I'm fine—just in the ladies' room. But we have to go. Axel, I got a call from Jordan. I can't go back to the table. Not now. I'm all right. But I have to try to remember this call. Please. Can you say goodbye for us? Can we go right away?"

"Absolutely. I'll say goodbye. Pick you up on the way out," he told her.

He strode back to the table. "Hey, guys, sorry. Call from some tech at Miami-Dade," he told them. "Probably more of nothing, but yeah. I'm always working."

"I can give Raina a ride home," Lucia said.

"That would be great, but I've got her dog and it's complicated." He decided to take a shot in the dark. "Titan is sick," he said. "We left him with a friend of mine."

"Titan! Oh, no, poor puppy. He's going to be okay, right?" Elly asked.

"Hopefully. Anyway, thank you all for a great partial evening," he said. He looked around, curious to the way her friends might react. Elly—truly concerned. Lucia—dismayed. Both Mya and Len appeared to be concerned. Tate...

Looking downward and then up. "Tell Raina we're hoping the best for Titan," he said. "And hopefully, sometime while you're still around, we can have dinner!"

"Thanks," Axel said.

He hurried inside. Raina was waiting by the bar.

He took her arm, leading her out quickly. As they headed for his car, he asked, "Where's Jordan? What's going on?"

"I don't know where he is. He doesn't know where he is.

Axel, he called and just started talking, babbling. He said he got away. I tried to ask from who—and from where. He said it was dark, so dark, and he was screaming about snakes. And he suddenly said, 'Oh, shit!' And then the line went dead on me."

"Dark and snakes? But he didn't say who or what was going on?"

"He just started talking. The call couldn't have been more than several seconds. I had just stepped in here. I couldn't get a word in. I tried. He talked so fast."

Axel called Angela.

"Anything? Have you got a location on that cell for me?"

"The phone is still on, but the signal's been in and out. I have people on it." She gave him the coordinates of the towers the signals were bouncing from.

He thanked her and hung up.

"Anything? Where is he?" Raina asked him anxiously.

"He's in the middle of the Everglades. Somewhere about twenty miles west of Miami and another five miles south of the Tamiami Trail."

"Oh, my God! By himself? Running from a killer?" Raina said. "We have to find him, Axel. We have to find him fast. There are all kinds of killer creatures out there."

"None quite so deadly as man," Axel said. "Yes. Jon Dickson and Kylie Connolly are on their way. Let's pick up Titan first and head out. I'll alert Andrew and he'll get the tribal folks moving. And Nigel can get the rangers and some of his people on it. We'll find him, Raina."

Dead or alive, he thought. But he didn't say those words out loud.

"He does know something," Raina said, staring ahead into the night. "He must. The way he was acting, that strange feeling I had. He knows something, but he's not a killer. I think he might know who killed Jennifer Lowry, and that's why he was so angry, why he kept saying she didn't deserve it. Axel, Jordan could be the key to what's going on. Maybe we should head straight there. Titan is great, but he's really not spent much time crawling around the Everglades."

He didn't want to suggest they should get her dog because it seemed the dog was someone's target, as well.

"We need him," he said simply. "There's no alarm on your house."

"Titan is an alarm. Oh, my God. You really think someone tried to poison my dog?"

"Yes."

"To get to me. But... I'm with you."

"And we need to keep it that way," he told her.

She swallowed and nodded.

He got on the phone as he drove, calling everyone with voice control. He spoke with Andrew first, then Nigel and Angela. Then he hesitated and called the lab.

"I was just about to call you," the head of the department told him. "We went high priority as you asked on that sample you gave us. And yes, it was laced. Common rat poison, available many places, but of course we'll get going on a list. But there's something else you need to know about the meat."

"What about it?" Axel asked.

"It was human. Human thigh muscle."

CHAPTER FIFTEEN

Raina had always thought she understood the meaning of "darkness."

But in the middle of the Everglades, in the middle of the night, darkness took on new meaning.

She stood in the back of Andrew's yard. He had a small army of Miccosukee friends, park rangers and a few other people who knew the area well, even some of the python hunters they were all so quick to disparage as being white-collar businessmen out for a spree or uneducated locals looking for a spot on a television show. Miami-Dade police and others were part of the group, as well; the search would be extensive.

She would never mock those wanting to look like hicks to get on a television show again. They were all there to help.

A couple of the python hunters had an idea of where to search. They'd seen an all-terrain vehicle moving in just about five miles south of Andrew's that day. That was very strange, because the terrain out there was lousy for fishing or sporting of any kind. Only airboats usually traveled the area.

Both Andrew and Axel addressed the makeshift search party, warning they had to be careful, as they all knew, at night. They all loved the Everglades, and they all knew even without possible danger from a killer there were plenty of predators to be found in the darkness.

The parties split up. Axel remained with Andrew. Nigel had arrived and apparently the three of them had a plan.

"She's coming—and the dog?" Nigel asked, referring to Raina.

"Safer than leaving her—and the dog—anywhere else," Axel said.

"And like hell you'd be leaving me. It's my friend who's out there," she said.

"We going to follow the route the python hunters suggested?" Nigel asked.

"It's as good as anything else," Axel told him. "And it jives with the placement Angela reported on the cell phone."

"Let's do this. Titan going to be okay on an airboat? Billie Osceola has one waiting for us."

"He'll be fine," Raina said with assurance. She paused a minute and then turned to Andrew. "Billie Osceola? A relative?"

He grinned. "There are lots of us Osceola—Miccosukee and Seminole. But Billie. Yeah, I think we're third cousins or something like that."

They drove the distance to the village where Billie Osceola was indeed waiting for them; he was going with them.

"I'm better at navigating an airboat than any of you."

"Hey!" Andrew protested.

"You want the airboat?" Billie asked.

"Take her away," Axel told him.

The moon suddenly broke from the clouds as they started out. It provided a glow over the Everglades—the hardwood hammocks and the wetlands, fields of sawgrass barely covered in water, deeper pools scattered as if by a casual hand.

The airboat had a powerful light, illuminating each area as they moved.

They saw all manner of creatures.

They woke sleeping gators, and at one point bounced over something.

"What the hell?" Nigel murmured.

"Python, I think. Damn things are getting to be just about everywhere down here. We have to kill them when we find them. It's kind of sad. It's not the fault of the damned creatures that they're out here. Found a rock boar in my yard the other day. Cool little dude." He hesitated. "I didn't kill it. I have a friend who's a science teacher in the city. Gave it to her. Didn't tell her where I got it—and she didn't ask."

They kept moving through the night. The powerful beam at the front of the airboat cut through mud and muck and foliage and trees.

"Stop!" Axel called out suddenly.

Raina hadn't seen anything.

And not for lack of searching.

"What?"

"There's something on that mangrove limb over there," Axel said. "Billie, can you get us a little closer?"

"Am I a driver extraordinaire or what?" Billie asked.

He maneuvered them into position. Raina saw there was a piece of clothing caught on one of the branches.

Axel reached for it, drawing it in.

"Oh, my God!" Raina breathed.

"You know what this is?"

"It's one of Jordan's jackets…he had it on the other day, when he was at my house," Raina said.

He studied her for a minute and handed her the jacket.

"See what you get," he told her.

"See what I get?"

"Put it on," he suggested.

She swallowed hard and then did so quickly.

"There's, uh, there's no mirror," she said.

"Close your eyes. Let your mind be the mirror," Axel told her.

She closed her eyes. For a minute all she felt was the humidity and the heat, slightly relieved by the fall of night. She heard crickets, something large slinking back into the water, somewhere.

A single cry from a night bird.

Then she saw a strange darkness. And she thought she could see Jordan. Something was covering his head.

She heard a harsh whisper.

"Sorry—you deserve this!"

"Bastard! Jennifer didn't!"

The voices were whispers in her head. She couldn't place them. She knew Jordan had to be the one speaking, the one in the strange darkness...

He started to run, and he ran and ran. She heard cursing behind him.

"Dammit, we need guns!"

"No guns, always traced..."

But she—Jordan—made it. She heard him panting desperately for breath. He was caught suddenly and barely kept himself from crying out. But he'd loosened the ropes on his wrists and they fell free. He struggled out of his jacket, leaving it entangled on the branch. He'd reached into his pocket for his phone, called Raina and then saw it—the large bull alligator on the path before him. He'd disturbed the beast.

"Oh, shit!"

His phone fell as he flew down another path—zigzagging. They'd been taught all their lives that an alligator could run with amazing speed, but that zigzagging confused them.

He zigged and zigged and zagged and then...

Nothing.

"Raina!"

She felt Axel's hand on her shoulder. He was standing over her.

"Tell us!" he said quietly.

"He, uh, ran into an alligator. Right down there, I think."

"He'd have had to have been on the hammock," Nigel said.

"Right. But it looks like there are a few trails through here, a few ways to go," Andrew said. "Billie, pull her up—"

"Already on it," Billie said.

He pulled the airboat up on something of a shore, jagged and filled with mangrove roots. Axel helped Raina out.

Titan, barking, leaped out on his own.

They looked around.

Then, slowly, Raina saw something appear before them—no, someone.

Peg-legged Pete.

"This way, I think, quickly. I heard the ruckus from here. I think he's in trouble now. Serious trouble! Hurry!"

They all ran, Titan bounding on ahead.

They twisted and turned, following the dog and the strange apparition who ran along with him.

Then they found Jordan.

"Oh, my God!" Raina cried.

She'd seen scenes like it in movies.

She'd never expected to see it in real life.

Jordan appeared to be dead—leaned against a tree, caught in the tightening coils of some kind of very large snake.

She went dead still, yelling at Titan to get back. Axel rushed forward with Andrew and Nigel. She wasn't sure who fired first. She knew they did so very carefully, killing the python while making sure not to hit Jordan.

Billie moved forward, as well. The four men wrested Jordan from the still-powerful weight of the snake.

"Is he alive?"

Her question was barely a whisper. But Axel heard her.

"He's definitely got some broken bones. I don't know how much damage. I've got a pulse—faint. We've got to get him help, quickly."

Nigel was already on the phone.

"Moving him is dangerous," Andrew warned.

"Not moving him is deadly," Axel said. "Help me make a carrier out of our jackets and those branches over there, enough vines to fashion it quickly."

Raina felt helpless. She stood there, watching. They were swift and efficient.

A makeshift gurney had been created out of the foliage. They carefully got Jordan on to it, and moved as quickly as possible back to the airboat.

Billie put out the report to the other searchers that Jordan had been found.

"I... I didn't know how to help," Raina told Axel, shivering by Jordan, careful not to touch him.

"What do you mean?" Axel asked. He took a moment to touch her face gently. "You led us straight to him."

"Peg-legged Pete—"

"Didn't know exactly which trail. And if we hadn't reached him when we did..." He paused and then added grimly, "Constrictors smother their prey. They tighten and tighten until the lungs can get no air. He had a minute or two left at best. You got us down the right trail."

Raina nodded. She looked back. Peg-legged Pete still stood by the mangrove. She lifted her hand to him and mouthed a thank-you.

She thought the ghost saw her.

Titan barked, whined and laid down by Jordan.

The night became a blur as the airboat sped back to Andrew's where a helicopter was waiting to bring him to the trauma center.

★ ★ ★

Jon Dickson called Axel while they were at the hospital, telling him that he and Kylie had arrived.

Axel brought him up to date on what had happened; Jon and Kylie would head out to the hospital right away.

He had opted to stay. Andrew and Nigel were back out in the Everglades, trying to find any possible clues, no matter how minute they might be.

Titan was with them. They were both aware of the attempted poisoning attack on the dog.

DNA was being processed. The piece of human flesh meant that there was another victim in the case. One they knew nothing about.

Jordan had not regained consciousness. When the doctor finally came out, he was sorry to tell them they'd been forced to put Jordan into a medically induced coma. Between the damage done to his bones and his organs, it was their only chance.

Axel thanked him. Raina stood at his side, anxiously looking at the doctor.

"But he can make it?" she asked.

"No promises, young lady, I'm sorry. But we are damned good here, and I do promise we'll be doing our best, and we'll be in contact the minute we can safely wake him."

Before they left, they met a party of officers, two in plain-clothes, two in county uniforms. Nigel was making sure no harm came to their victim while he was in the hospital.

"We can leave, safely," Axel assured Raina.

"But Jordan," she whispered.

He understood. The man had been her friend forever. And no, he didn't believe Jordan was a killer.

But Jordan had known something.

And he hadn't shared that information. And now, someone had tried to poison Titan.

If Jordan had just spoken...

He didn't say any of that to Raina. She surely knew it; she didn't need to hear it from him.

Jon and Kylie arrived when they were about to leave the hospital; it was nearly 2:00 a.m.

Raina was polite, though she still seemed shell-shocked. Adding more law enforcement officers into the game didn't seem to mean much to her, though he had told her a bit about Kylie. She might have been too dragged out by the day to remember or for it to even register.

"We've both got cars. We'll meet back at Raina's place?" he suggested.

"We'll follow," Jon said.

"Meet outside the garage," Axel said.

For once, there was almost no traffic on the streets.

They made it to Raina's in about twenty minutes. She seemed to start to come alive a little as they reached her house.

"Are they staying here? Are you staying?"

"I'm not leaving your side until we've got this solved," Axel told her. "Ultimately, it's up to you. Do you have room?"

"Plenty. It's a three-bedroom house. I'll get clean sheets."

Jon had parked and he and Kylie were walking up the steps when Axel quickly warned, "She usually has her dog here, but Andrew kept him when we headed into the hospital. I didn't want him alone," he added.

"Titan!" Raina said. "I'm horrible. How could I forget? Should we go back out to Andrew's house and pick him up?"

"Hopefully Andrew is sleeping, and if I know Andrew, he's cuddled up with your dog," Axel told her. He took her by the shoulders. "Please, trust me. Andrew will protect him."

"And he'll surely protect Andrew, though I have a feeling, from what we've been briefed on, Andrew has a slew of good people watching over the area now," Kylie said. She smiled at Raina. "We don't mean to be a burden."

"No, not at all! I'm delighted to have you," Raina assured

her. "Help yourselves to anything in the kitchen. Just give me a minute."

"We can certainly help," Jon said.

"He was a military man. Makes a bed like the best-trained nurse in the country!" Kylie said.

"It's a talent," Jon said lightly.

"No, please. I'll just be a minute," Raina said.

She disappeared down the hallway.

"Let's sit, shall we?" Axel suggested.

They did. Axel knew it was good to have them there. He'd liked Kylie the minute he'd met her when she moved to the DC area to be with Jon. Her love of the past had made her invaluable to the Krewe, though she hadn't opted to go to the academy, join the FBI and become a member.

That didn't keep her from helping. They often brought people in as consultants.

Kylie was a talented consultant. First, she had a natural ability with people. Kylie could draw them out easily. And she was so calm, cool and casual in her manner that she could bring forward extraordinary memories, or things people knew that they didn't know they knew.

She and Jon had only been together a few months. Jon had long ago proven himself an ace agent; Kylie had quickly shown she was an incredible asset in both his life and his work.

"You know," Jon said, "Kylie and I met in Salem, a place I know like the back of my hand. The Everglades? Not so much. Not at all."

Axel smiled. "This goes a lot further. The reason for whatever is going on has nothing to do with the Everglades—that's just the dumping ground. And now, well, Nigel wouldn't have put anyone on guard at the hospital he didn't trust implicitly, but I'd still be happy if one of us was around and available at the drop of a dime. I don't want Raina left alone. Someone did try to poison her dog."

"With human flesh," Kylie said, shaking her head.

"You've both been briefed," Axel suggested.

"Yes," Jon said. "Well, you know Adam Harrison, Jackson Crow and Angela Hawkins. We wouldn't be here without being as briefed as humanly possible. And one would think, if they're trying to poison the dog, they're trying to get rid of him to make Raina vulnerable."

"But tell us about the beginning," Kylie said. "With Raina... it's a matter of touch? I mean, we've all heard often enough about 'mediums'—some so-called and some who must be somewhat real—who are given the objects of a missing person in the hopes of finding them. We know dogs go by scent, but..."

Axel looked up. Raina was standing in the arch that led to the hallway and the bedrooms.

"I think maybe Raina can best describe it herself," he said. "And then, well, hell, we're all going to be worthless without sleep."

Axel had spoken the truth about one thing—sleep. She was exhausted. She didn't remember feeling so exhausted, or so worried at the same time.

Titan.

She was never away from him.

Someone had tried to kill her dog.

With poisoned human flesh.

Jordan was in the hospital. He'd nearly been killed by someone, and then a giant snake had tried to finish him off.

It had all begun with that dress...

She still needed to burn the damned thing.

"Raina, are you up for this?" Special Agent Jon Dickson asked her politely, empathy in his voice. She liked him. A tall man with steel blue eyes, he seemed to be no-nonsense, and he seemed to be imbued with the same confidence and air of authority that Axel wore as easily as a cloak.

Kylie was comfortable and self-assured.

She was an attractive woman with chestnut hair and really beautiful eyes—blue and green with little gold spikes streaking out from the pupils.

She had a great smile.

"Are you okay?" Kylie asked her.

Okay? Hell, no. Her world had gone to hell.

But admittedly, she felt a strange sense of both determination and purpose. She wanted the killer caught. She'd never thought she'd be part of something like this, but she was.

And her friends were being affected. Maybe they—or one of them—was involved.

It didn't matter. She was in it, and she was damned well going to see it through.

"I'm just fine," she said. "And, Jon, I'm sure you're a great agent and I'm willing to bet that you'll easily meet Peg-legged Pete and see the pirate ship, but, Kylie, I think you're both here because of you."

Kylie glanced at Axel before speaking.

"I don't know if I can help anything or not. I mean, what we seem to have is different, but I learned something from the terribly slimy man who almost killed me. I can help talk you through, but I think we should start in the morning."

"And we need to get back on looking for common ground. It exists somehow, somewhere," Axel said to Jon.

"Almost 3:00 a.m. now. Call it quits till morning?" Jon asked.

Axel nodded gravely. "Windows and doors," he said.

"We're all on it!" Raina said.

The four of them went through her house. All windows and doors were securely locked.

Jon and Kylie bid them good-night. Axel followed Raina to her room, but she paused in the hallway.

"What?"

"I've had Titan in this hallway every night since he was a pup," she said.

"All right, in all truth, I'm not as good as that dog. But between Jon and me, we do wake at just about anything."

She smiled at him. "I know that I'm well protected. I was just missing my dog."

"Oh, well, of course, but he's in good hands. I swear it."

"I know that, too. And I can't help thinking…"

"Yes?"

"Oh, God, Axel, someone tried to poison him *with human flesh*! How horrible could someone be?"

"It's a warning."

She shuddered. "And someone out there is missing that flesh."

"It's horrible," Axel agreed. "I know. The thing to keep in mind now is that we put an end to it."

She nodded and walked into the room, shedding her clothing as she did, heading straight for the shower.

He didn't join her. She stepped out of the stall and poked her head out the door. "Okay, no offense, but tramping around the Everglades…"

"I just thought you might like privacy, that you were tired."

"All that's true. Get in here. Sorry, please get in here."

He did. She hugged him while the heat and the water raged around them. He held her in return. She was so glad he was there. Glad for the tremendous warmth and vitality of his body and the strength of his hold.

"I know it was a horrible day," he said quietly.

"It was. Make me forget it. Please, just for a while."

His mouth touched hers. His hands began to move.

And he did make her forget.

If only for a time.

Axel's first order of business was to call and check on Jordan Rivera's condition.

He was stable; the doctors believed they would be bringing him out of the coma within a few days. His bones would take a long time to heal but the internal organs were doing well and, importantly, his heart was holding up.

Axel called before even rising. He saw Raina was watching him, waiting for an update. He quickly repeated the info. "He's going to make it," he assured her.

"He's going to have survived a python attack...and lived to tell the tale. Was it a python?"

"I believe it was a Burmese python and I'm thinking the damned thing was close to eighteen feet." He hesitated, watching her. "You ready for today?"

"Damned ready." She hesitated, ready to swing her legs off the bed. "Axel, it's like something out of a slasher movie. Someone tried to poison my dog with a hunk of human flesh."

"There's another victim, I'm afraid. And whoever did it intended for Titan to die, too."

"Thank goodness your quick thinking saved him," she said, rising quickly. He noted the ease and agility of her movements, and loved the fact they were so comfortable together.

She paused suddenly, diving into her closet.

"Your friends are up!" she said.

"I'm pretty sure they know we're both in here."

"Yes, I know, but we should be out there. And we have to get to Andrew's. I know that a dog's life isn't a human life, but—"

"You love your dog. Yes, you're right. Let's move."

She wagged a finger at him. "Separate showers—fast ones."

He laughed. "Hey, I'm well behaved. You're the temptress."

They showered—separately—and dressed and emerged from the bedroom within minutes to find Jon Dickson on the phone. Kylie was pouring coffee.

"I found the pot and figured we should start off awake," Kylie said. "I hope you don't mind me just making myself at home in your kitchen."

"I'm grateful you made yourself at home," Raina told her. "I love coming out to coffee that's already brewed."

"We need to get over to Andrew's—he says he has plenty of food. Nigel is meeting us out there," Jon said. "He's gathered everything he can and thinks we should all go through the dossiers on the victims. They're working on the DNA from the piece you found in the yard, and will hopefully come up with a match." He studied Axel for a minute. "I'm not sure your friend believed in your theory that this has been going on a long time until yesterday. Now, well, he's wondering just what else might be found, or what unsolved cases might have ties. He said someone named Vinnie Magruder is coming out, as well. Who is Vinnie Magruder?"

"He was a Miami-Dade patrolman when I was a kid. He had the county beat, covering what wasn't federal or tribal out here. But then, federal lands, county lands and tribal lands are often hard to determine. I know there have been places where tribal police and county deputies or federal agents have had trouble, but not with Andrew and his officers, and not in any of my dealings. Helps that Andrew, Nigel and I were friends all our lives. Plus, there isn't a soul I know of who doesn't want this solved and put to rest."

"So, we need to do it!" Kylie said, handing them all paper cups.

Axel smiled at her. He hadn't known her that long, but he liked her a lot. He knew she'd been about to start a dream job in New York City when she and Jon had met; she had given it up to move to Northern Virginia with him. She was a brilliant historian and had quickly found work she loved, doing research on a Revolutionary-era building near their home in Alexandria—work that was exactly what she wanted, done on her own schedule. Adam Harrison had seen the historic property and determined to buy it, with Kylie continuing her work on the research, and starting the process to open the old home as a museum, circa the late 1700s when it had been built.

She also embraced what Jon did and loved the Krewe.

And it just so happened that she herself was unusually talented, like the rest of the Krewe.

He was counting on that now.

"You need the dress, right?" Axel asked her.

"I'm working in the dark here, too. I haven't figured myself out yet," Kylie told him. "But yes, I'm thinking we should have the dress."

They left soon after, taking both cars just in case they discovered later in the day they might need to move separately.

As he drove with Raina, Axel asked her, "You're seriously all right with all this?"

"I'm not just all right, I'm anxious. I want to do this. I want Jordan to be all right. I want to believe I helped stop whatever is happening, that I've helped to save lives, maybe."

He nodded. "Last night, you saw things. Amazing things."

She nodded slowly. "That's what I mean, though. It was like Kylie said. I don't understand myself, either. But I want to test the limits and hope it can take us where we need to be."

They drew down the off-road path to Andrew's house. Jon and Kylie were right behind them. Andrew and Nigel came out as they arrived, ready to greet the four of them.

But first out was Titan. He ran to his mom as if he were a toddler who'd been left at day care for the first time.

A happy dog. Bending down, Raina greeted him lovingly, and then introduced Titan to Kylie and Jon, who luckily had not lied.

They seemed to like the dog immediately and Titan returned the affection.

Then Andrew cleared his throat, looking at Nigel.

"Check your messages," Nigel said. "There was a quick hit

on our interagency system. The thigh material belonged to a young man named Brandon Wells. He went missing about a week ago, from the St. Pete area."

"St. Pete?" Axel murmured. "Interesting. And until now, our killer hasn't done any slicing."

"For now, we have to treat it as if it might be a separate case," Nigel said.

Axel stared at Nigel. "Unlikely someone would try to poison Raina's dog without there being a connection." He looked around at the silent group. "Kylie, Raina, any place in particular you'd like to be?"

Raina looked at Kylie. "Where are you most comfortable?" Kylie asked.

"Where we are out of the way?" Raina suggested.

"Anywhere you want to be is fine," Andrew assured her.

Raina smiled ruefully. "Believe it or not, I'd love to be in the stables with the horses and the smell of hay, and yeah, I'd be comfortable there."

"Okay, going to try the dress on in a stall?" Kylie asked.

She was serious.

So was Raina.

"Sure. Sounds fine. Just—"

"I'll be there. Ready to catch you if you fall."

"I don't think I will," Raina said.

"Jon, want to join Andrew and me?" Nigel asked.

"I'm here to help. Where are we starting?"

"We're looking at relationships in the life of our latest victim. Presumed victim. Though it's unlikely the young man is still alive if he's, er, missing that much leg material. Possible, but under the circumstances…"

"It's strange, though," Andrew said. "How do you go from a swift, practiced kill to slicing and dicing someone?" He shook his head and started toward the house.

"We won't disturb you—unless you need us," Nigel said, looking from Axel to Kylie and, finally, to Raina.

"I'm going to be fine," Raina said.

She did so with confidence. Axel hoped she was really growing as comfortable with her strange visions as she claimed.

Then again, what choice did they really have other than to exploit them in any way they could?

CHAPTER SIXTEEN

Axel was headed inside with Andrew, Nigel and Jon to quickly discuss their course of action for the day.

That left Raina to introduce Kylie to Wild Thing and Jacob. Kylie apparently liked horses as much as she liked dogs. It was hard to fake affection for dogs and horses. They instinctively knew who did and didn't like them.

"How did you get into animal training?" Kylie asked her. "It's not one of those careers that comes up when you're speaking with a school counselor."

"I think I wanted to be a veterinarian—except I found out animals died and there might be a lot of blood. Anyway, I always had a dog, even when I was young, but my dad was with a friend who had an old horse and was thinking glue factory. It turned out the horse wasn't so old, he was just a bit wild. Anyway, I worked with him and someone at the ranch was impressed and said I should be a trainer. So, I went to college and did all kinds of courses in science and psychology, and luckily, a lot of people need their pets trained."

Kylie grinned. "People are animals. I know a few who need to be trained." She laughed. "Sorry—that sounded horrible.

I just mean there are a lot of people out there who need to learn about manners and behavior."

"True, people are animals. But I prefer to deal with the furry kind."

"Easy to see why sometimes," Kylie said, stroking Jacob's nose.

"What about you? How did you come to be with Jon? I know you had a strange experience with a regression."

"I went on a bachelorette party with a friend who didn't want strippers or wild nights, just fun with her closest friends. And then," she said, pausing and smiling dryly, "everything kind of went to hell, horrible at first. I witnessed a murder, and I had a hard time dealing with that. But then things got better because I was able to do some good. Anyway, it's all worked out for me."

"And you're here now," Raina said.

Kylie nodded. She looked at Raina. "I was like you—everything was just normal. Four of us…we were just spending time doing what the bride loved to do, which was explore Salem, Massachusetts, something we'd all done together dozens of times. And we'd done tarot and palm readers several times—mainly just for fun—so we went to this man who had a reputation for past-life regressions and, just like that, my life was suddenly different. I'm no hero of any kind but I felt like you did. That I had to stop what was going on. Make a difference. And now, of course, I'm hoping to use my experience to help you. Of course, you don't have to do this. If you feel—"

"Oh, I do have to do this! I want to do this," Raina told her. "And I hope I'm smart enough to be frightened and wary, the kind of frightened that makes me careful and watchful."

Kylie smiled at her. "I like it." She was quiet a minute. "I think whoever is doing this knows you or Axel or maybe someone in law enforcement. How has Titan been acting around everyone?"

"Titan was around a lot of people. He was at the fundraiser with me. But he didn't behave oddly around anyone. Of course, that night, there were hundreds of people there. He also knew he was 'on duty,' more or less. The only thing was a strange feeling I had after Jordan had been at my house. And then, finding Jordan and remembering the way he had behaved." She looked at Kylie. "Think there's any possibility Jordan will come out of his coma and tell us everything we need to know?"

"There's always the possibility. And there's the possibility others who know something or suspect something might disappear quickly, as well—and not be found alive. It's pretty amazing Jordan escaped whoever had taken him."

She was right. Raina looked around the stables. For a moment she thought about how great Andrew's house was— modern, sitting on the edge of an ancient world. She loved the history of Florida's Native Americans, their run deeper and deeper into a no-man's-land, conquering it to survive. The Everglades, deadly, yes. Beautiful, too, and unique.

"I'm anxious to get started—with whatever we're going to do."

"The dress."

"Yes, the dress is the key. Let's see if Axel is ready to join us. He's not going to be happy if we start without him!"

"We're lucky that DNA testing can move so swiftly and we have priority with all this," Nigel said. "Not that long ago, we'd have been waiting for weeks to get anything on the flesh you found."

Axel studied the papers they had on the missing man whose DNA had matched up with the piece of thigh left in Raina's yard.

"Humdrum job," Andrew said, reading a dossier. "Computer tech with a big company. No records suggest he'd driven or flown down this way, or been in the Greater Miami Area or even Broward County. Credit card statements for the last six months keep him in his own area—St. Pete, Tampa and one drive down to a restaurant in Sarasota. His girlfriend reported him missing. They'd been together about a year and a half when he disappeared."

"We've found the remains of Fran Castle, dead thirteen years, most likely," Nigel said. "Dr. Carlysle can't say, but it's likely she was killed when she went missing. Then, Hermione Shore, rich widow, but again, known for being a kind humanitarian. Next, we have the man who was found, throat slit, first in our recent history—Peter Scarborough, separated and living here while his wife was far away in South Dakota. He's liked by all his coworkers. No one can think of anyone who would want to harm him. Then, Alina Fairfield, a clothing designer who traveled a lot. It took several months to identify her. Then, quickly discovered, Jennifer Lowry. And now, we believe we're going to find Brandon Wells, another victim. Loved by his girlfriend, who again, according to all records and reports, never left home in the days before he was reported missing. They'd all been living here—or working here—except for Brandon Wells. The only thing they seem to have had in common was that they were nice, well-liked people. No criminal activity in any of their backgrounds." He looked at them, frustrated. "Maybe this last incident— the human meat meant to kill a dog—does give us what we need, since the person responsible knows Raina Hamish has become involved in this search."

"Raina is the key. Listen, you guys keep at this," Axel said. "I'm going to head out to the stables. I want to use Kylie to guide Raina."

"She'll be good," Jon said.

"I've gotten ahold of Vinnie Magruder, retired," Nigel

said. "He'll be out here tonight and we'll see if he remembers anything at all."

"I'm not sure he can help us—unless it's with old cases we don't know anything about," Andrew said. "Still, anything that might help."

"That first young lady, Fran Castle. From what we have—and what we remember, though memory could be faulty—she must have been at the casino. Her car was found just a little farther west on the trail. That suggests to me she'd been playing…and maybe then she was headed over to Naples. Someway or somehow, she stopped there and was picked up. And killed."

"No one seemed to protest when they were taken—though, of course, we don't really know. But we do know that with Jennifer Lowry, there was no sign she'd fought, that she'd been knocked on the head or given a concussion. She was just taken. That suggests someone powerful," Nigel said.

"Or someone who might have had a strange hold like a bribe, blackmail, something like that," Axel suggested.

"They were all blackmailed?" Andrew asked. "If you're blackmailing someone, don't you want them alive so you keep getting those blackmail payments?"

"Maybe. But maybe that's the answer when you haven't made your blackmail payments. There's got to be something that ties them together. And I think we're looking at more than one killer. More like a team. Maybe it's more than two people, or two people always, but a different two people, somehow involved with one another—and a plan to get rid of someone. However, when you have a quiet neighborhood, it would be easy enough to stalk someone—know their schedule—and wait to seize them quickly and in the darkness. You do risk being seen by a neighbor, but if you've observed someone's habits long enough, it's certainly possible and likely. The Fran Castle case, though…right on the Tamiami Trail."

"Someone had balls," Nigel noted. "Or, if she was the first, they were just learning. Maybe taking risks because they didn't really know what they were doing yet."

Axel's phone rang and he answered quickly.

Angela Hawkins.

"I found something," she told him.

"You did? Great! What?"

"Not sure how great, but Jennifer Lowry had an aunt who died about forty-eight hours after the medical examiner determined Jennifer had died. The aunt—Elizabeth Lowry—left behind a considerable fortune. Jennifer died before her aunt, so according to the will, none of it would come her way or go into any of the charities she embraced. It would go to the other nieces and nephews—there were three more of them. Now that might mean nothing, but—"

"It might mean everything. She needed to die before the aunt, and unlike the others, the killers needed for her body to be found immediately."

"That could suggest a couple of things. Copycat killers, or killers who had been hired to make sure her body was found quickly. Which may be why she was found in a more obvious, well travelled part of the Everglades."

"Murder for hire," Axel mused.

"I'm digging into other finances, other family members," Angela said. "I'll get back to you."

"Thank you."

Axel told Jon, Nigel and Andrew what Angela had discovered.

"Executions. You said it from the beginning," Andrew said.

"A business machine that's been running for years, and God knows just who it might employ," Axel noted.

"Let's see what we get from Angela on the others. The finances on Jennifer Lowry didn't pop up because she was never involved with the money. She would have been out of the aunt's will before the aunt died because she was dead already," Jon said. "I think we're on to something now, but the who and why is still missing."

"We need Raina and Kylie," Axel said.

"We need anything we can get," Jon agreed.

Axel started out and the others followed him. Maybe, Axel thought, they all needed a break from staring at data and trying to figure out what it could all possibly mean.

Their timing was good. Raina and Kylie seemed to be coming from the stables for him.

"We didn't want to start without you," Kylie said. "We need to figure out a way to own horses in Alexandria!" she called to Jon as he headed back toward the house with Andrew and Nigel.

"Sure! Everyone has a few on the beltway!" Jon called back.

"Spoilsport—we're near tons of good land!" Kylie told him. "Okay, a bit of a drive, but doable."

In the stables, Raina paused again to speak to and assure Wild Thing and Andrew's sturdy and dependable buckskin, Jacob.

Then Raina ducked into the tack room to disrobe and don the little blue dress that had started it all.

Axel stood just outside the door to the tack room, waiting with Kylie.

After a while, he grew anxious and he opened the door.

Raina was clad in the dress. Standing barefoot, she was staring straight ahead at Axel and Kylie, but not "at" them at all. She was seeing something distant, something they could not begin to fathom.

At Axel's side, Titan whined softly.

Axel reached for her hand, then hesitated. She still didn't see him.

"It's all right. I think. This is the blind leading the blind," Kylie said softly. "Take her hand, lead her out here with us.

We can have her sit on the grain chest over there and be next to her."

Axel grasped Raina's hand and led her over to the grain chest, easing her down to sit, and went on his knees before her. Kylie stood just behind him.

Titan found a position by Axel, setting his nose on Raina's knee. Her eyes didn't change, but she set her free hand on the dog's head.

"She didn't scream this time," Axel commented.

"In my experience, you stop screaming once your mind kind of accepts what's going on," Kylie said softly. Then she spoke in an even, level tone to Raina.

"Raina, it's Kylie. You're safe. You're with Axel and me. We're in the stables. Titan is here and the horses are here and Jon and Nigel and Andrew are just inside the house. Whatever you see, it isn't where you are. But it's good to see what you see. Can you talk to me?" Kylie asked.

"Yes," Raina said.

"What are you seeing? Remember, you're with us. You're safe. But we need to know what you're seeing. To try to help."

Raina nodded, again, doing so without her eyes changing. She stared straight ahead.

She didn't blink. "Right now..." She paused.

"What?"

"I see Jennifer. She's happy, she's excited, and she's feeling daring. She's trying on the dress for a special occasion. She likes it. She thinks she'll buy it, but she'll wait. She'll check her finances. She'll make sure that..."

"That?" Kylie prompted softly.

"That he'll be there. She likes him. And she knows he likes her. She's been hurt before. She means to be careful..."

Her words broke off.

"Raina?" Axel said softly.

"It's growing dark. It's night. She was so happy. She saw

him. She knew she'd see him again. And she's hurrying and she's careless and she doesn't see..."

"See what?" he asked her quietly.

"What's coming around from the side of her house. The person. So dark. Because there's no face. It's all dark and then...

"Then the bag. The burlap bag over her head. And even while she's terrified, she's still thinking it has to be a joke. Her coworkers, trying to surprise her, trying to make her have fun. They don't think she gets out enough. Still, she tries to scream. She can't. She can barely breathe. Her scream is just a sound, so weak. And she isn't strong enough to save herself from being dragged. Her hands are tied and she's suddenly in the back of the car, and she wonders if it's him..."

"Him as in Jordan Rivera?" Axel asked.

"Yes. Whoever it is, he's tall. Tall and strong and..."

"Jordan?" Axel said.

Raina slowly shook her head. "No. She can't see him, but she knows. It isn't Jordan. It can't be Jordan."

"How does she know?" Kylie asked.

Again, Raina shook her head slowly. Her eyes remained staring straight ahead. Wide open.

Still unblinking.

"Because she knows how Jordan smells. No cologne or aftershave. Nothing bad. Just something unique that is Jordan. And this isn't Jordan."

"Can she sense anything? See anything? Is it definitely a man?" Axel asked.

"She's trying to tell. The person who took her, she doesn't know, but she does know someone else is driving. She tries to cry out, make someone in another car see her. No one does. No one stops them. She tries to tell herself it's a prank, that it's all going to be okay, and then..."

Neither Kylie or Axel spoke.

Titan whined softly.

Raina's hand moved automatically over his head.

"She is terrified. She's being dragged out of the car. She feels high, wet grass all around her ankles. She can smell the earth and its rich aroma and the ground is soft, muddy or mucky. And in a flash, she feels something, something move across her throat. It doesn't even hurt at first. She just becomes aware of the warmth. Sticky warmth sliding down her throat and through her blouse and down her shirt. She can smell something awful and she starts to feel the pain and the smell at the same time, the pain at her throat, the smell of her own blood."

Raina's eyes closed at last.

Axel was about to rise when they opened again.

Titan whined softly again.

He turned.

The barn was in shadow. No lights turned on, just a bit of the sun filtering in through the wooden structure and the open doorway to the stables.

In those shadows, something appeared, slowly taking form.

It was Jennifer.

She was not ripped or torn or covered in the thick grasses or dense mud of the Everglades, of the embankment where she had been found.

She was in a flowered blouse and jeans, the outfit she had been wearing that day, fresh as it had been before she had been killed. Her eyes were wide and full of gratitude. There was a pained smile on her lips.

She reached out to Raina.

And, in turn, Raina reached out to her.

Then, just as it had appeared, the ghost of Jennifer Lowry disappeared, and as it did, Raina blinked and stood and stared and then sighed softly.

Axel stood, as well, and waited, ready to steady Raina, to

speak, to hold her, to try to make better what had to have been hard and painful.

But Raina was fine. Steadfast. Straight as a ruler, dignified and in complete control.

"She so desperately wants to help us. Everything was stolen from her—life, a promise of happiness. She was excited about Jordan. She liked him—really liked him. I mean, we saw the picture Jordan had snapped of the two of them on his computer. He liked her, too. It was the first time in a long time she'd dared to think someone might really care for her. But she's given us what she can. She just doesn't know anymore."

Axel nodded. "She'll grow stronger. We'll see her again. And there may be something she'll recall later—just like a living witness. Raina, thank you," he said softly.

Titan let out a woof. He had either sensed or seen the ghost. Dogs tended to be far more perceptive than people.

Raina looked at Kylie.

"Thank you so much!"

"I didn't do anything," Kylie told her. "You really came to it all on your own. And it gets better, honestly."

"You've regressed again?" Axel asked Kylie.

She shook her head. "No, but I'm getting to be more like Raina. And I don't think I'd be afraid to try much of anything—if Jon was there, of course, or perhaps other Krewe members."

"I'm not sure we've learned much," Raina said. "I mean, we knew she cared about Jordan. We know Jordan cared about her. He didn't kill her. And now, he's in a coma, and he can't talk."

"But we now know there was one kidnapper—and one driver," Axel said. "That's more to go on than before. Now we have to find out just how Jordan is related to those he might have suspected. He didn't know Jennifer had been killed—and he was angry, incredibly angry. He knew the method and he evidently knew how to escape once they were in the Everglades." He smiled at Raina. "We have the connection. Now, we're going to find out where it leads."

"Money," Nigel said, looking up.

It had been quiet awhile. They were all—Axel, Nigel, Jon, Andrew, Kylie and Raina—going through files.

Every file they had on the murder victims.

On those around them.

"Motives for murder. Revenge, hatred, jealousy—money," Axel said suddenly. He leaned forward. "Jennifer Lowry died just before she might be one of a number of people receiving a large inheritance. We need to be looking for a similar motive with the other victims."

"But didn't you all look into Peter Scarborough's estranged wife? He had no money—he left no money," Raina said.

"I'm looking at her finances, and I don't see anything. Then again, he was cremated, and his ashes were finally picked up by a coworker. His stepchildren didn't come. What the hell?" Nigel said.

Axel gritted his teeth and looked at his file. Nigel touched his arm. "Hey, this has been going on for years. We're not going to get an easy answer."

He nodded and stood. "There's money somewhere. A money trail we can't find. Raina, want to go riding?"

"Sure."

"Good idea. Get out and clear your head," Jon said quietly.

"You're starting to drive us all stark raving nuts," Andrew told him.

"What the hell? I'm not doing anything," Axel protested.

"Breathing," Nigel said.

"Gritting your teeth," Andrew told him.

"There's an annoying sigh now and then," Jon said.

Raina smiled. "I'm happy to go for a ride."

They headed out to the stables again. The blue dress was still there, thrown on a shelf in the tack room.

Raina ignored it.

"Saddles or bareback?" she asked Axel.

"Bareback. I need to do something!" he said.

They headed out, following the trail they had followed before.

The crew from the forensics team were gone, but some of their tape remained, trampled to the ground.

"I guess they found all they could of Fran Castle?" Raina asked Axel.

He nodded. "Some bones. Not a complete set. At least we know where she wound up and her family has something to bury. Closed coffin," he added dryly.

Raina nodded. "I wonder if…"

"What?"

"It's really horrible."

"What is it?"

"Well, I didn't try to get anything off what we found." She hesitated. "What I thought was some kind of leftover steak in the yard. The poisoned…meat."

Axel was quiet. "Raina…"

"I know it's a strange idea, but anything that would help. I mean, horrible, yes, but I'm more than willing. Though I foresee a problem—trying to tell a medical examiner or someone else you want to hold someone's sliced-off flesh…"

He looked at her. "It can be arranged," he assured her.

For a moment, he remained reined in on the trail where the leftover crime tape littered the scene, where the bones of Fran Castle had finally been found.

"Anything here?" he asked her.

Raina closed her eyes. She heard birds, something sliding in the mud, the chirp of some kind of insect.

A mosquito landed on her arm, giving her a good bite.

She slapped at it and looked at Axel. "I'm sorry," she told him.

As she spoke, someone stepped around one of the trees. Peg-legged Pete with another of the ghostly pirates.

"Axel, Miss Hamish!" Peg-legged Pete said, sweeping off his feathered pirate's hat and bowing low before her.

"Hi, Pete!" Raina said.

"What a sweet lass, and a beauty," Pete told Axel.

Axel grinned. "I do agree," he said. "Joshua!" he added, addressing the other pirate. "Has Joshua met Raina yet?"

"Miss," the other pirate said, stepping forward. He was wearing a knit cap, blousy shirt, vest, breeches and high boots. Puffs of long sandy hair escaped in long tendrils from his knit cap. He was very thin, and as he greeted her, he swept off his cap, bowing low.

"I was hoping to see you…thought I'd take a walk on to Andrew's place, but you never know who might be there, and you know me, I don't like to be causing trouble," Pete said.

"You have something for us?" Axel asked.

"Joshua, tell them," Pete said.

Joshua, his cap between his hands, nodded anxiously. "Strange, it were, in my estimation, that be. People out here. Several of them. They came in an automobile, parked on the trail where it ends to our west there. They were shouting, angry. Someone was saying the situation had to be stopped. I couldn't see anyone clear, but I'd say there were three of them at least, running around. And the dress…so strange. Looked like they were in trousers and handsome coats of some kind…not what you often see out here. But I could see no faces. I hid, and then, sometime later, I saw people, lots of people, crawling around. Not here, deeper in. Then I heard a man screaming and then airboats, and then, well, you were there, and you know the rest."

"Wait—men in suits were out here right before we arrived in the airboat?"

"No, they were gone. Only one remained."

"Was he tied up, then? Did you see him running?" Raina asked anxiously.

Joshua shook his head sadly. "I don't know. I just heard when he started screaming. When the snake took him."

"Thank you," Axel said.

"It's not much," Joshua told him.

"Well, I'm truly grateful," Axel said.

Raina echoed her thanks. Peg-legged Pete and Joshua nodded grimly and Pete told Axel, "We're headed deeper in. Watching the airboats. Lots of them moving around. The usual tourist trade, and it seems like more. Python hunters."

"That's a great idea," Axel said. "You have been incredibly helpful, Pete. Joshua."

The pirates looked pleased. They started off, moving like fog through the foliage.

Pete stopped and turned back. He lifted his hand in the air and gave them a hearty "Arrrr!" which seemed to provide Joshua with a great deal of amusement.

"They were really brutal once upon a time?" Raina asked when they were gone.

"Some men find a time when they regret the evil they've done," he said quietly. "I wasn't there, of course, but I know the legends. I know the dead. How deeply they were involved in cold-blooded murder, I don't know. But—" he grimaced, looking at her "—being passive when evil is happening is just as bad sometimes. Maybe the pirates I know are the ones getting a second chance."

His phone rang and he answered it.

"We should head back," he said to Raina. "Vinnie Magruder made it to Andrew's. God knows what he might remember, if anything."

"Everything is something," Raina said, lifting Wild Thing's reins.

Everything, indeed, could be something. She was learning.

CHAPTER SEVENTEEN

"You know," Vinnie said. "That poor girl, Fran Castle, disappeared over thirteen years ago. Now, I know you're coming up with more corpses, and that anthropologist medical examiner person is certain she found a slash on the hyoid bone, but that was over thirteen years ago." He shook his head. "A shame, a crying shame, what's going on."

Vinnie Magruder had the look of a grizzled old Floridian, skin bronzed and wrinkled by endless years in the sun, gray hair worn a little long now and matching a gray beard and sideburns. He wore old jeans, battered by the years, and an open cotton shirt over a T-shirt. He was a big man, tall and broad in the shoulders, polite, but skeptical about himself, and seemingly about the ability of anyone else to do anything to stop the killings in the Everglades.

"You came out here when one of the school camps was going on," Axel said, studying him intently. "What I need to know is if you remember timing. It was night when you arrived. You found the car at about 2:00 p.m. I know about the events registered in the records, but that doesn't mean something wasn't going on before."

Vinnie sighed and looked at Raina. Titan was sitting next to her, and Vinnie smiled. He'd heard Axel perfectly clearly and he would answer, Raina thought, in his own time.

"Great dog," he told her.

"Thank you," she said.

"He's always with you?" Vinnie asked.

"As much as possible," she assured him.

He nodded. "Good. A dog is better than many a man. Or woman." He looked at Axel again. "She's special, huh?"

Raina smiled; she knew he was referring to her.

Axel nodded gravely. "Very."

"Another of you spooky types, huh? And your friends?" He looked down the table where Jon and Kylie were sitting.

"My spooky friends?" Axel asked.

Vinnie waved a hand in the air. "Oh, in the best way!" he said. He glanced at Nigel Ferrer and said, "You know these guys and their ghost stories about the Everglades. Oh, wait! I think I've heard you tell a few, too!"

"There are some good stories about the area, Vinnie, you know that. And we all enjoy the ones from way back, right?" Nigel said easily.

Vinnie shrugged and nodded at the same time. "Ghost ships, ghost planes...the land can claim a lot. Anyway, these murders. I came out here back then to get search parties started up because the girl was missing and her car was parked where it shouldn't have been. And when I found the registration and called it in to headquarters, they already had her name. Well, her friend, it seems, started with the casino security at about noon and then demanded that the police be notified. Now, you know, that's not a great deal of time for an adult to be considered missing at all—but I found the car, and the cops had already heard the young woman's name."

"Noon?" Axel said. "You're saying the friend reported her

missing at noon. Do you know how long before that she had last been with the friend?"

"We have surveillance video of her at the entrance around ten thirty. They'd met out there early. Seems they had a theory that if you hit the machines early after the night before, they paid out better."

"But you found her car abandoned about 2:00 p.m.," Nigel noted, frowning. "People are on the Trail during the day. A two-lane highway. And nothing weird was reported."

"Right. People all in a hurry. If anyone saw anything, they didn't call it in. And yeah, 2:00 p.m. is when I saw the car and checked on it. The car was open and no one was around. But it was where it shouldn't have been—that must be in the report. Anyway, I called in about the car after I checked it out, a little after 2:00 p.m., so that would be correct. Again, Fran Castle had been at the casino with a friend. When the friend couldn't find her...they hadn't come together, you see. But they'd planned to spend the day together. Play some machines, have something to eat and then maybe head back in or play bingo or I don't know. They were supposed to spend the whole day together. The woman who reported her missing—Terry Highsmith—said they'd gotten into a little tiff over some kind of animated machine."

"This Terry Highsmith was checked out, right?" Nigel asked.

"Thoroughly. She never left the casino. Cameras everywhere, you know."

"What about Fran Castle?" Andrew asked.

"She got a phone call and then left the casino. That was at 10:30 a.m. Then there were no more cameras. After Fran went missing, Terry waited there all morning, growing more and more anxious."

Vinnie had told them he didn't remember much. He did.

In his mind, Raina thought, Vinnie remembered it all well—he just didn't remember anything he thought could be of use.

Vinnie was still deeply bothered by what had happened.

Haunted by it.

By the failure of law enforcement or anyone else to find Fran Castle before she'd been killed.

Twelve noon.

Raina glanced at Axel, who gave away little of his thoughts. But she knew him. And she knew his next move would be to find out just where Frank Peters and Loretta Oster had been between 10:30 and noon on the day that Fran Castle had gone missing.

Again, the question rose in her mind.

Why?

Why kill someone like Fran Castle?

Or any of the others for that matter, including Jennifer Lowry?

"I just don't know anything more about that day. Terry couldn't understand why Fran would have left the casino. They had a spat—but just a really little tiff because she'd been at the machine, and Fran had sat down, and the bonus had come in. It hadn't been big. Fran had just moved over to another bank of machines…"

And then disappeared.

"Normally, it takes time for an official missing-persons report. But her having just walked out, with her car abandoned, and Terry Highsmith so insistent that something had to be wrong, well, it got things moving. Sometimes idiot folks start walking around along the shore of the canal looking for birds or even trying to snap pictures of sleeping gators. Made sense for us to look. Never made sense that we couldn't find her."

"What about her friend?" Axel asked. "Terry Highsmith? Was there ever a time she was able to tell the police anything more? Fran's friends, her enemies, was she in debt?"

"I talked to her after I found the car. She was babbling,

mostly. Very frightened because I'd found the car abandoned. She was the one to suggest Fran might have just gotten angry and headed up to the Seminole casinos. The abandoned car was what made that theory a little wild. Terry was trying to think of reasons Fran might've left. But she was scared for her friend. Just disappearing like that wasn't the kind of thing Fran did. And she hated bugs and mosquitoes and alligators and snakes. There was nothing wrong with the car—it was just parked off the Trail. We all wanted to believe there had been a problem, that she'd called another friend, but she was never seen again. Until now," he added softly.

"Maybe talk to Terry Highsmith again," Jon suggested.

"Dead," Vinnie said. He paused. "I kept up on it, you know. Couldn't forget the way Fran Castle had just seemed to vanish. I'd call Terry every few years and just check on her, and, well, she died five years back. An aneurism or some such thing—just dropped dead at work one day. She'd been a manager at one of the big grocery stores in Miami. Anyway, we tried everything. Everything and everyone. And never found Fran Castle or any reason for why she disappeared."

"What happened to her estate?" Kylie asked.

"What estate? She didn't leave any kind of estate. Maybe a few thousand dollars. She was never declared dead, so… I don't know," Vinnie said.

He looked old and sad. Raina was next to him and she set a hand on his arm.

"We can only imagine how much of yourself you gave to trying to find Fran Castle," she said softly. "Thank you."

He looked at her strangely, probably wondering what a dog trainer might have to do with the search for a killer. But he did know Axel had "spooky" friends, so he might not be as confused as he could have been.

"Thank you," he told her. "There's always that one lingering case that follows you forever. I don't know if I've helped—"

"You have," Axel assured him.

"Then I guess I'll head on out. But if you need me again, in any way," he told them, looking from Axel to Nigel and on to Andrew, "you know I'll do anything. Search, dig, go through records. I'm retired, but if you need it, call me." He offered a rueful smile. "Like that song title, call me. I'll be there."

They all thanked him, and he left.

For a while, they were quiet. "So, no estate for anyone to get. A well-liked person. She and her friend—also dead now—had a little spat over a game machine. But Terry said they had those little spats all the time—they were part of the day. They didn't bet big amounts or lose big amounts or win big amounts. They would vie for different machines, and then laugh about it later."

"Thirteen years ago," Jon reminded him. "And if you're right, it's damned chilling. A murder-for-hire enterprise that's been going on for all these years possibly starting before Fran Castle disappeared."

"She left the casino after a phone call," Raina mused.

"Lured out," Axel theorized.

"It's late. We need to start fresh in the morning," Andrew said. "Maybe Jordan Rivera will be out of his coma by then. And when there's light, we can start searching again."

They were all silent. Then Axel stood up. "Right. We won't get anywhere without some sleep. And Angela is busy on records." He hesitated. "We might even have to take a quick trip to South Dakota. I'd like to meet Peter Scarborough's wife and find out more about their split."

"So far, no money trail," Jon said. "I've read and read and... I'm not seeing anyone giving or receiving large amounts of money."

"Maybe the reasons for murder differ," Raina suggested. They all looked at her.

"I mean…maybe someone just hated someone. And then, in another case, maybe money was involved. And then, in another case, there was a job out there that was coveted by someone else and they were behind. I mean, I don't know…"

"It would still be murder for hire," Axel mused. "And if that is the case, someone had to be getting money from somewhere. Angela has to find something—offshore accounts. Murder for hire. Money. Unless…"

"Unless?" Nigel asked, leaning forward.

"Unless payment is in a different form," Axel said.

Nigel sat back. "What kind of form?"

"I don't know," Axel said. "A favor done…for a favor? We can look at the victims and those close to them and see how their lives might have changed."

"I can hop up to South Dakota and see the one-time wife of Peter Scarborough," Jon offered.

Axel nodded. "Tomorrow, we'll start here with the most recent victim, Jennifer Lowry. We'll head back to the dentist's office."

"And maybe the doctors will be able to wake Jordan Rivera by then," Raina said. She hesitated, wincing inwardly. "Because he might well know something."

There was silence again.

Axel stood up; it was time for them all to leave. Frustrating to have to break for the night.

As they left, Raina looked up at the sky.

Night. It made such a difference out here. Andrew barely seemed to notice, but this was his home. He had always known the darkness and shadows and simple *eeriness* of the Everglades by night. There was, of course, still a moon. It seemed to ride higher in the sky here than it did above the city lights.

Stars themselves seemed different. Brighter. And yet all around her, the darkness was more complete, and nature's light allowed for strange shadows, making the sound of the creatures that lived and died in the ever-flowing river frightening at every turn.

She seemed to be the only one who noticed. They exchanged a few more words as they all headed to their cars.

They drove in silence, but as they neared her house, Axel looked at Raina and said softly, "This has gone on for years, you know."

"I know," she said. "And I know things aren't solved easily."

"Hey, this is it. We're on track. We will get where we're going."

They reached the house. Titan jumped out of the car and ran ahead. Jon and Kylie had just pulled in ahead of them.

Raina quickly stepped out of Axel's car, anxious.

But she needn't have worried.

Titan was ready to greet them, convinced already they belonged there. She lowered her head and let out a soft sigh, relieved, and then hurried up to open the door and let them all in.

Night.

She found herself more distracted than ever, confused and lost.

And wishing she'd never tried on the blue dress.

But then they said their good-nights to Jon and Kylie, and she set Titan up with a treat in the hallway.

But in her room with the door closed, Axel took her into his arms, and suddenly strength seemed to flow back into her.

She didn't know exactly what it was. Maybe that they could laugh together, maybe the feel of bare flesh touching, seducing, bringing such sweet and vibrant heat. The way his lips could move over her flesh. Or the way he kissed her, or the way his eyes fell upon hers right when he rose above her and they came together, the feel of him in her.

Sex.

It wasn't that she could call herself an expert, but life had brought a few lovers her way.

Sex, and then…

Sex with him.

And falling in love. And loving everything about him, about his touch, rising like a whirlwind, buffeted by lightning into the heavens, drifting again on the most gentle breeze.

Seeing his eyes again.

Feeling the way he held her.

Maybe it was just so much more. Really making love.

And the night, even darkness, even shadows, were good.

She wondered what it would be like to live like that, always.

Axel's first call was to the doctor.

Jordan Rivera was stable.

But not good.

The doctors were unwilling to bring him out of his coma, despite the stakes at hand.

Axel knew the doctors were good. They followed the oath they had taken. The patients entrusted to them deserved their care to the best of their abilities, and that was that.

But it was frustrating.

He knew Jordan was safe. He believed in Nigel and the police.

County officers remained on guard—two at any given time, allowing for necessary breaks, coffee, staying awake and being aware and, most important, alert.

Jon and Kylie had left at the crack of dawn. He had dressed and come out to tell them goodbye and thank them as they headed on out.

"All is good," Kylie told him. "I'm not an agent—"

"You're an important consultant," Axel interrupted, grinning. It was a title many people took on when it was necessary for work with the Krewe.

"Yeah, well, this case is important. Not that I don't love the work I'm doing with Adam at the new museum he's opening, but I'm good at what I do, at hiring the right people, and we're moving along fine in the right direction. We'll have a great fall opening. For now, they're good without me."

"And I'm grateful."

She gave him a kiss on the cheek. "As long as you show up for the wedding!" she told him.

The two were getting married in New York in October.

"I intend to make the wedding," he assured her.

"With a real date, I think," Jon teased. Then he grew serious. "Let's get going. South Dakota isn't close and I'd like to get some bearings."

The Krewe members were lucky. Adam Harrison had seen to it they had a private jet, and it was available to get Jon Dickson and Kylie Connolly to South Dakota. They would be seeing Melissa Scarborough; she'd agreed to meet with them during her lunch break.

With those two gone, he'd checked on Titan, giving him a treat, and returned to the bedroom to quietly make his phone call.

When he'd finished at the hospital, he'd lain beside Raina, staring at the ceiling, thinking. She stirred at his side, but he hadn't realized she'd fully awakened until she spoke.

"We're going back out to Andrew's?" Raina asked him. "Are we looking for the remains of Brandon Wells?"

"I think we're going to head back to the dentist's office and talk to Dr. Wong first. Then, maybe, take a trip downtown."

"Downtown?"

"Law offices."

"Like where Tate Fielding and Jordan Rivera work?"

He nodded.

"But Jordan's not there," she said. "Jordan's in the hospital."

"Right. Tate will be there."

"What do you think Tate could know?"

"Well, you're all still good friends, right? And there was a time when Mya dated Jordan and you dated Tate, right?"

"Ancient history."

"That's not what I'm getting at," he said, smiling. "I'm thinking if you're all still friends, then Jordan and Tate are probably really good friends, and Tate might know more about Jordan and his activities than we do."

"Okay. Tuesday at a law office. We might have some trouble seeing Tate."

"I don't think so," Axel said. "It's amazing what an FBI badge can do, especially in a law office. Attorneys have to be on the up-and-up at all times, and if they're not, they have to appear to be."

"The firm has been around forever."

"Trust me, Tate will take the time to see us." He glanced quickly at his watch. "We can be there for nine. That will leave us hours and hours to try the trails out around Andrew's house. Or," he added dryly, "opt for another airboat ride."

"Okay, then, I'm up," she said.

He glanced her way, grinning. "So am I."

"It's morning."

"So it is. I have nothing against light."

She laughed softly and curled into his arms.

Eventually, she was the one who rose, sprinting into the shower. He used the time to call Nigel and Andrew.

Search parties would start up again soon. This time, the police and others on call would be looking for the remains of Brandon Wells.

Nigel sounded weary and frustrated. "I just don't get it. Eventually, there's some kind of a money trail. There's something. Anyway, I'm going to go out to some of the police stations in the different cities, just make sure everyone is on the same page, and aware, if nothing else. Tomorrow, my captain has asked we have something of a task force meeting early. So, anything we get today will be of great help."

"Good," Axel said, and told him his intentions.

"A plan is a good thing," he said. And they agreed again, late that afternoon or early evening, they'd meet back up at Andrew's.

Raina emerged from the bathroom, not just showered but dressed and ready.

He headed in, showered in very hot water very quickly, and came out. She was in the kitchen with Titan, telling him he'd be in for the morning, but out with them later.

"Downtown," she said. "Should I call Tate?"

"Let's surprise him," Axel said.

They headed out, taking US 1 down to Flager and a few blocks in from Biscayne Bay, to the impressive new high-rise building and the law offices of Fielding, Brockton and Emery.

"There are more attorneys in the firm," Raina said, whispering in the elevator, even though they were alone in it. "About ten of them, and legal assistants, and other office workers. Jordan is a whiz at their civil cases, so I understand. And he's not even thirty. I know one day he's hoping the name 'Rivera' is going to be added to that of the partners."

"What else do they handle?"

"Civil and criminal cases. And apparently, they're known to be especially good with their criminal cases. They work diligently for their clients, but also know when to advise a plea deal. They don't handle maritime law, but they do personal injury. For the clients, not the insurance companies. But from what I understand they're respected because they don't represent anyone who spreads honey on the grocery store floor to fake a fall. They go for the real thing."

"Commendable," Axel said. But he found himself thinking they were careful and didn't handle any cases when a client might have been caught on camera doing any such thing.

The firm had the entire twentieth floor of the building. The receptionist was an attractive woman in her late thirties or early forties, handsomely dressed in a business suit, her dark hair neatly queued at her nape.

She knew Raina and greeted her warmly.

"Christmas party a few years back," Raina whispered to him, before greeting the woman in return. "Karel, I'd like you meet an old friend, Special Agent Axel Tiger. Axel, Karel has been with the firm for years. They'd never manage anything without her!"

"Well, that's pushing it!" the woman said, smiling. "What can I do for you?" she asked pleasantly, and then her expression changed. "Oh, dear, it's about Jordan. He's not worse, is he? Tate told us the doctors have assured him Jordan will be okay eventually. He's a great guy, truly. We're all praying for him!"

"No change with Jordan. They're keeping him in the coma," Axel told her. "We were hoping to talk to Tate and perhaps anyone else Jordan was close to here."

"I'll call young Mr. Fielding immediately. I still can't believe it. I mean, someone attacked Jordan and left him out there to die. I assure you—he didn't go out there alone! But it certainly wasn't anyone here!"

She didn't wait for a response; she picked up her phone and informed Tate Fielding they were out in the reception area.

A second later, Tate—suave and impressive with neatly combed-back hair and an expensive designer suit—appeared, a look of concern on his face as he urged them to follow him back to his office.

It was a corner office, nice and high. The buildings next to it were older and not as tall. His office looked out over those buildings, all the way to the water.

He had a handsome chrome-and-glass desk with a computer set up on it, and matching filing cabinets that accented the ultramodern look of the office. Even his desk phone was framed with chrome. Comfortable but businesslike chairs sat in front of the desk with his swivel chair behind it, with wall cabinets lined up in easy reach.

He indicated they should take the chairs in front of his desk.

He looked at them anxiously. "I went by the hospital this morning before I came here. They say Jordan's stable, and I guess that's all that they'll say officially, but the nurse I spoke with seemed optimistic. Nothing's changed, right?"

He looked at Raina worriedly as he finished speaking.

"Nothing has changed," Raina said softly. "Not that we know about, anyway."

He frowned slightly. "What do you think he was doing out in the middle of the Everglades alone? I can't even fathom how he got out there. I mean, the only logical thing is that someone took him, probably against his will. Do you think this is related to the case that brought you here, Axel? Do you think someone meant to slit his throat? But no, it was a python! I know a dog or a small child could be a nice little morsel for a snake, but Jordan isn't small. I'm sorry. All of this is just so bizarre."

"It was a damned big snake. Close to the largest found out there, I'd bet," Axel said. "Frankly, I can't imagine how that constrictor might have gotten such a huge meal into his mouth, either. I just know he was wrapped around him. But no, we can't figure out how he got out there in the first place."

"Jordan is really one of the nicest guys in the world," Tate said. "They like to mock lawyers, call us sharks, but that wasn't Jordan at all. He fought hard and passionately for people. And I can't imagine why anyone would want to harm him. Me, maybe. I've defended some people who probably deserved more than they got. I could see...well, I've defended a few murderers. Drug dealers. No matter what the crime, by our justice system, everyone deserves to put up the strongest defense the law allows."

"You don't know of any cases where there might have been some bad blood? Someone who wanted to come after Jordan?"

Tate sat back, shaking his head and looking baffled. "We have a meeting once a week. We all go over every case that's been brought into the firm. Criminal and civil. Jordan's recent cases have been against corporations, ones with enough money to make settlements. He has gotten the best for his people. But seriously, I can't think of a situation where anyone would want to come after him."

"What about his personal life?" Axel asked.

Tate gave him a quizzical look. "Well, you know as much about that as I do. We were all joking at dinner the other night. Jordan hasn't been serious about anyone in a long time. He does usually show up at events with someone different each time."

"Did you know he knew Jennifer Lowry, the young woman whose body we found on the embankment just into the Everglades?"

Tate frowned. He shook his head.

"No. I didn't know he knew her. I mean, he never brought her anywhere. He might have met her at this club he liked to go to. Jordan never liked really loud places. Well, Raina, you know. He loves music, has always loved music, but hates DJs who go from one pounding beat to the next. I can't think of the name of the place he liked. I went there with him once. He talked to all kinds of people that night. What was it? Oh, Sunshine and Moonlight!" He was proud of himself for remembering the name of the place, but then he paused again. "Oh, God. That means I might have met her, too."

"He cared about her," Axel said. "You don't remember him introducing her to you by name?"

Tate thought a minute and then shook his head slowly. "No. But I only went there with him once. He might have seen her at another time."

"What about anyone else here?" Raina asked him.

"I think I'm as close as anyone here," Tate said. He frowned suddenly. "I did just think of something. Sorry—not associated with any outing. Well, yes, I guess in a weird way. The night I was out with him, he did meet someone at the bar. I wasn't paying that much attention." He was quiet a minute. "I do wonder if it might have been the poor girl who was murdered. Later that night, he mentioned he might have landed a new client. Jordan handles civil cases, you know, so I didn't think too much about it. I was going to ask him, but he wandered away again, and I started watching the girl onstage. Solo act that night. Boy, did she have pipes. And she could play a guitar something fierce! I wonder if Jordan ever put anything into the record about a new client? I can look, but honestly, I believe he'll be able to answer these questions himself before long."

"Do you mind checking the record?" Axel asked. "It could be important. Jordan was attacked by someone, we're convinced. Anything that moves this along more quickly will be great."

Tate nodded to Axel but flashed a smile to Raina. "Anything for you kids," he said. "I'll check the records." He spoke into the intercom. "Karel, will you get me all of Jordan's most recent files, memos, notes. Anything, please."

"Of course, Mr. Fielding, I'll bring his files, but they should all be in the computer, too. They're password-protected, but—"

"I know his pass code, thanks. I'll just bring his files up," Tate told her.

He ended his conversation with another press of the button, frowning as he keyed in what he needed on his computer.

"Come on around," he told Axel and Raina. "Maybe you'll see something I don't."

They walked behind his desk. Raina read the file as Tate used the touch screen. Jordan kept excellent notes. He was dealing with a case, defending a man with a dog. Two young men had jumped the fence into the defendant's yard, and the dog had bitten one of them. The young man was suing, and Jordan was defending the dog owner. Countersuing. Why was the man in his yard?

"Strong case here. I met the dog when the man was in the office. Mutt was just defending his home. Jordan will make mincemeat of this," he said.

He scrolled on.

"Stop!" Axel said.

A notation had caught his eye. Jordan had begun conversations with JL.

Jennifer Lowry? The date seemed right.

"Workplace harassment?" Raina murmured aloud.

She looked at Axel. "At Dr. Wong's office?" she asked. "They all claimed to love her!"

Axel didn't answer.

"Hey, get around, get around!" Tate said worriedly, standing.

Axel comprehended why instantly—the elder Fielding was coming. He grasped Raina's hand and walked around quickly.

The three of them were standing—Tate behind the desk, properly, and Axel and Raina in front, where they should be—when Jefferson Fielding walked in.

"Well, hello, Miss Raina, and Special Agent Tiger, is it? You are finding out what happened to Jordan Rivera, right?"

"We are, sir," Axel said. "And Tate has kindly spoken to

us. We were hoping he might have an idea of anyone who threatened Jordan in any way."

The older Fielding looked at his son and smiled grimly. "Well, they are good friends, yes. But of course you know neither Tate, nor anyone in this firm, can give you information on cases. Attorney-client privilege. As much as we'd like to help you, there might be situations in which we are morally obligated to keep silent."

"Of course, sir," Axel said. "We would never want anything that wasn't completely within the law. As a matter of fact, we were just leaving. We do believe Jordan will be out of the coma soon, and when he is, well, he'll give us whatever we need."

He turned to Tate. "Thank you for seeing us and we do understand you couldn't give away any of his client information. Mr. Fielding, good to see you."

"Thanks, Tate!" Raina said. "Mr. Fielding," she added, starting past him.

"Amazing," Jefferson Fielding said.

"What's that?" Raina asked politely.

"A dog trainer out asking questions with the FBI. Is that legal?"

"Raina is consulting with us on this because of the animals involved," Axel politely improvised, taking her arm. "Good day, gentlemen, and thank you again."

The door was open. They left it that way.

As they started out into the hall, they heard Jefferson say to Tate, "What, she's sleeping with him now? She's something to look at, but pure bitch, son. You're well out of anything with her!"

"Dad, we dated for two minutes years ago," Tate replied wearily.

Axel saw that Raina's cheeks were burning. Of course the elder Fielding had meant for her to hear his words.

"I'm tempted to go back and deck him," Axel said.

"No. He's just an ass," Raina said. "I broke it off with Tate, and I guess in Jefferson's mind, no one does that to his son. Tate and I remained friends. His dad can't seem to accept that." She looked at him and grinned. "I'm grateful you were ready to rush to my defense, but seriously? He's just an ass, and not worth the trouble!"

He grinned at her, and then his grin faded.

"We've got to get back to the dentist's office," he said.

CHAPTER EIGHTEEN

They left downtown and headed back toward South Miami and the dentist's office.

As they drove, Raina sighed. "Poor Tate."

Axel glanced her way, lifting a brow. "Poor Tate? His dad will have him made partner in a matter of a few years. He's a very handsome young man, pretty much has the world at his feet. But poor Tate?"

"He was ready to help us. His dad is a jerk." She was quiet. Then she spoke softly. "Jefferson Fielding himself was around that day, thirteen years ago, and he was no kid at the time. He even followed Tate out to the campground, making sure it was safe for his son. I know he embarrassed Tate a lot, always making it sound as if he was elite, being groomed to be an incredible attorney and maybe politician. Tate was okay on his own. Like you said—good-looking, charming. He managed just fine."

"He's also grown now. Out of college, well over twenty-one. He could leave, if he chose."

"I can't imagine that kind of pressure. My parents were

more like belated flower children. They wanted me to do whatever would make me happy," Raina said.

He shrugged, and then smiled. "Mine were pretty good. They wanted me to know the culture of both the Seminole and Miccosukee tribes, which was fair. According to my dad, the Seminole is a little more liberal and the Miccosukee is a little more determined to hang on to history—and whatever the rest of my mixed-up background might have been. They were great. Belated flower children, too, believing we were all entitled to grow up to be whatever we wanted to be, as well. I guess you're right. I knew what I wanted from a young age, and they did nothing but encourage me. Maybe it is 'poor Tate.' Anyway, he tried to help us. And I saw the 'JL' and the note Jordan left. It could prove to be very important."

Raina gazed out the window as they drove. They were soon back in her general neighborhood, South Miami, and about to park by the dentist's office.

"Wong seemed truly beloved," Raina said. "Patients and staff seem to be crazy about him. Do you think it could be true someone was harassing her? It seems the only time she went out was with her friends from work."

He didn't answer right away. They'd pulled into a parking spot on the street near the office and his phone was ringing. He glanced her way apologetically and answered it.

He talked for a minute and then hung up, looking at her thoughtfully.

"What?"

"That was Jon. He and Kylie saw Melissa Scarborough, who is about to become Melissa Newton. She was very well dressed and she had them meet her at an upscale restaurant. She was, in Jon's opinion, determined to help them in any way she could. Too determined. Very nice, crying over Peter, and claiming while they'd been split up, she still loved him, of course. She'd never imagined such a terrible thing. They both thought she was trying too hard. She hadn't wanted him down in South Florida—too many criminal elements. He was a nice guy, but if he drank too much at a bar, he was prone to get into fights. She was afraid he finally managed to anger the wrong person."

"Angela checked out all her records, right? She never did come to Florida?" Raina asked.

"We can't find any records that suggest she came to Florida anywhere near the time he disappeared and was then found. But about a year before they split up, they were here as a couple, vacationing. They spent time in Miami and then over in Naples. Which meant they went through the Everglades, driving from east to west."

"You said they met at an upscale restaurant and she was very well dressed?" Raina asked.

"Kylie said her clothing was designer and very expensive."

"But they had been people who made moderate incomes."

"Right. I'm going to call Angela and tell her there has to be a money trail somewhere," Axel said.

She was quiet. "If she hired someone to kill Peter Scarborough, wouldn't that mean she'd have less money? Maybe the guy she's going to marry is wealthy."

"Maybe. Jon told me he and Kylie just smiled and accepted everything she said, but they didn't feel it was sincere. Melissa Scarborough was almost smug, as if she were playing a part. And even if they knew it, there was nothing they could do about it. She suddenly has money, and I'm willing to bet it somehow came from her husband. She had a reason to want him dead. And now, we have Tate letting us see the notes Jordan had in his file. I think someone—no matter how loved Jennifer Lowry might have been—wanted her out of the way. Let's check out Dr. Wong's office."

He turned and she followed him as they entered the building and headed up in the elevator. Axel opened the door and

Raina stepped in before him. The reception area was filled with waiting patients and Marci was at the desk. She looked at them with surprise and then frowned, rising and coming around from her desk to greet them.

"Has anything else happened? Do you need something… that can wait? As you can see, we're really busy!" she said anxiously.

"We went to the club and talked to some people there," Axel said, smiling. "Sometimes, when a bit of time passes, you think of something more, so we wanted to check in."

"Of course you're busy," Raina said. "How are you managing? You must be short-staffed."

"Well, thankfully, Roger has been able to step up and fill in on a lot of work Jen always did, and he has a cousin who has been a dental assistant and she's come in to help. It's been a godsend, really. Dr. Wong was saying the other day not only were we mourning the loss of an amazing friend, we were down an amazing woman who was like his right hand."

"Now is a tough time. We understand. We'll make arrangements to talk later," Axel said.

He gave Marci a sad smile, completely understanding the situation.

"Thank you!" she whispered.

He had Raina's hand.

They left the office. Axel seemed grim but reenergized.

"We're on track," he said. "I know it."

"Axel, do you think Roger Martinez arranged for Jennifer to be killed to take her place, to bring his cousin in? There's just not much money in it. Murder for hire must cost! I don't think the rewards would equal the cost."

"It's not always money. It's what a person really wants. You've seen it before, I'm sure. We all have. Someone who claims to love someone the world seems to idolize—when resentment is brewing beneath."

"That's possible. But enough to want someone dead?"

"It's impossible to tell what people might do or what they might think something is worth. Is it possible to want someone dead? Sick, cruel, yes. But possible. At the moment, we're looking at two people who might have somehow benefited from the deaths of two others. It's more than anything else we've got, and definitely worthy of pursuit. Come on. Let's pick up Titan and head out. I want to get to Andrew's and talk to him and make some phone calls. Get more facts and figures. Look into the lives of the others, find out just who might have benefited from the deaths of Alina Fairchild, Fran Castle and Hermione Shore."

"Do we think Roger Martinez had something to do with Jennifer Lowry disappearing because he's gotten a better job and brought his cousin in? If so, why are we just politely walking out of the office?"

"I'm on a theory right now. We need a lot more legwork and brilliant computer tech people who can find money trails and so on before I can make an arrest. You know that—your brother is an attorney."

She nodded. Robert always wanted hard evidence he could give a jury. She knew, through her brother, that what you knew didn't matter unless you could prove it.

"We still don't know about Brandon Wells," Axel said. "And tomorrow, kids are coming back out to the Everglades for an overnight camping trip. I want to get Andrew with us, out to the camping area. And Nigel if he can do it. I don't want a bunch of kids finding the remains of Brandon Wells."

"Okay. But can we get Titan now?" she asked.

He smiled. "Oh, yes, definitely. We can get Titan."

The school camping program was popular. It had been since its inception.

There were dozens of programs in the Miami-Dade and

Broward counties on the eastern side of the state, but this particular program happened only once a year.

The same people had been involved forever with others
joining in over the years.

By the time they picked up Titan and got to Andrew's,
collected Andrew and reached Nigel, it was after three, but
they still had several hours to search the general area where
the young people would be staying before darkness fell.

When they arrived after taking a long snakelike backwoods
trail off the main road, they discovered Jeremy Gray was already there, among others, setting up his tent and his displays
and maps. He greeted them with a bit of surprise, looking
from Axel to Andrew and then Raina and the dog.

"You're early!" he told them.

"Yeah, we're going to go over the place with a fine-tooth
comb," Axel said.

Jeremy nodded. "The dog will certainly help with that."

"There's nothing like a dog," Raina assured him.

Axel offered Jeremy a shrug and a rueful smile.

"Kids are coming," he said. "We want to teach them about
the incredible and unique wonder of our river of grass, and
the history of the Seminole and Miccosukee tribes. This is
an important program. Fun ghost stories are one thing, but
potentially stumbling upon a body is another matter."

Jeremy nodded strenuously, having grown serious at Axel's
words.

"I hear you, my friend. I can help you in another thirty
minutes if you'd like."

"Every bit helps," Andrew said.

Jeremy pointed to one of the chickees down something of
a straggly path. It was built up with a platform several feet
above the ground as they had been in the past, a bit of safety
from the things that wandered the Everglades at night.

"That's still the storyteller's space. All yours."

"Thanks!"

"The old concrete-block-and-stucco structure has been kept up through the years. Bedrolls, blankets, stuff you might need—all still in there in case you want to hunker down for the whole shebang," Jeremy told them.

"Great. They still have showers, right?" Axel asked.

"Is it still ninety degrees plus on many a day?" Jeremy said. "Hell, yes, there are still showers!" He smiled at Raina. "Not sure about dog food, but I'm guessing Titan would be fine with some frankfurters! We do weenie roasts. Not to worry—we still do native cooking demonstrations."

"We should get to it," Axel said, waving to him, and heading out.

"They're already here, you know," Andrew said. "The teacher chaperones, Loretta Oster and Frank Peters."

"Yeah, I noticed," Axel said. "You think it's them? Angela checked out their individual finances—neither seems to be living above their means. Then again, I don't always think money is the motive for those who want people dead—maybe getting ahead is the motive."

"For the people who want people dead. Possibly, as you told me, Peter Scarborough's estranged-wife-now-widow, and the young fellow working at the dentist's office. I know your Krewe offices are scouring records." He hesitated. "The only ones with real money are the attorneys."

"Attorneys," Axel said. "If Jordan Rivera would just come to, we'd know more. Andrew, I know you know this hammock like the back of your hand. Six finger areas heading off the central site, the dirt road entering through the largest, to our west?"

Andrew nodded. "Storms come and go and the landscape changes. But yes, basically, same six finger areas you know. How do you want to do this? Clockwise and counterclockwise?"

Axel nodded. "You start with the rear southern finger, I'll take the rear north, and we'll meet up back at the main road."

"It will be dark by then," Andrew noted.

"Then we'd best be really careful," Axel said. He looked at Raina. "You going to be okay? The ground is going to be soggy. Out by the swampy areas, we could encounter all kinds of things."

"You do know how to shoot that gun you carry, right?" she asked him.

"I do," he said.

"Then let's go."

She hunkered down and talked to Titan, stroking his head.

"Now, don't you go after anything out here—they can be dangerous. You bark, let us know what's happening."

As she spoke to the dog, Axel's phone rang. He answered it and then swore softly.

"Hung up on me," he said, shaking his head and looking around. "Cell phones are still iffy out here." He frowned, looking at the number.

"The hospital!" he told her, dialing the return number.

She waited, saying nothing.

He was put on hold several times. Then he listened, nodding.

He looked at Raina. "They're going to bring Jordan out of his coma tonight or tomorrow morning. He's doing well. They'll let me know when he's able to talk."

"There's a break!" Raina said.

"Yeah, hopefully," Axel agreed. "Okay, Titan boy, see where we are now? Decent-size area. There's lots of solid ground beneath us here, and out into those little snippets of land. Don't try to bite an alligator if you see one. And give a wide berth to any snake you see. Most of the time, they'll slither away from you, and there's been a lot of activity going on here, so any of the big guys should be off. That leaves the rattlers and the pygmy rattlers and little coral snakes and the moccasins. Sometimes they bask in the sun, so walk around them, too, huh?"

Titan barked as if he'd understood, word for word.

"Let's do this. We'll check back with the hospital as soon as we're through. The doctor said that he may be talkative soon after he's brought out of the coma—or it may take some time. But we may be taking a drive back tonight."

"I'm up for anything," Raina assured him.

And so they started out.

An hour later, Raina was hoping they didn't have to go anywhere in public anytime soon. She surely smelled worse than any living creature.

She thought she'd done fairly well, ignoring the heat, swatting away mosquitoes and even managing not to scream when she was convinced a low-hanging branch was an evil reptile.

They did see a large snake sitting in the middle of a path, but she and Titan dutifully skirted it and all was well. The snake just continued to bask.

They searched, and they searched. And there was nothing. They finally reached the spot where they were to meet back up with Andrew.

Titan let out a little growl, but just settled at Raina's feet, close to her, as if uncertain. Axel didn't notice; he was looking for Andrew.

She looked around but didn't see anything. Then she felt a touch. Soft as the breeze against her cheek. She closed her eyes tightly, not afraid, but trying to understand.

Jennifer Lowry?

Andrew met them along the road, shaking his head as he approached them. He looked tired, hot and worn, as well.

"Nothing," he said simply. "Nothing I could find."

"I think that's good, isn't it?" Raina asked. She looked from one man to the other. "Do you think that maybe, just maybe, Brandon Wells is still alive?"

Neither man replied.

Axel sighed. "Let's head back, see how the setup is coming along."

"What's the possibility of a shower?" Raina asked. "Not that I have clean clothes, but..."

"If you can live with the jeans, we have some fantastic Indian blouses," Andrew said. "And skirts, too, but out here, I tend to suggest pants for everyone. Mosquitoes can bite through denim, but it's a little better than simple cotton."

"I'm down with that. I love the patterns and the colors and the beading," Raina assured him.

When they arrived back, there was a fire going in the pit just outside Jeremy Gray's chickee. Folding chairs had been brought out. Frank and Loretta and Jeremy and a few of the other Miccosukee volunteers had joined them.

"Hey there!" Loretta said, lifting a glass of something as they walked up. "I heard you all were out here, making sure the grounds were safe."

"Walking—and sweating," Andrew said. "It was great."

"Hey, you live out here," Loretta reminded him.

"So I do. In a house. With air-conditioning."

"They just redid the village a few years back," Jeremy told them, "making the gift shop bigger, with entry tickets being bought there. But way back, the village was more open and we did our crafts and slept in the same chickees where we were selling our goods. New is nice, old is—"

"Must have been hot," Loretta said, laughing.

"Miccosukee kids all learn the old ways," Jeremy said. "Sons go with their fathers and learn to fish and hunt. Daughters learn to farm and cook and sew, and families matter."

"Which is wonderful," Loretta said quickly. "Just curious—what if a daughter happens to be a great fisherwoman? Or wants to grow up to be a doctor?"

"Then she fishes or goes to school and does well and heads on to college and med school and becomes a doctor," Jeremy said. "The past isn't about stopping the future—it's about remembering culture and valuing it."

"Oh, of course," Loretta said.

"Raina would love a blouse, Jeremy," Axel said. "Would you mind? She's going to take advantage of the showers first."

"Sure." Jeremy studied Raina, then hopped up to the platform of his chickee to go through a rack of clothing he'd set there. He chose a blouse, beautiful with rows of different colors and designs and beadwork.

"Okay?" he asked her.

"Okay? It's beautiful!"

"Please," he said, presenting it to her.

She wanted to offer to pay; she looked at him and knew he would be offended.

"Thank you."

"I'll show you to the showers," Axel told her.

Titan barked and hurried along as she and Axel gave the others a wave and started out.

His phone rang again. As he stopped to answer it, Raina looked around.

Darkness had fallen. There were electric lights in the main house and they cast a good glow out on the night. She could see the area where fires had been prepared for the next night and little tents had been set up for the students.

She remembered her own excitement when she had come as a student. Staring to the southwest, with the sun falling and the moon rising, she thought she could see the pirate ship, sailing now eternally across the river of grass.

Axel ended his call and smiled at her. "That was Jon. He and Kylie just landed back in Miami."

"Wow. South Dakota for lunch and they're back already."

"They had the use of the private jet."

"Now that must be the way to fly!"

"I like it when I'm on a case that requires fast action," he told her. "They'll come out here, so they'll be back fairly soon."

"Great!"

"Let's get you clean. When they arrive, I'll shower. That way, it will be me, Andrew and the two of them and I'll know I have someone with eyes on you."

They entered the main building where a young, light-haired park ranger was working with an older Miccosukee woman, setting up name tags on a table and remarking on the schedule. Both looked up as they entered. The Miccosukee woman smiled and opened her arms. Axel walked over to her, accepting a warm hug. The park ranger smiled on benignly and Axel introduced everyone—the woman was a distant cousin, Tiger clan, as well. She was happy to show Raina the hallway to the showers and assure her she'd be quite alone for a while.

Both women were introduced to Titan; Titan seemed to like them.

"I'll be here, waiting," Axel assured her. He made a face. "I'm going to check on Jordan Rivera's condition again. If we can't see him until tomorrow, I was thinking we might stay out here tonight. If you're game."

"Definitely," she assured him.

"Titan, you're with me for a few minutes."

Titan obediently sat at his feet. Axel smiled. "Go ahead," he told Raina.

She hurried down to the shower stalls.

She remembered being there before, but it had all been updated. Back then, there had been four shower stalls and they had been rustic. Now, there were eight stalls, all with little sitting areas, hooks for clothing and a pile of clean towels.

Nice. Time did make for some much needed improvements.

There was also plenty of water, deliciously hot. And soap and shampoo and conditioner, all in dispensers. She didn't realize just how great the shower felt until she opened her eyes and realized that steam was rising all around her. She'd washed every conceivable inch of her body. Time to get out.

She turned off the water and stepped toward to the little sitting area where she'd left her clothing. And there, in the fog, she saw a woman appear.

Jennifer Lowry.

"A voice. I heard a voice. And I recognized it. One of them is here now," the ghost whispered.

A call broke through the air.

"Are you all right in there?"

Raina thought it was the park ranger checking on her.

"I'm fine! It was just a great shower," she said.

The voice came again. "We're stepping out for a minute, grabbing some food. You're welcome to anything here. Axel is right out in front with Andrew. They were on a phone call, trying to get good reception!"

"Thanks!"

The image of Jennifer Lowry before her was fading, disappearing as if rising along with the mist from the shower.

"Wait! Please!" Raina said.

But the ghost was gone.

Raina stood frozen for a minute, despite the heat around her, naked and dripping. But the ghost didn't return.

She dressed again quickly, grateful for the clean blouse.

Then she paused, frowning. She heard a door, she thought. Coming from the rear of the building, near where she was, not from the front.

She stepped from her little stall, dressed and ready to hurry out.

She started to smile.

Then her smile faded and she tried to scream.

Too late. The burlap bag was already over her head, and the best she could manage was a gasping, choking sound.

"We brought him out of the coma. But if you want him awake and aware and responsive, I suggest you come in the morning," the doctor told Axel over the phone. "He was intubated so he's really not responsive yet."

"Thank you. It's important. I'll probably come in tonight, anyway. Sit and wait," Axel said. "If that's all right."

"It's fine. He's doing well. We brought him around several hours ago now, but sometimes they sleep."

"Understood. I appreciate it. He may be all we have."

Andrew was standing next to him. He repeated what he had learned.

"Well, here's hoping he does know the truth. He could have just been another victim. Upset because he lost someone who had enchanted him, making a fuss and, therefore, somehow, ended up being a danger?"

"One way or another, we need him to tell us what the hell happened."

"If he knows."

"I'm sure he knows."

His phone started ringing again and he answered it.

It was Angela.

"I think I might have something. Maybe a link that means nothing, but a bit of a link, anyway."

"And that is?" Axel asked. He frowned, trying to pay attention. Titan was with him, had been following every step.

Now, he was suddenly whining.

"Titan, shh!"

"What's up?" Andrew asked, frowning, and watching the dog's behavior.

Angela was still speaking, unaware Axel's attention was

then divided. "A patient of Dr. Wong was one of your 'people of interest,'" she said. "At least, I think it was him. I called Wong himself for his old records. And about a year ago, he had a patient named F. Peters. Now, there could be several, but I have a feeling it might be your man, Frank Peters. Which would, at the least, connect him to Jennifer Lowry."

The dog was really whining, tugging at his leash. And though they'd told Axel they'd be in the building until he returned, his distant cousin and the park ranger were outside the building, chatting as they headed toward Jeremy's fire pit.

"Hey!" they called.

He stuffed his phone into Andrew's hand and shouted out to them. "Hey, where's Raina?"

"Oh, I checked on her a few minutes ago. She was just fine—but we're starving," the park ranger called to him.

Axel had been right outside the damned building. The women leaving Raina on her own shouldn't have been so unnerving. But Titan was suddenly pulling and snapping at his leash.

And Frank Peters had been at the fire pit.

He grabbed the phone back, gave Titan his lead and raced after the dog as the animal flew toward the building. He had to wait for Axel to open the door.

Axel did.

He was barely aware of Andrew shouting out to him, demanding to know what was going on.

The dog made a beeline along the hallway to the showers, but then came to a dead stop, barking in confusion.

Then Axel saw it—new, along with several refurbishments to the building.

A door marked Fire Exit.

Titan raced in that direction.

Axel's mind raced, too. It could be something else. Frank

could still be sitting by the fire. Raina could still be dressing after a long shower...

He screamed her name. There was no answer.

Titan was barking furiously.

He burst through the emergency door.

The second he stepped out, he heard the loud whirr of an airboat, a gigantic fan burning its way over water and swamp grass, heading deep into the Everglades.

CHAPTER NINETEEN

The burlap was itchy, suffocating.

And Raina couldn't understand why she was wearing it.

She had seen one of her captors.

One of them. There were two. Well, she had known there were two…and maybe more.

Maybe different people at different times.

Or maybe the same.

She didn't know. Maybe she never would. Or maybe they would tell her—before they killed her.

How far were they going? Where were they going? On the one hand she knew her dog well, and if Axel didn't realize she'd been abducted, Titan would.

They'd be coming for her.

How? They were in a tangle of hammocks and water and swamp and sawgrass. She thought about throwing herself over the side. But now, her hands were bound. If she threw herself over the side, she could die a more dreadful death. Things she knew streaked through her mind. She was unlikely prey for a gator—not really bite-size. Since the python and boa invasion, food was scarce and all creatures were going for what they could get.

Then, of course, there were the snakes...

What the hell, why not make it difficult for them?

The airboat began to slow; they were coming to a stop somewhere. Did they predetermine their places of murder? Or were they random?

There was a bump.

An aggravated voice rang out.

"What the hell? Can't you drive? Damn it, you're going to do this!"

Raina pitched herself toward the side. Even if her hands were bound and she was wearing a burlap hood, she was determined to draw it out.

"Shit! She's going to make us capsize!"

She felt herself grabbed roughly, but the hold wasn't strong. She jerked violently—slamming her head forward, as she'd seen done in the movies.

It hurt! It hurt to bloody hell!

But oddly, it seemed to have done something. She heard cursing. "Now I'm covered in this fetid water, and shit, oh, shit! There's an alligator over there—"

"Leave it the hell alone!" another voice said.

This time, when Raina was grabbed, it was with strength. And she suddenly recognized the second voice as it said, "Oh, please. I don't want to be here. I don't want to do this."

"It will all be thrown on you, so grow up! Or you'll have a witness against you, and you know damned well, the rest of us will come out okay. Even Daddy will be forced to testify against you!"

The burlap bag was wrenched from Raina's head.

She was glad to see that, at the very least, she had head-butted Loretta Oster. The chubby-cheerful teacher was

drenched in the swamp water, trying desperately to free herself of the grass and muck clinging to her.

She was stunned to see the face of the man holding her. The
miserable, tearstained face of her once-upon-a-time flame,
Tate Fielding.

It made no sense.

She stared at him, astounded. If he wasn't about to kill her,
he would be truly pitiable. He was sobbing softly.

Tears were streaming down his face.

"Tate?" she said.

"I'm sorry. Oh, God, I'm so sorry!"

"Toughen up, frat boy!" Loretta snapped. "Come on, we've
got to get this over with. I have to get back, and now, how
do I explain this? I tripped into the damned water?"

"Wait!" said Raina. "Who killed Fran Castle?"

"Why, honey, your friendly neighborhood chaperone,"
Loretta said. "You kids were too full of yourselves to realize
I wasn't there until the damned buses arrived. But of course
I wasn't alone." She paused, still angry and irritated over her
condition. "Tate! Damn you, come on. Grow a pair of balls
and finish the stupid bitch!"

"Wait!" Raina demanded. Tate would listen to her, she
knew. Tate wasn't a killer. He was being forced into this for
some reason. "Hey, you're going to kill me. So, humor me!
Tell me, please, tell me what has been going on. Did the two
of you kill Jennifer Lowry?"

"I've never killed anyone," Tate said. "And I'm so sorry,
Raina—"

"Shut up you ball-less wonder!" Loretta shouted. "If you
can't do this, give me the damned knife. I won't have a problem, I assure you!"

She had a chance, Raina knew. She had a chance because
Tate Fielding wasn't a murderer. He might have known what
was going on, but he wasn't a murderer himself.

And Loretta…

Could she take her? The woman didn't even have the knife yet…

"Who started all this and why?" she demanded.

Loretta laughed. "Why is it they just never want to believe it could be a woman?"

"I know!" Raina said. "And you are so good—or so it seems. I mean, there's no money trail. I'll admit, you naturally fell under suspicion, but what I can't figure out is, why? Did you know Fran Castle—did she do something? I mean, Tate is here now, and Jordan obviously knew something, but they were kids then, so… Oh, I get it! Jefferson Fielding. It was him!"

"No, you don't you get it. Jefferson is as big an ass as the rest of them! I knew Jefferson because his son was in one of my classes. That idiot needed to get rid of a witness—at the time, it wasn't Fran Castle. It was a man named Gabriel Mercury several years before Fran. But as to the money, well, you'll never find it. Jefferson is great at hiding money, but he's such a wuss that he regretted what happened to the witness."

"What happened?" Raina pressed. Loretta seemed to be on a roll.

"The man sort of fell off a building. I say sort of because, well, Jefferson was yelling at him. Accident? Maybe. But I was there, and I saw it happen—and after that I had the man in my pocket. Once I had him, well, I had a way to wash some money, you know? It's amazing how much can go through an attorney's office without raising any suspicion."

"You always had help. I know you had help. Two people attacked and then killed Jennifer Lowry," Raina said. "Frank Peters? You were a pair of murdering teachers? I mean, it's obvious the man is horrible, but I'm learning. Being a bad person doesn't make you a murderer. So who was with you

when you took Jennifer Lowry? Jennifer said there were two
of you."

"Jennifer is dead! She couldn't have said anything," Loretta argued.

"There were two of you."

"Oh, and how do you know that?" Loretta demanded.

"Like I said, she told me."

Loretta stared at her, and then started laughing. "You're
crazy as a loon. This might well be a mercy killing. Damn
you, Tate—give me the knife!"

She still didn't have the knife.

It was now or never.

Raina took off at light speed, slamming into Loretta so that
she fell, and raced straight into the brush and muck surround-
ing the hammock, seeking a trail through the firm ground.
She staggered onto one and kept running.

Straight into another man.

Straight into the arms of death?

He needed an airboat.

Axel knew he needed to follow as quickly as possible. He
spotted one and ran toward it, seeing Billie Osceola was just
coming in.

"Hey!" Billie called cheerfully. "You're already here, too.
Great!"

"I need the airboat," Axel said.

"You—what?" Billie was stepping out.

"I need the airboat. Sorry!"

Axel jumped on, followed by the dog, and took the helm.

"Hey!" Billie called again. But Axel already had the vessel
geared again. It shot out over the shallow water and grasses.

He vaguely heard his phone ringing. He concentrated on
only one thing—reaching Raina as quickly as possible.

But it kept ringing, shrill, even against the thunderous whirr of the airboat.

He pulled it from his pocket. Andrew.

"Andrew, get out here. He took Raina. Frank Peters took Raina."

"Frank Peters is sitting by the fire."

"What?"

"Frank Peters is sitting by the fire. But Nigel just reached me. He tried to get you, but you weren't answering."

"She's gone, Andrew. She's gone. Someone got to her. Raina is gone."

"So is Jordan Rivera."

"What? He's just out of a coma, hadn't moved."

"Oh, he moved, all right. He knocked out a male nurse, stole his clothing and left the hospital. They don't know when exactly. Possibly hours ago."

"So, it may be Jordan?" Axel asked incredulously. He kept one hand hard at the helm. He was crashing through low water and high water, over roots and other obstructions. He stared ahead, desperate to find the course of the airboat that went ahead of him by minutes.

"Maybe, but..."

"But what?"

"Do you know who isn't by the fire?"

"Who? Andrew, just talk to me. And get the hell out here!"

"It's Loretta, Axel. Loretta is gone."

"Just start searching. Whoever the hell it is, they have her. Andrew, get anyone—anyone we trust."

He hung up, looking ahead desperately.

And then he saw the ghost.

The ghost of Jennifer Lowry. She stood by a massive tree that boarded a narrow strip of deep wetland.

She beckoned to him, deep sorrow in her eyes.

Titan began to bark. That was the way to go.

He gritted his teeth, ducking beneath the limbs of an out-stretched tree.

Then he saw Peg-legged Pete and Joshua and a whole lineup of pirates, waving and guiding him through the maze of little islands.

He wasn't sure if it was the ghosts, or his own heart beating in his ears. He heard a word, repeated over and over again.

Hurry. Hurry, hurry, hurry.

Jordan was in bad shape. He caught Raina, but could barely hold her.

"If they killed Jennifer," he said. "If they killed Jennifer..."

"Jordan, did you...?"

"Did I kill Jennifer?" he asked. "No! I was falling in love with her. I didn't want to be in love. I didn't. But I knew something was wrong, oh, God, I knew. There were things said at work, money that went into strange accounts. And Tate's father. He'd meet with Loretta Oster. So I started to wonder, and I didn't want to wonder..."

He staggered back, falling against a tree, slipping down to the ground, barely conscious.

"Jordan, why did you leave the hospital?" she asked anxiously.

"Had to. I hit the nurse. I took his uniform, and I just walked out and they didn't see."

"How did you get here?" she demanded.

He didn't answer; his head fell.

She hunkered down by him, searching his pockets, hard going with her hands still tied. Nothing except a wad of bills in the nurse's aqua tunic he was wearing.

"Taxi," he mumbled. "Stole...airboat." He managed to look up at her, his eyes vacant and watering. He was fading. Either exhaustion or medication or the fact he'd awakened from a medically induced coma to make his way out to the Everglades. "Had to come. I couldn't let them kill again."

"Brilliant," someone said.

Raina shot to her feet and stood; Loretta was there, just twenty feet from them.

Now, she had the knife.

And she was done talking or listening. With the precision of a circus performer, she drew back an arm and sent the knife flying.

It would have hit Raina. It would have hit her cleanly in the chest.

But it didn't. Because Jordan somehow thrust to his feet and launched himself forward, pushing Raina back.

"No!" she cried.

But Jordan was on the ground, bleeding. And Loretta Oster was still staring at Raina with a smile on her face.

In the distance, Raina thought she could hear the whirr of an airboat.

"Know that saying? Never bring a knife to a gunfight? My opinion on that is simple—you bring both."

She drew out a gun. Raina didn't doubt Loretta's ability to fire the weapon.

Loretta took aim.

Axel was where he needed to be. Tate Fielding lay on the ground, moaning and bleeding. Titan raced to him, sniffing and whining. Axel rushed over, ducking down to see where the blood was coming from. He needed the man alive.

He didn't know Tate Fielding's part in it all, and he was evidently in bad shape now, but he was damned well going to lead him the rest of the way to Raina.

"Where is she?" he demanded.

Fielding wasn't bleeding from the throat. He'd been stabbed. But he was alive. Shaking, he reached up and pointed.

He hadn't really needed Tate.

Titan was ahead of him, already racing through the trees and foliage. Axel drew out his gun and followed.

Axel burst through a pile of leaves and saw Jordan Rivera had made it out to the Everglades.

He'd made it out there, apparently, to die.

He was on the ground, a knife in his chest, eyes open, staring blankly ahead.

Raina was at his side.

Facing her, Loretta Oster held a gun.

Titan let out a growl that sounded more like the roar of a lion. He was going to race forward, tackle Loretta.

But it would be too late.

"Drop it!" Axel roared, raising his Glock.

Loretta broke her stare from Raina to look quickly at Axel, assessing the threat. She wasn't going to listen to him. She was going to fire, no matter what.

He couldn't let that happen.

She might know her weapon; he knew his better.

He fired and Loretta dropped to the ground.

Titan was still in motion, flying across mud and muck and grass, landing atop the fallen woman. Axel rushed forward.

Raina stood still as rock, staring at Loretta where she had fallen.

"Raina!"

She turned to him. Staggered toward him. But she couldn't put her arms around him. Her wrists were bound. He dug into his pocket for his knife, freeing her.

She fell against him.

"Jordan… Tate…" she cried. "They knew. Axel. Help— Jordan needs help. He saved me, stepped in front of me. He needs to get back to the hospital."

She was shaking. He nodded; she didn't realize Jordan was already dead. Tate, however, might live.

"Andrew is right behind me. He'll get Tate to a hospital."

"Tate was supposed to kill me. He couldn't do it. But he was fine when I ran—"

"I'm afraid he's not fine now."

"Jordan needs help desperately."

He drew in a deep breath.

"Jordan is… I'm sorry. He's gone, Raina."

She stared at him, eyes wide, then she turned, rushing back to Jordan. She fell on her knees by his side, touching him. "Oh, Jordan!" she whispered.

Axel heard the whirr of an airboat. Andrew.

But suddenly, shots were fired, ringing out wildly.

He dove for Raina, drawing her back with him behind a crooked old oak. More shots exploded.

Axel drew a finger to his lips.

"Titan! Get over here!" Raina said, and the dog obediently came to her call, whining softly as he joined them behind the tree.

Axel expected to see Frank Peters.

But it was Jefferson Fielding who walked carefully toward them through the hardwoods, ducking down by Loretta.

"We're out of it—thank God, we're out of it," Jefferson whispered.

Axel didn't know what alerted him. They hadn't made a sound. The dog hadn't even made a sound.

But Jefferson Fielding didn't see him; he just looked straight at Raina.

"It was an accident," he said to her. "It all started with an accident, but then she blackmailed me. She used the firm. Used me to find people. Don't you see? I'm sorry. Tate couldn't do it. I have to do it. I have to because it will all fall down, like a house of cards. I hated Loretta for what she did to Tate, teasing him and then using him, but I never wanted to dirty my hands. To make a kill. Jordan and Tate couldn't take it. Especially after they killed that Jennifer girl. Jordan—he loved her—he was going to ruin it all. You have to understand. It's one of the most prestigious law firms in the state, in the country. I'm sorry."

He took Loretta's gun from where it lay beside her body, and he took aim. Axel jerked Raina back, raising his own gun.

Jefferson Fielding's shot hit the tree.

And he didn't get a chance to fire again.

Titan was on him like a mountain lion, snarling, his jaw clamped around the man's forearm. The gun fell to the ground, and Jefferson was dragged to his knees by the animal.

Axel darted forward, covering Jefferson with his weapon, and shouted at him. "Don't move!"

Raina stood, calling to the dog. With a final shake, Titan let go and came to her side.

Andrew reached them at last, his boat pulling up with another behind his, bearing Jon and Kylie and emergency medical technicians.

Axel shouted quick warnings and explanations.

Jon went to handcuff Jefferson Fielding while Andrew hurried with the EMTs back to Tate Fielding.

Loretta Oster was dead.

That much was clear.

And Jordan...

Raina was moving to his side again when Axel caught her arm.

"Wait," he said softly.

Because the ghost of Jennifer Lowry was there again. She stood by the fallen form of Jordan Rivera, then knelt down beside him, laying her cheek against his back, weeping softly.

Then something happened.

Something Axel had never witnessed before, with all he had seen.

Jordan was dead; he couldn't rise.

And yet he was rising. Some part of him—his soul. His spirit.

He stood as if confused for a moment. Then he saw the ghost of Jennifer Lowry down by his body.

He said her name softly.

She looked up and saw him, and a smile lit her face. He offered his hand to her. She took his hand and stood and went into his arms.

They were locked together in an embrace for all time.

Then they moved apart just a bit and Jordan turned and saw Axel and Raina.

He smiled.

"You died for me," Raina whispered. "Oh, Jordan, I'm so sorry."

Jordan smiled and managed to speak. "No, I died for me. Because I could not bear what was being done. Because I did not stop it."

He turned back to Jennifer.

"We're together," he said with amazement.

She nodded, the love in her eyes obvious as they stared into his.

They locked hands, and started to move.

The airboats were providing light, but the sun was almost completely down.

And the moon was rising.

A strange, soft, yellow-gold light seemed to shine just between a few of the trees edging against an overgrown trail.

Together, the ghosts seemed to disappear into the light.

"Does that mean…?" Raina asked.

"I don't know," Axel told her. "It might mean they have moved on, together at last. Or it might mean they will now become another legend of haunting in the Everglades. I'm not sure. But I do know they really loved one another, and they're together now."

She nodded.

"I'll have to believe that he's happy."

"I do believe he's happy," Axel said.

Andrew walked over to them. He hadn't seen any of what had gone on with Jordan; he'd just seen to it that Tate Fielding was on his way to the hospital.

Jon had the other Fielding in custody. He was cuffed now, and a Miccosukee police escort had come to take him away.

"And so it's over," Andrew said. "And just beginning."

Axel nodded.

"Just beginning?" Raina asked.

Andrew glanced at Axel and then explained, "There are going to be a lot of arrests in this case. Angela reached me again. They've made a money connection in the matter of Peter Scarborough's murder. His widow will be going to prison—murder for hire. From what she's gotten in the Jennifer Lowry case, Loretta managed to meet up with Roger Martinez while Frank was seeing the dentist. Martinez was the second killer in Jennifer's murder. He wanted her gone because, in secret, he hated her and coveted her position. He hated the way the patients and the dentist loved her. Meanwhile, Loretta wanted Jennifer dead. She was a rather jealous person, it seems. Frank had wanted to buy Jennifer a drink. That had clinched the deal for Loretta. All she needed was a second so she could carry out her plans."

He hesitated, looking at Raina. He cleared his throat and continued. "Angela has been talking to your brother, who is putting together dossiers that will have to do with the case. He isn't going to be the prosecutor—he has a personal connection to you, and Robert won't risk a mistrial. But he'll be on the team for the county charges. And by the way—he's really distressed all this has gone on and you haven't kept him in the loop. But we've assured him you're all right, so he's grateful. He says he's going to throttle you himself when he sees you, but he loves you."

Raina smiled, feeling guilty.

She hadn't kept Robert up to date.

"Will they get all the co-murderers? Have we even found all the dead? We know Brandon Wells is out there somewhere."

"We'll do our best," Andrew said.

"And trust me, we will find all those who kept Loretta in business, who paid her and joined in her murder duos," Axel said. He looked at Andrew and smiled. "We never stop."

"None of us," Andrew replied. "Not from a tribal viewpoint, country viewpoint—or federal viewpoint. We won't stop. I promise."

He walked away.

For a moment, Axel just stood by Raina's side. Then, heedless of the medical personal and all others standing around, he pulled her into his arms.

"I need to do this while we're alive," he said. "I love you. I want my life to be with you—I want to say and do and feel everything while we can, while we're breathing, and then years from now, into eternity. I realize this is fast, that it's been intense, that—"

She pressed her fingers against his lips.

"I love you. And I'll be incredibly grateful just to breathe beside you. To hear your heartbeat every moment we're alive. And I hope we have years and years and then eternity."

He smiled. It seemed so strange, here in the darkness, in the heart of the Everglades, with death around them.

But there was no better place to realize life was meant to be lived—and love was something that shouldn't be lost.

The moon kept rising.

Police came and went. They watched Jordan's body as it was gently taken away, followed by the body of Loretta Oster.

Titan stood by them all the while, and then it was time for them to step into an airboat themselves.

Back into the dark tangle of the past.

Where they could put together the pieces.

And look into the bright promise of the future.

EPILOGUE

"When the wind blows and the fog swirls over the great river of grass, you can look out over the miles of long grass, cypress trees and more, and then, as the moon rises, casting its glow out over the landscape, you can see it, riding high on the horizon, the pirate ship, great sails white beneath the glow of the moon, and you know the pirates are roaming the Everglades, ever eager to atone for their sins!"

Raina watched Axel with the children gathered around him.

They were standing in the vast and elegant entry of Adam Harrison's historic theater. It was a Sunday afternoon, three weeks after the events that had brought the strange killing spree perpetrated by the least likely of killers to an end.

An hour ago, on the theater's stage, Jon Dickson and Kylie Connolly had been joined in marriage. Now, tables cluttered the entry and a band played to the side where there was most customarily a T-shirt stand celebrating whatever play was being performed each night.

The food had been catered in.

Raina had met Kylie's friends and family, down from the DC area for the occasion.

And bit by bit, she was meeting more and more members of Axel's Krewe of Hunters, and loving all those she met, exchanging stories with them and finding she was happy with herself. What had terrified her before now seemed like something wonderful. A unique and special sense that could help others.

Axel had spun a few more local ghost stories he'd learned before one of the kids at the wedding had begged he tell them about the pirates who supposedly roamed the Everglades.

They'd also wanted to know if he'd wrangled alligators. Axel had explained they didn't really wrangle alligators—they handled them and learned about them, sharing a special environment with them.

She smiled as Angela Hawkins, the lovely blonde wife of Jackson Crow, field head for the Krewe, sat down beside her.

"I'm imaging one day he's going to be a great dad," Angela said. "He definitely has a way with children."

The groom, fresh off the dance floor with one of the older guests, slid into a chair, grinning. "That's one of Kylie's great-aunts! Spritely lady—octogenarian, and I think she can outlast me!" He grew serious. "Raina, you're doing all right here? Enjoying the area— Oh! How are Sheila the cat and Titan getting along?"

Raina smiled. "Believe it or not, cat and dog are doing all right. They were a bit suspicious of one another at first, but now, it's pretty cool. You can even see them curl up to sleep together sometimes. And they're very protective of one another."

"You doing any training?" Jon asked her.

"I am! Adam Harrison very nicely introduced me to a friend who deals with police dogs—a special group of police dogs. Rescue animals we're training to seek out drugs and bombs and work with officers. I'm loving every minute of it."

He nodded. "And you? How are you doing, after everything?"

She smiled. "We're still following up regarding people involved. They've now arrested a cousin of Alina Fairchild—he assisted in her abduction because there was family money that wasn't on the table at the time of the murder, but would be a windfall when the last great-grandparent died. Melissa Scarborough is awaiting trial, but my brother was able to get his investigator on her and discovered she'd met Loretta Oster by chance at a club when Melissa and Peter had been in Florida the year before—they have an email connection. She didn't get the windfall of his money until he'd been dead several months. It had been a legal settlement for an injury on a job he'd done several years earlier, and with Peter being dead, it went directly to her, long enough after the murder to keep anyone from noticing. It will take police and legal teams a long time to sort it all out."

She was quiet a minute.

"I have to admit," she went on, "I didn't care much for Frank Peters—but he was a jerk, not a murderer. And Tate's dad! They're still trying to get to the truth. He was a real jerk—*and* possibly a murderer. That night in the Everglades, he claimed he didn't like to get his hands dirty. But my brother believes he did assist Loretta in some of the kidnappings and murders. Now, they just have to find proof. We know he was accommodating exchanges of money, through a bank in the Cayman Islands. We know he was aware of Loretta's activities, and blackmail doesn't excuse him. What the exact charges will be against him, we don't know yet. Jordan, of course..." She paused. It still hurt. And it was still oddly... good. She'd seen Jordan walk away, hand in hand, with Jennifer. "I still feel badly for Tate. I don't know what the charges against him will be. I know I'm grateful. He was being pressured, but he refused to kill. So, in that, I hope all goes well."

"Complicated, but you're here. And you're happy here?"

"I am," she assured him.

Axel, drop-dead gorgeous—in her mind, certainly—in his tux, had evidently finished with story time for the younger guests.

He joined Raina, Jon and Angela at the table.

"Good stories," Angela told him, a slight smile on her lips. "You almost make me believe in ghosts."

"Ah, well, Angela, at some point you must come and meet the pirates!" he said.

"Hmm. Maybe I'll get to do that one day," Angela said.

"Miss Hamish, would you be so kind? The band is playing a lovely tune. Would join me on the floor?"

She smiled, excused herself and stood.

There wasn't much of a dance floor. And now, the children who had been avidly listening to ghost stories were playing on the bit of space designated as dance floor.

"All right, a little awkward," Axel said, skirting around a boy of about three who had decided to do some kind of break-dancing number to a Paul Williams ballad.

She laughed. "I will dance with you anywhere!" she told him.

"I think the party is starting to break up," he told her. "Want to dance on home with me soon?"

She did.

As others began to file out, they joined them. She hugged Kylie and Jon warmly, grateful to have known them in Florida.

Axel's home was a single family dwelling just a mile or so southwest of the Krewe offices, an easy jaunt almost anywhere on the nearby metro system.

He might have only had Sheila, the cat, before he met her, but Raina had been delighted to discover he had a large fenced yard—one that delighted Titan, too.

They returned to the cat and dog, fed the animals, settled them and headed to bed themselves.

"Perfect wedding," Raina said. "They were beautiful. Friends and family, coworkers, children. It was great."

She had just set her bag down on her dressing table as she spoke. He was behind her, turning her around to face him.

"I'd love something similar for us," he said softly, kissing her lips.

"Is that a proposal?"

"An assumption, but an educated guess," he said.

She grinned. "I think you're supposed to be on your knees, and maybe have a ring to offer me, something like that."

"Really? You don't get down and ask me?" he asked.

She grinned. "Hmm. Cocky, aren't you?"

"Well, no, not really. I mean, well, I don't have the ring— yet. The thing is, I know why nothing else has worked all my life. I know what I want. Being with you. Dealing with the complicated, the good and the bad, handling the painful together, and all that's good and sweet and wonderful, as well. I like to believe you feel the same way—without being too cocky." He suddenly fell to his knees with a dramatic finesse. "Marry me, because you are the love of my life, my soul mate, my heart mate, and…"

"And?"

"Frankly, because you just might be crazy enough to be with me—for all of our lives."

"The first part was the best!" She laughed. "Sure. I'll marry you. Who else would be crazy enough to marry me?"

"At least I started out being eloquent!"

"Eloquent." She shook her head. "I'll teach you eloquent."

She kissed him. The kiss deepened, and they were breathless when they parted, ready to tear off their clothing and take that kiss where it was destined to go.

"Hmm," he murmured, eyes golden and teasing. "That was a deliciously eloquent kind of silence."

"I can demonstrate it some more if you'd like," she said.

"Please do!"

She did.

And that night, she remembered back, when she had wondered if lying beside him each night could be her life, how much she had yearned for this, a lifetime with him, sleeping beside him, waking with him, learning his thoughts, being a part of his life.

She curled into his arms, and she was saddened as she thought about Jennifer and Jordan again.

Saddened, and grateful. She had learned from them.

They had the gift of life. And the gift of love.

The future would bring hard times, new cases, puzzles, trials, work and more. Ups and downs.

Life.

Love.

And the unique and precious beauty of both.

★ ★ ★ ★ ★